BLACKTHORN

Chronicles of the Dark Sword Book One

DeWayne M. Kunkel

Copyright © 2011 DeWayne M. Kunkel
All rights reserved.
ISBN-13: 978-1461060819

ISBN-10: 1461060818

*This book is dedicated to my children.
Without them,
Tel'Ganduil would never have set sail across the
Darkling Sea.*

DMK

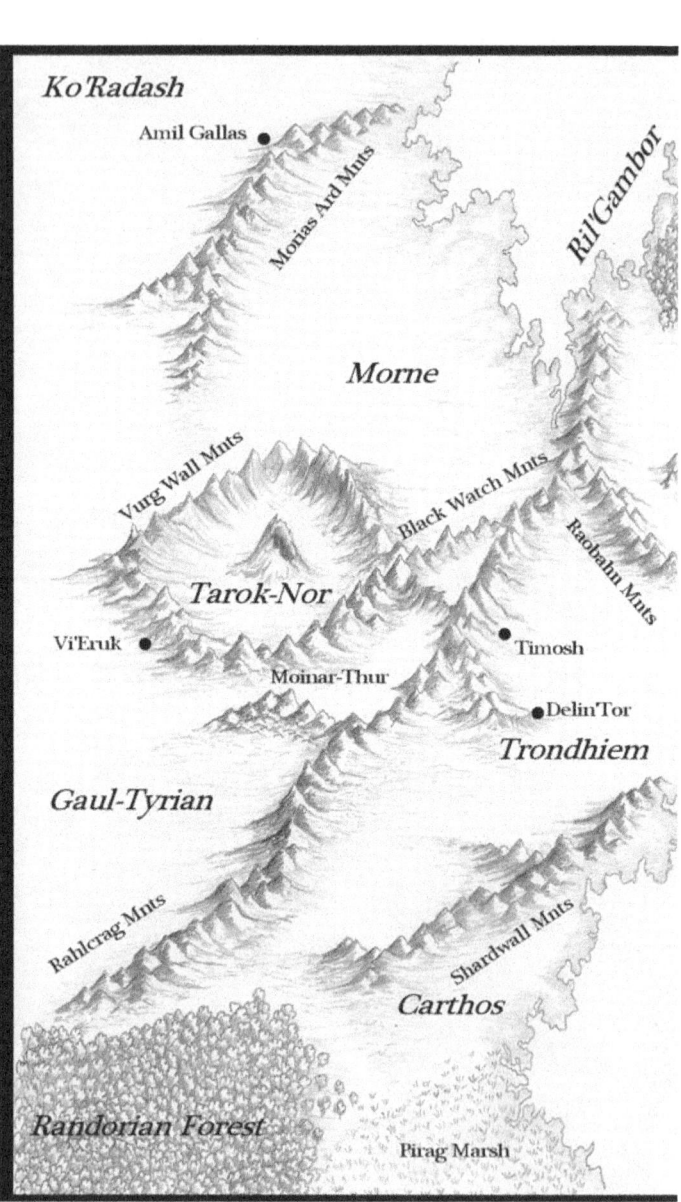

The Eastern Kingdoms

PROLOGUE

Three thousand years ago the world stood on the brink of destruction. An age of peace and prosperity had come suddenly to an abrupt end. For more than two hundred years, brutal war had ravaged the once fertile lands. Laying waste to the great cities, entire nations fell beneath the sword.

The last remnants of free men had assembled upon a plain of scorched earth. At their side were the immortals, the Tal'shear. The tall fey beings stood defiant, resplendent in golden armor and brightly colored tabards of blue and silver.

A lone Mountain loomed over the plain, its roots seated amid barren hills of broken rock. Gaping black chasms that leaked poisonous vapors into the air opened on the plain. The Mountain's ragged crown was lost in a billowing cloud of fire and smoke, obscuring the sun and casting the land into darkness.

Along the Mountain's flanks flowed thin ribbons of orange light, molten stone vomited up from the fiery depths. It crawled slowly forward. Flowing about an immense fortress built upon a high knuckle of stone at the peak's base. The lava disappeared into thick clouds of black smoke rising from deep crevices in the heat blasted rock.

The Keep was offensive to the eye, constructed of dark stone, its crenellated walls surmounted by four high towers that resembled the jagged fangs of some wild beast. Three massive gates of iron were set into the thick walls. Dark openings from which crept a foul mist, reeking of death and decay.

Vi'Erud it was named, the keep of the damned. For more than two hundred years it had endured. Guarding the sole entrance to Sur'kar's sanctum. Many times it had been attacked, but the dark fortress had never fallen, and within its daunting ramparts lurked Sur'kar's accursed horde.

Amid the host from the east, eight Tal'shear had gathered upon a low hill. They were unlike the others of their kind; each emanated an aura of power and wisdom. They were known as the Warders, a group of powerful mages sworn to the protection of the world.

Horns sounded, and the black gates of Vi'Erud slowly swung open. From within the darkness a great host of Morne marched out onto the plain. They came by the tens of thousands, pouring forth as a dark tide that stained the land. Bearing before them crimson standards held aloft upon spears capped with the skulls of slain men.

From the fuming maw of Trothgar a great explosion of gas and fire erupted. Shaking the earth with its vehemence.

Drums pounded and out from the center gate advanced giants. Huge one-eyed brutes that waded through the assembled Morne brandishing iron cudgels, cruelly barbed with long spikes.

The Trolls towered over their allies; the Rock Trolls easily twice the height of a man while the Ice Trolls stood even taller. They were massive beasts, cruel and wild. One Troll could instill terror in the heart of any man, but here had gathered more than two thousand.

The drums grew silent as two figures left the keep. They rode upon reptilian creatures with horned crests. The beasts spewed fire from nostrils that flared widely as they caught the scent of their enemies.

The Riders wore armor of deep black. Upon their great helms, brass horns gleamed brightly in the deepening gloom. From within the shadow of their visors an emerald fire burned, the feral glow filling all who looked upon them with fear.

They were the Balhain, Sur'kar's most powerful servants. Twisted by his might until all that remained was nothing more than murderous spirits endowed with great power. Even the Warders feared them, and with good reason, for the Balhain had once stood among their number.

The Morne continued to flow from the gates, the army swelling in size until its number became all but uncountable.

The Warriors of the east knew that they were hopelessly outnumbered; their foe would easily overwhelm them. Fear spread throughout the ranks, and many of the men felt despair darkening their hearts.

There were many heroes in those days, both Tal'shear and of the race of Men. Mighty warriors who bore enchanted weapons of great power. They gathered before the assembled army and rallied their spirits. Fire shone along enchanted blades, and they stood boldly before the enemy without fear.

Lightning flashed in the darkness overhead and resonating booms of thunder split the silence. A hot fetid wind blew down from the burning mountain reeking of sulfur.

Twice more the horns of Vi'Erud called, the discordant sound reaching far across the plain. The Trolls lumbered forward, their long legs quickly outpacing the charging Morne. The ground trembled beneath their weight.

Sur'kar's forces slammed into the Eastern army. Swords flashed and the cries of the dying contested with the clash of weapons.

The Trolls shattered the lines, and waded through the ranks reaping men as if they were wheat. Their iron cudgels growing slick with gore as they pulverized their enemies.

Arrows filled the dark sky; iron tips reeking havoc among the combatants wherever they fell. The Tal'shear engaged the giants, at great cost they slowed their progress and with long bladed spears the tall warriors began to slay the fearsome juggernauts.

Emerald sheets of fire rained down upon the armies, slaying friend and foe alike. The Warders rallied their power and engaged the enemy turning aside many of the attacks the Balhain hurled at them.

The Balhain became incensed by the arrogance of the Warders. They ceased attacking the soldiers, turning their attention to the hilltop. Bolts of power lashed out, and the Warders were hard pressed to defend themselves. The hilltop glowed with power and the eldritch forces being wielded there killed any who stood too near.

So'san, mightiest of the Warders was driven from the hilltop by the Balhains' attacks. He staggered through the field of combat protected only by his Anghor Shok, a man sworn to give his life in his defense. The Warrior fought valiantly, slaying any who would dare attack his charge.

So'san climbed a jagged hillside and stood above the combat. He watched in horror, as the army of the east was being overrun. Looking on helplessly as brave and powerful heroes fell and rose no more. The Balhain were pounding his companions mercilessly, their might setting the very air ablaze.

He knew they had lost; their brave ploy had failed. For Sur'kar yet remained in his tower within the volcanoes heart. He would not come out this day and they lacked the strength to enter.

His Anghor Shok was slain by one of the few remaining Giants, struck from behind, his body exploding into bloody fragments by the force of the blow.

Rage filled the Warder, an emotion he was unfamiliar with and could not fully control. Power filled him and he threw down the Troll with a bolt of searing energy. The Troll cried out in anguish as his body burst into flame.

Horrified by what he had just done, So'san fell to his knees weeping. He had violated the most sacred of his oaths. To use their strength to kill was against everything his order stood for. In the blink of an eye he had become akin to the evil that they now fought.

Tears clouded his vision and despair filled his heart. He knew today, right now, upon this field. Was their only chance to save this world and its people.

There was but one choice remaining, a desperate plan that would kill millions but it would slay Sur'kar as well. It offered a slim chance for the survivors to rebuild a new world without the darkness of the Kin Slayer.

He closed his eyes and called upon all the power he could master. He cast aside his barriers and allowed the might to build within him to a level he had never dared before. Pure power raged within him. He jumped to his feet. All of his restraints now gone, he felt as if he could simply close his fist and grind the world to dust.

The energy built within him until his body could hold no more, and as he burned away, he sent his final casting out into the darkness above.

The hilltop on which he stood exploded in a ball of golden light, so bright that it rivaled the sun. A blast of tremendous force raced out knocking nearby combatants from their feet. The soldiers closest to the blaze simply vanished consumed by the hellish energies So'san had unleashed.

The Balhain were caught in the open and the light burned them, shrieking in anguish they disappeared into the shadows. Dissolving into a dark mist driven by the wind.

The Warders looked on in shock, they knew not what So'san had done, but it was a violation of every law they lived by.

The glow subsided and a profound silence reigned upon the field of combat. Broken only by the groans of the dying and the rumble of the fire crowned mountain.

A new sound came on the wind, a deep rumbling screech that grew to deafening proportions quickly. The cloud of ash and fumes above raced off to the west as if it were simply wiped away by a giant hand. The sun shone brightly and a terrible hot wind raced across the landscape.

The sky brightened and a flaming sphere fell from the heavens, trailing a dark roiling cloud behind it.

There was little time to react; it struck with such force that it nearly split the Earth. A huge blinding fireball erupted from where Trothgar had once stood. A wall of searing flame and gale force winds flowed out from it with unbelievable speed and power. The hills were flattened, and the Keep of Vi'Erud vanished, the dark walls exploding into dust.

The Warders used their strength to hold back the conflagration, but they were not strong enough. Much of the army was destroyed, the men dying horribly as their bodies burst into flame.

Great crevices opened in the plain and magma rose up covering the landscape. The sky once more darkened, and fiery debris fell from the clouds to strike the tortured land.

A great crater had formed, and jagged mountains of glassy stone erupted out of the soil ringing the hellish pit. Through the haze of smoke and fire, the great volcano still stood at its center. It had been reduced to a mere fragment of its original size, but the power of Sur'kar had spared it from total destruction.

Within the maimed Calderas the great tower V'rag was no more, and with it Sur'kar's throne. Few were the survivors of that great battle, only those who had stood close to the Warders lived to tell the tale. The heroes and their weapons of power were forever lost in the destruction.

The world was cast into darkness for many years. An age of ice had settled upon the land, where only the strongest would survive.

*"The challenges of tomorrow are often
rooted in the deeds of antiquity."*

Lenar, Bard of Ril'Gambor

CHAPTER ONE

Casius stood facing into the wind, watching the gulls soar gracefully in the sky. Their plaintive calls a sharp contrast to the wind blown chimes ringing in the graveyard behind him.

Seventy-two Cairns of piled rock lay in orderly rows. Each with its own marker of carved wood that had turned gray with age. Here rested New Hope's dead, securely surrounded by a low wall of dry set stone, blanketed with thick patches of dark moss.

The graveyard had been built on the highest point of the island. A flat-topped hill of dark stone rising high among the eastern crags that bordered upon the vast expanse of the Southern Sea.

One hundred feet below him, powerful waves crashed onto the jagged rocks of the cliff's base. Striking with such force that they often sent spray high above the cliff, where it drifted down in tattered patches of fog, giving the whole area a surreal look.

A lone tree grew here. A hoary old pine moaning as the wind blew through its sparse needles. From its lowest branch hung the ringing set of chimes. Once, when new they had shone brightly in the sun as they moved in the breeze. The silver metal was now a deep tarnished green from years of exposure to the salt laden air. Their soft silvery notes still rang out, believed by many to keep the unsettled dead from rising.

Squinting his eyes against the afternoon sun, Casius let his gaze wander northward, where he could see a distant line of dark ominous clouds. Up thrust like an angry fist they rose above the horizon. He had little doubt that the approaching storm would strike the small island as many did during this time of the year.

The same wind that drove the clouds had also turned the day bitterly cold. Casius shivered, the icy air cutting through his thick wool shirt. He grimaced at the thought of the freezing rain, and deep drifts of snow soon to come. Gone now were the long days of summer and winter was fast approaching.

The Island of Kale lay north of the tropics, fifty miles off the eastern tip of Ao'dan. Winters here were long-lived and often brutal, testing the limits of both man and beast to survive.

Tiring of the wind's relentless fury, he turned his face away from its cold clawing fingers. Remembering at the last moment to ring the small brass bell he held to frighten any lurking spirits away. To look upon the dead was a dangerous thing for the living to do.

Gazing on the cairn that held his mother, he remembered how she would laugh at the superstitions held by the villagers of their home.

These hardy folk earned their livelihood from the sea. It was an arduous life, often perilous. The deep was capricious and scores of myths had grown around it. The fishermen often told tales of legendary creatures, both benign and malignant. Strange beings that populated the mysterious depths of the dark abyss, who at times would rise up from the deep and pull a ship and crew down to their doom.

Casius rang the battered bell. He did not believe in the tales of ghosts that would steal a man's spirit. To him it was nonsense, a belief grounded in ignorance. He carried it though, as did his father when he visited her grave. I am my father's son he thought, pragmatic to a fault.

He set the bell down upon the low wall and stepped easily over the barrier. A narrow path lay before him leading down the steep slope of the hill. He paused at the trail's head looking out over the island. From where he stood one could almost see it in its entirety.

A mile away, stretching to the west, lay a sea of gold and red, the Nahl Wood. The stately trees having changed their colors, heralding the beginning of the lean months yet to come.

The wind swirled through their tops scattering loose leaves high into the air. The skeletal branches swaying as if clawing at the escaping flecks of color, seeking desperately to hold onto the last remnants of their foliage.

The Wood was old and forbidding. Few men ever ventured far within its verdant confines, and fewer still ever came out again. When Casius was eight years old he had brazenly walked into its shadowy depths. His ill conceived plan to prove his manhood to his friends went terribly amiss when he had become hopelessly lost. Twisted about in a maze of snarled undergrowth, he wandered beneath the looming trees for two cold and lonely nights.

Tired and hungry he eventually staggered out of its clutches. His sudden emergence from the gloom of the wood startled a group of nervous woodcutters who were laboring nearby.

The people of New Hope considered him to be blessed by the gods; his father however insisted it had been nothing but good luck. To this day the sight of the wood still filled him with dread, although he has no clear recollection of what had happened to him during his time within it.

To the south, less than two miles away stood the settlement of New Hope, surrounded by fertile fields and orchards. It was a small village of stone cottages clustered closely together, thin tendrils of smoke rose from their chimneys above newly thatched roofs.

The village was well protected by a surrounding earthen bank crowned with a palisade of sharpened logs, through which a narrow gate allowed entry. Along the bank livestock meandered, eating at the lush grass to be found growing there.

The town had been built around the only beach on the island. A shallow cove that sheltered a crescent shaped shore of small water smoothed pebbles. The remainder of the island was ringed by low rocky cliffs that would tear a ship to pieces should one venture too close. The Settlers had chosen this island well; it was remote and easily defended.

Casius took one last look at the row of graves before starting down the narrow footpath. At its bottom stood his father's horse, an old gray gelding named Fleet. He was one of only three horses on the isle. A gift from Lord Baln, given to his father the day he was granted the title of Ship Thane, an honor even in such a small community as New Hope.

Fleet snorted when he noticed Casius was on his way down the slope. Tossing his head the horse pulled at the yellowed grass growing from between the lichen covered rocks.

The booming thunder of the waves lessened as he descended. A new sound was borne upon the wind. A deep resonating tone that repeated itself twice more before he realized what it was that he was hearing. It was coming from the village; someone was blowing the brass horn at the watchtower that over looked the bay.

Casius dashed down the slope, excitement making his heart race. The horn was never blown lightly; it was only sounded in emergencies, a call to arms for the men of the village.

He swung up onto Fleet's back; the old horse refused to budge, as it was busy eating. A heel to his flank and a light twitch of the reins got the recalcitrant animal moving.

Down out of the crags they raced, Fleet running as if he were a young colt. Leaving the last of the hills they sprinted through dormant fields, between rows of steaming haycocks. The wind roared in his ears, thick clods of muddy soil flying from Fleet's hooves.

Without slowing they plowed up the earthen bank scattering a group of chickens. Amid a flurry of squawking birds and flying feathers the horse bolted through the thick gate. The men standing behind it were just beginning to push it closed. A few of them cursed the reckless boy as they leapt from the charging horse's path.

He reined Fleet in as the gate boomed shut and the cross bar was slid into place. The village was in an uproar and through this chaos of running and shouting he led the horse. He still had no idea what was happening, but from the looks on the faces of the armed men scurrying about it was serious indeed.

The men bore axes, swords and bows. A few farmers even carried the sharp scythes they had been working with when the alarm had sounded. They took positions along the palisade their faces grim. Women, Children, and those too old or sick to wield a weapon went to the Long House, where armed men would protect them.

Securing the horse's reins to a post, he watched as men were being directed away from the wall and down towards the small beach.

As Casius joined the trail of men a thick-fingered hand fell upon his shoulder, stopping him before he had gone very far.

"Here now," a deep voice said merrily. "Where are you off to?"

Casius knew the voice and was not surprised to see the village butcher grinning down at him. Lon Hawsell, he was a burly man that smiled almost constantly. He wore his grin as often as he wore his bloodstained apron. "To see what's caused the alarm," Casius answered.

"That is no concern of yours, into the Long House with you," Lon's powerful grip turned him about.

"I am not a child," Casius said insulted by the butcher's suggestion. "In another month I will be sixteen."

Lon removed his hand and laughed, "My apologies good sir." He looked Casius over with a critical eye. "You have grown, now that I look at you." He held up a well-honed cleaver. "But you're not armed, besides your pa would be skinning me if I let you come." He pointed to the Long House with a wave of his weapon. "Now go," he said with a smile. "There's always next year."

Casius knew better than to argue the point. He went back up the road towards the Long House. He walked slowly, and once Lon had disappeared around the corner of one of the storehouses, he turned and followed after the big man.

Down the narrow lane he sped keeping close to the buildings. On his left he could see the wooden watchtower rising above the rocky outcrop of the cliff. The sounds of the waves smashing into the breakwater grew louder and the tang of salt was in the air.

As he circled around the smokehouse he could see out onto the waters of the cove. Small waves washed up the pebble beach, falling short of the flotsam left behind by last night's high tide.

A line of thirty men stood shoulder to shoulder just above the high tide mark, their axes and swords gleaming brightly in the sunlight. They were dour faced and anxious, the air heavy with tension. Casius could not see what it was that held the their attention. Skulking down the beach for a better view he moved among the overturned hulls of fishing skiffs. What he saw stopped him dead in his tracks.

Just inside the breakwater a lone vessel was making its way to the shore. It was a long ship, a raiding vessel from Cythera. Sleek and low the ship was built for speed; it sported a single mast from which only a tattered white pennant flew. Snapping in the brisk wind the standard raised a few eyebrows among the villagers.

Casius had heard the tales told by the sailors. These men had the reputation as bloodthirsty cutthroats. All who lived near the sea feared the Raiders. Although Kale was a poor target, with little gold, the men of the island still dreaded them.

The sleek vessel's oars rose and dipped with precision, slowly driving the ship towards the beach. A human skull yellowed with age was mounted upon the bow. The grotesque trophy swaying with the rocking of the ship, as if its empty sockets were scrutinizing the waterfront.

The men on the rocky beach stepped back as the bronze clad prow scraped up onto the shore. The ship ground to a halt and the oars were lifted out of the water. A line was thrown over the bow into the surf. The rope lolled about in the waves, no man on the shore moving to secure the vessel.

The men aboard the boat stood along the railing dressed in tattered clothing, defiantly staring down at the men on the beach. Heavily armed with swords and battle-axes these were men to be respected. A few of the sailors wore blood soaked bandages that drew black flies from the drying nets nearby. They had seen combat recently and from their appearance it would seem that they had lost the battle.

Casius noted movement down the beach behind one of the smaller boats that lay on its side, awaiting repair. He turned his head to look when Lon hissed from the line drawing his attention.

"Keep your eyes on the boat," he whispered glaring from the corner of his eye.

Casius nodded heeding Lon's command. He had seen the group of warriors moving into place. They were concealed, ready to ambush the Raiders should they attack. Casius relaxed somewhat for among their number he had seen the flame red hair of Baln Longwyrm himself, dressed in gleaming armor with his enormous ax in hand.

Casius's father stepped forward a broad bladed ax held casually at his side. Urold Rhaine was an older man nearing his fifty third year. His complexion was dark and his skin weathered from a lifetime lived within the elements. A mane of gray hair crowned his head, merging with a thick beard that hung to his chest.

He had a stern visage that was enhanced by his deep-set dark eyes, making him appear menacing. Despite his advanced years there were few men foolish enough to challenge him. Standing well over six feet he was a giant of a man with a barrel like chest and arms thicker than most men's legs. He looked up at the sailors with distrust. "What is it you want here?" He asked somewhat hotly, he was still wearing his leather apron and was not pleased at having had his work disrupted.

One of the sailors stepped to the vessel's bow. His hair was cut short and greased. An old scar ran from his temple, across his right eye and ended in a large lump of flesh at the corner of his mouth. It pulled at his lip giving him a permanent sneer. "I am G'relg Halmfist," he shouted a bit too loudly. "Who is lord of this place?"

"Baln Longwyrm," Urold replied. "What are your intentions, G'relg?"

"I would address him or his regent," the Sailor replied swinging his leg over the bow and dropping down into the shallow water lapping at the shore. He scooped the mooring line up and nonchalantly walked past Urold and through the line of men. Making the rope fast to a wooden post sunk into the earth. He crossed his arms and looked Urold over, evidently not impressed by what he saw.

Urold ignored the man's show of arrogance. "We have no house of nobles here, G'relg. I am named Urold, Ship Thane of New Hope, Speak your case with me or leave my shore." Urold shifted his grip on the haft of his ax, putting emphasis to his statement.

G'relg caught the thinly veiled threat and his face reddened in anger. He was a man not accustomed to being treated in such a manner. With an apparent great amount of effort he held his temper in check and chose his next words with care. "Very well," he said slowly. "We have escaped from the slave pens of Cythera, and are seeking your lord's protection."

The men on the beach whispered among themselves at the news. This was unheard of; no one had ever escaped the Raiders' clutches. The Isle of Cythera was a veritable prison, heavily guarded by evil men. The twin towers of Torinth protecting the entrance to the island's only harbor.

Urold cursed, "You bring with you the very ship stolen from Bjorn's harbor! Are you daft man? We are not a large nation who can withstand the Raiders. Look about you," Urold indicated the men behind him with a wave of his hand.

"Farmers and Fishermen, not warriors trained for battle." Urold shook his head, "Those black hearted bastards will be out in force searching for you, and they will not stop until you are found. You have brought danger down upon all our heads with your recklessness."

"Many good men died in the taking of this vessel," G'relg snapped. "I would not see their lives wasted, we will not go back."

Urold reexamined the group of refugees. There was something about these men that did not strike true. He exhaled slowly before he spoke. "I did not ask you to return," he said. "But you cannot remain here with that vessel."

G'relg nodded in agreement, "Look Urold, we do not wish to bring harm to your people. We are tired and hungry, the raiders are combing the seas about the larger nations and we cannot hope to confront them. We have come here as our last hope, seeking only the protection of your lord's banner, the ship can be burned for all I care."

Urold grunted at the mention of burning the vessel. He thought it a fitting end to such a craft. Try as he may he could think of no honorable way to be rid of these men. Despite his misgivings they had come under the flag of truce and have openly pled for sanctuary. By all the customs and laws of his people, Lord Baln was honor bound to grant it. Still he did not like the looks of these sailors. They appeared to be too proficient in the weapons they carried.

It was G'relg that concerned him the most. The man was willful and proud. He had the eyes of a man who has killed often, and has found it to his liking.

Lord Baln was no fool; if there was a way to send this lot back to sea he would find it. Urold shouldered his ax his mind made up.

"Very well then G'relg," he said with a shrug. "Leave your arms with your shipmates and I shall escort you to the long house where Lord Baln will hear your petition."

After a moment's hesitation G'relg removed his sword belt and tossed it up to one of the men along the rail. "I am ready," he said facing Urold.

"Your men are to remain on the ship," Urold ordered. "Should they leave the vessel before our return, my men will cut them down." Ignoring the grumbling complaints from the ship he looked to the men of the village to ensure that they had understood.

As his eyes fell upon his son, a flicker of anger crossed his brow. The boy quickly lowered his eyes knowing he had done wrong. Urold looked past him to one of the men, a young farmer named Jaren. "Go and inform Lord Baln that we are coming."

Jaren nodded and sprinted up the beach, tossing the club he carried to another as he passed.

"Lead on good Ship Thane," G'relg said with a smile, the scar on his lip twisting it into a scowl.

Urold whispered to Lon, "Guard that ship well. I do not trust these men, there is more here than what they have told us."

"There will be no mischief from the crew while we hold the shore." The butcher answered flipping his cleaver skillfully.

"This way," Urold said leading G'relg up the narrow lane towards the Long House. Several men followed keeping a watchful eye on the sailor.

Casius gave his father an apologetic look as he passed, and was relieved by the wink he got in response. His father understood what it was like to be a young man and would not punish him for coming to the beach.

He fell in step behind the group of men following them up the lane. This was the biggest event that had ever happened in his lifetime and he wanted to see everything that was going to take place.

CHAPTER TWO

They walked into the square at the village's center, across the open ground stood the Long House. The building served as the meeting hall of New Hope and the seat of Lord Baln's power. It was an impressive structure, fashioned in the manner of the old ways.

Constructed of massive split logs, it spanned fifty feet in width and three times that in length. Rising nearly sixty feet from the ground to the top of its steeply peaked roof, it was the village's largest building, and unlike the others, the long house sported a roof of split cedar shingles.

With intricately carved wooden pillars depicting various mythical beasts framing its doorway. It was the only building in town to have any form of decoration.

People crowded the entry, and more were coming across the square. It seemed to Casius that every citizen of the Isle was on hand to witness the novel event.

The men of the town eyed G'relg warily, not trusting any man who would willingly sail upon a raider ship. They reluctantly moved aside as Urold led the man into the building.

Once through the doorway Casius stepped off to the side and joined a group of boys who were gawking at the proceedings.

Two large fire pits stood within the Hall's center, each holding a cheery blaze that drove back the cold. The thick smoke from the fires filled the upper vault of the ceiling enshrouding the large beams supporting the roof. The haze drifted slowly about until escaping through the four large smoke holes cut into the ceiling above.

The walls were covered with panels of polished dark wood. From which Brightly colored shields hung, running the length of the Hall.

At the opposite end of the Hall hung a dark red banner embroidered with a coiled serpent in white. The ancient symbol of the house Longwyrm, A flag that had a long history and had been carried into many a battle.

Below the standard a large Battle-axe rested in bronze mounts, its razor sharp blades shone brightly in the flickering light of the fires. The haft of the weapon was of dark iron and five feet in length. The weapon was immense, and few were the men who could lift it, let alone wield it in battle.

Below the axe set a large table. Fashioned from thick planks of oak, its top marred by many years of use. Ten high-backed chairs of dark wood and leather lined the side facing the Hall's center. It was of simple construction, the carpenter choosing strength over beauty in its creation. Twenty other tables of similar construction lined the hall. In place of chairs these had benches on either side.

Baln stood behind the table, his ax at his back. He watched the men enter impassively, his hands resting on the back of his chair. At just shy of seven feet tall he made even the Ship Thane appear small in comparison. He was a figure of heroic proportions dressed in glittering chain mail with a cloak of dark scarlet hanging from his shoulders.

His hair shone in the gloom, a blazing red mantle that fell to his shoulders. Unlike the men of the village he kept his beard trimmed short enhancing his firm jaw. His eyes were bright beacons of ice blue that burned with intelligence. They locked with G'relg's as Urold led him down the Hall's center.

The chamber hummed with a hundred conversations. Lord Baln raised his hand and the talking slowly stopped. The silence grew and was only broken by the sound of an occasional cough and the popping of the fires, outside a dog barked in the distance.

"Urold," Lord Baln spoke in a powerful voice that carried through the chamber with ease. "Who have you brought before me?"

The Ship Thane tipped his head slightly as a sign of respect. "I bring G'relg, Leader of the raider ship that has come to our shores." Urold waited as a burst of excited conversations filled the hall. Once the talking had died down he continued. "He and his companions have come under the flag of truce and seek sanctuary under your protection."

"A Raider seeking sanctuary?" Lord Baln mused.

"Not raiders Lord Baln," G'relg corrected, taking a bold step forward. "We are free men who have escaped from Cythera."

Lord Baln shook his head. "No one escapes from Cythera G'relg. You and your men have come in a raider ship, and you have the bearing of a raider." He raised his hand cutting off any response that G'relg would make. "Your tale is weak, I cannot find it within me to believe that so few men have managed to steal one of Bjorn's prized ships."

"We numbered over two hundred on the eve of our escape," G'relg interrupted. "Four vessels in all were taken. We alone survived the tempest that covered our flight."

"Then fortune favored you and your men," Lord Baln said his voice still filled with skepticism.

"Fortune had little to do with it." G'relg snapped his patience wearing thin. "The men on that ship are accomplished seamen, stripped of their livelihoods when their merchant ship was taken off the coast of Alcedoria."

"Where were you taken captive then, G'relg?" Lord Baln asked.

"I was seized off the coast of Arn by the same raiders a few nights earlier." G'relg replied without hesitation.

Lord Baln leaned against the table the wood creaking in protest. "G'relg, we have avoided the raiders eyes for many years." He paused looking over his subjects. "Your arrival has placed all that we have built here in jeopardy. Bjorn will not stop in his search until you and your men are found. He will make an example of any who have been foolish enough to have given you aid. That is the price of granting you sanctuary, a price I would not care to pay."

The people in the Hall agreed with their lord, and a boisterous few yelled for G'relg to leave immediately.

Lord Baln waited for silence to return. "As holder of these lands and its sworn protector. I am bound by both honor and law to grant you your request."

The Hall erupted with cries of protest. A few of the men pounded the tables in anger.

This time, it was Urold who stilled the protest. "Silence!" he shouted above the din. "Do not forget in whose Hall we stand!"

The crowd grew quiet. The faces of the people burned with anger as they glared at the Raider.

Lord Baln gave Urold a nod of thanks. "I am no fool G'relg," he continued. "Do not make the mistake of thinking of me as such. Your tale has flaws, Cytherans brand their captives." Baln touched his forehead, above his nose. "Here is where the slaver's mark is placed. I see no such mark on you. This is just one part of your tale that makes me wary."

"We escaped before the brand was put to us," G'relg replied hastily.

Lord Baln walked around the table and stood facing G'relg. His eyes burned with anger as he looked down on the roguish man. "Listen well, I will grant your request and give you what protection I can." A look about the room stilled any protest that was arising.

"While in my lands you and your men will never again possess or bear arms of any kind. You will tend to the needs of livestock and till the earth. No voice will be given you in this Hall, nor shall you enjoy the rights of property ownership. Your home will be the stables, and your beds the fodder within."

Lord Baln lifted his finger and pointed it at G'relg's heart. "It will be by my charity alone that you live among us, violate any of the laws of this land and you will find the hangman's noose about your necks." He crossed his arms as if daring the man to attack him. "Though my terms are harsh, the law has been followed and thus my honor is served."

The sounds of barely contained laughter drifted through the Hall. The villagers approved of their lord's decision, for the proud men upon the ship would never yield to such terms.

G'relg was furious and it was through clenched teeth that he spoke. "You offer us nothing more than Bjorn offers his slaves."

Baln shook his head. "I have offered you far more than Bjorn ever would. I offer you freedom, you are free to stay or go while you still have your ship. Decide tonight for in the morning I will have it hauled ashore and burned. I will not long suffer such a foul craft on my beach." Without waiting for G'relg to reply Baln turned his back to the man. Leaving the Hall through a small doorway that led to his private chambers behind the serpent banner.

Chaos erupted in the Hall as a hundred people shouted at once. Many approved of their lord's judgment for they too did not trust the shady men. There were a few dissenters but their arguments were soon lost in the din as people began filing out of the Long House.

G'relg turned and faced Urold. "You seem pleased by the insult handed to us by your lord." He spat onto the hard packed earthen floor.

Urold shrugged his shoulders, "I am only wondering how long your vessel will burn."

G'relg glared, "I would not light your torches just yet, Ship Thane." He turned and stormed out of the building.

Urold followed him across the square and down the lane to the beach. As he walked he noticed Casius following a short way off, with a wave of his hand he beckoned for him to catch up.

Casius picked up his pace until he walked beside his father. "Do you think they will stay, Father?"

"Not likely," Urold said with a smile. "Lord Baln judged them rightly, and has kept the law. Sparing New Hope the trouble of having the likes of them living among us."

"Are we so certain that they are more than what they claim?"

Urold thought about his response for a moment before speaking. "These men are more than simple sailors. I doubt that they have ever served as crew on a merchant vessel.

"They carry themselves as warriors, and are marked by the scars of swordplay." Urold gripped his Son's shoulder. "When a man is captured by raiders he is beaten and the mark of Bjorn's towers is burned onto his brow.

"I have heard it said that they even have an enchanter who binds the slaves. So that they can never attempt escape should the chance arise. Our friend G'relg here has never felt the weight of a slaver's shackle, men like him would die before succumbing to such a plight."

"Then if they are not escaped slaves," Casius said puzzled by the day's events. "Who are they, and why come here at all?"

"That's the question that has me worried." Urold replied. "They may be nothing more than a mutinous crew of raiders who have fallen from Bjorn's favor. It matters little, for they will be gone on the morning's tide. The terms Baln offered will not sit well with this lot."

"What if they were sent here simply to spy on us? Once they leave they will return and tell Bjorn all they have seen." Casius said giving voice to the nagging thought in the back of his mind.

Urold stopped walking and gave his son and approving look. "You are growing into manhood fast son. Those are my very thoughts on this matter as well.

"Were we cut of the same cloth as these men, I would slay them and burn their ship." Urold shrugged, "Let Lord Baln worry this bone, he is a wise man and will do the right thing." He picked up the pace to catch up with the stiff-backed sailor.

When they reached the shore Urold motioned Casius to come no further. Casius stopped and watched while the two men walked to the ship's bow. He did not hear the words G'relg spoke or the replies from his men. Their faces however clearly displayed their anger at Lord Baln's offer. G'relg stood glaring at the villagers for a moment before climbing on board the beached vessel.

It appeared to Casius that his father had been correct in his assumption. There was no way that these men would subjugate themselves to the life Lord Baln's conditions would grant them.

Urold added to the insult by posting sentries. Twenty men guarded the beach within plain view of the ship. They built a large fire. Intending to stay the night until the vessel left with the morning's tide.

The remaining villagers wandered away, the excitement now over. There was always work to be done with winter fast approaching.

Thick clouds blew in that afternoon and a light rain had begun to fall making the day all the more colder.

It was late in the afternoon when Casius returned home. The small two-room cottage he shared with his father was ice cold, and he quickly set a fire in the hearth. The crackling logs shed light and warmth making the small cote comfortable.

After his mother's death from fever two years ago he had assumed the duties of the household. This mostly consisted of keeping it clean. Casius and his father never cooked; instead they took their meals at Lord Baln's table in the Long House.

Their neighbor, a comely widow took in their wash for a small fee.

For many months some of the single women sought to catch Urold's eye. His intentions became clear over time. The Ship Thane would never again wed. His heart belonged only to one woman, Cewyn. The memory of her could never be replaced.

Casius straightened up the room and opened a cedar-lined chest at the foot of his bed. Beneath his clothing at the very bottom he kept his two prized possessions. Leather bound books, a gift from his mother when she had taught him to read.

Lighting an oil lamp he settled down into his father's chair. He knew his father would not be home tonight. Duty would keep him on the beach with the men guarding the unwanted ship.

He turned the pages carefully, books were rare on the Island, and few of the villagers could even read. His mother had been educated and had insisted that Casius would be as well. In fact she had named him after one of the more colorful characters found in one of Lenar's tales.

The book was not new to him; he had read it a hundred times over. Of the two he owned this was his favorite, a tale of the heroic deeds of the armored knights of Ril'Gambor. The stories although familiar, still thrilled him and sparked his imagination.

For a short while as he read, he too would become encased in polished steel thundering into danger on a horse's back, his lance tip glowing in the sunlight. He would scale the heights of the Dragon Spine Mountains and slay the Giants that haunted the snow-clad peaks.

As the hours passed, his eyes grew heavy, until he could no longer focus on the handwritten letters. He closed the book and returned it to the chest. Adding more wood to the fire he blew out the lamp and lay in his bed. He was asleep in moments, the glow of the fire dancing on the plaster walls.

Urold stirred the fire into life, sending a swarm of golden embers skyward. The tiny sparks swirled up the beach riding on the stiff wind. It was well past midnight and had grown freezing cold. The rain had stopped several hours ago. A thin film of ice was now forming on the shallow pools where the water lay.

Heavy clouds blanketed the sky, cutting off any light from the moon and stars above. The men sat huddled around the fire, their eyes never straying far from the ship. The men aboard the vessel no longer looked out over the gunwales. They had hunkered down seeking what warmth they could find.

"Damn!" The village's blacksmith cursed, swatting at the flying embers that had blown into his clothes. "I get enough of this at my forge."

The men about the fire grinned at his antics.

"Sorry, Wahlen." Urold apologized. It was his stirring of the fire that had sent the sparks onto the man. He smiled as the smith tossed a small piece of driftwood at him.

"It's cold," Wahlen said stating the obvious. "Coldest night of the year I'd wager."

Urold nodded in agreement, "Just keep alert." He warned the men. "Cold or not it's all too easy to fall asleep in the coming hours. The tide is turning, and our guests will soon be gone. Then we can go to our homes and get our rest."

"Tis a pity that," The Smith said exposing a mouthful of broken teeth when he smiled. "I was looking forward to a good fight." He twisted his fire-reddened face into a pout that best suited a small child.

"You are a nasty bastard, Wahlen." One of the men said in a fair imitation of Urold's voice.

The men about the fire laughed loudly, each hoping to disturb the rest of those aboard the boat.

G'relg muttered a curse. Let them laugh now, he thought. He slid away from the gunwale, back down into the darkness between the rowing seats. He pulled his share of the canvas sail over his shivering body.

"What are we supposed to do now G'relg?" Dulrich complained. He was the largest and most vocal of the group, a real threat to G'relg's leadership. "Freeze to death while we await the dawn?"

G'relg drew his dagger, and in the blink of an eye he had its keen edge pressed hard against the man's throat. Holding it tight as a thin bead of blood seeped out along its length.

"Quiet fool," G'relg hissed. "Do you want to face Bjorn with the news of our failure. I was told that should we fail to gain their confidence, to lay low and wait."

Dulrich's eyes shone with hatred, "I am not as stupid as you would take me to be. But what is it we are waiting for, a sign from the heavens?"

G'relg relaxed the pressure on the knife, "I know not, only that Bjorn had said our way would be made clear enough, just stay silent and wait."

Dulrich nodded, "For now G'relg we will wait." He said threateningly while leaning back rubbing the thin cut on his throat.

G'relg mulled over Dulrich's tone; sooner or later he knew he would have to kill the man. Dulrich was a natural leader and the men followed him. G'relg could not allow this threat to his command to continue.

"If you have finished playing children. Perhaps we can return to the work at hand." A thin voice spoke, barely a whisper above the sighing of the wind, and the distant rolling thunder of the waves slamming into the breakwater. It came from the darkness, soft and filled with malice, a voice that froze the hearts of those who heard it.

Caught by surprise the men drew their weapons and turned to the ship's stern from where the voice had emanated. Their faces lost all color and their eyes widened with fear. Steel rang upon wood as they hastily cast their weapons aside.

Vool, the enchanter had come and where the dark one traveled, death followed in all her glory. He was tall and thin, wrapped in a voluminous cloak of purest black. The stiff wind that tore at the men's clothing did not touch Vool. His robe lay perfectly still only stirring as he moved.

He stood with his arms crossed, his hands tucked within the sleeves. The hood of his robe was up hiding his face within the inky darkness of its shadow. A sickly emerald light shone from his eyes. Even in the torchlight nothing could be seen of his face. There were stories of people who had looked upon Vool's face. In all the tales, they had died a horrible death.

For once in his life G'relg was speechless. He had heard of the horrible power this man wielded, if such a being could truly be called a man. It was rumored that even the touch of his shadow could render you insane.

The men scurried backwards, much to Vool's amusement. They fought with each other to put as much distance as possible between themselves and the shadowy figure. The aura surrounding him filled them with uncontrolled fear. A few of the men had actually soiled themselves in their terror.

Vool stood motionless, a patch of darkness in the night. "Do you forget your station G'relg?" he asked in his whisper like voice.

G'relg hastily bowed his head, motioning for the others to do likewise. "Nay Lord Vool," He stammered feeling the loathsome touch of those malevolent eyes. "Your sudden appearance simply startled me." He added in explanation. "How did you come to be here? There are no hiding places on this ship." he cringed at once, realizing he was treading upon dangerous ground. No one ever dared to question Vool. It was a quick way to meet your end.

"That is of no consequence," Vool replied. "Heed my words well, you are to kill every man in this village. There is no room for mistakes, fail to accomplish this task and you will spend the rest of your life begging for the release of death." He left the threat to their imaginations. No explanation was needed, as his reputation was enough.

"We are outnumbered and under heavy guard, how are we to accomplish this task?" G'relg asked flinching; he expected death to strike him at any moment.

When Vool answered his voice had grown menacing. He was beginning to lose his patience with these men. "Ready your blades, the way will be opened for you."

Vool turned his back to the men, raising his arms he began to chant softly. The sleeves of his robes fell back, revealing hands so thin they appeared to be nothing more than pallid skin stretched over bone.

The words he spoke were in a language that no human tongue could emulate. The incantation sent searing waves of pain through the sailors' bodies. It was as if a knife was tearing at their very souls. They collapsed unable to stand, watching in horror as a faint blue fog fell from Vool's hands.

The strange mist filled the boat and seeped out over the railings, flowing smoothly down the hull of the ship. As with Vool's attire, the wind simply passed through the mist, leaving it unchanged. The fog's vaporous tendrils drifted slowly up the beach towards the encamped men. Writhing as it went growing thicker until it spread out along the entire shore.

G'relg rolled in agony completely covered by the mist. Every hair on his body stood on end, his skin burning at its touch. He opened his mouth to scream but no sound would escape his lips.

On the beach Urold leapt to his feet. "What madness is this?" He shouted a warning to the others that something was amiss. From the ship he could hear the sounds of soft chanting. "Sound the alarm!" he said raising his ax. "This is a ruse of some sort."

Vool smiled maliciously from within his robe's shadow. He clapped his hands together with a resounding boom that shattered the peace. The earth heaved, rocking the ship violently. The fog raced outward in a rolling wave, encompassing the entire village in a shroud two feet deep.

The pain disappeared with the shaking of the ship. G'relg rolled onto his side and slowly drew his dagger. For a brief instant he actually thought about driving it between Vool's shoulder blades.

Urold flinched as the unnatural mist washed over his legs. Its touch was freezing and sapped his strength. He fell to the ground fear filling him as his consciousness faded. Fight it! His mind screamed as he slipped into darkness.

Vool spun about his left arm pointing to the town. "Go now!" He commanded the stunned sailors. "Their slumber will last less than one hour. Be quick about your task and remember let no man survive this night." Vool crossed his arms and faded away into the darkness.

G'relg stood for a moment staring at the now vacant deck. He tested the edge of the dagger with his thumb a grim smile coming to his lips. "Let's go," he said to the dumbfounded men. "There are throats to be cut." He vaulted over the ship's side. Upon landing he searched for his first victim, the Ship Thane.

The men followed G'relg, not out of eagerness but out of fear of Vool's power.

They moved through the town rapidly, slaying every man that they came across. Vool's fog had put to sleep the entire village. The animals remained unaffected, stray hogs rooted around the buildings, excited by the smell of blood in the air.

Dulrich caught up with G'relg as he worked along the palisade, slitting the unconscious guards throats. Both men were bloody, their knives dripping with gore.

"This is grisly work we're doing," Dulrich complained. He was a marauder, but this was pushing his limits. "Bjorn has damned us all to hell this night."

G'relg laughed, "And just where was it you think you were going?" He asked wiping the blood from his blade. "All Bjorn has done is make our work easier. His bargain with Vool has spared us the prospect of facing these men in armed combat. Or would you rather have faced Baln in a fight?"

Dulrich shook his head, "Of course not." He knew there were few men who could have done so and lived. "But this is murder most foul."

G'relg slapped him on the shoulder, "Be thankful that Bjorn has our best interest at heart."

Dulrich failed to catch the sarcasm in G'relg's voice. "Now that's a cart of dung," he replied. "The only thing on Bjorn's mind is gold and how to get more of it. If it means selling his own mother he would do so without hesitation or remorse."

"That's right," G'relg said. "Wealth and power, remember he gets the lion's share but we will still profit from this escapade."

Dulrich had seen much of the village he knew there was little of any worth here. "Slaves," he suggested.

"Only women and children," G'relg reminded him. "There's a fair number to be had here for Bjorn's Black Trumpet fields. At a gold Talen apiece this trip should set us up nicely."

Dulrich smiled at the thought of the wealth to be had. "Perhaps I'll find me a handsome woman, tis a long voyage home after all."

"Cold as well," G'relg added.

Both men laughed and returned to their murderous foray through the town. They took great care ensuring that Vool's instructions were followed.

When the hour had passed, the streets of New Hope ran red with the blood of her citizens.

Vool stood upon the watchtower's roof, unfazed by the cold. He watched the men as they combed the town, satisfied by their diligence and speed. If his master's divining had been accurate, then the God Slayer was here. An unfamiliar feeling passed through Vool. It was the touch of fear. His master had ordered the God Slayer's death and Vool was to see it done.

The Balhain had lived far too long to risk his own death. The raiders were the answer; these greedy men would do the deed, and by their own hands ensure their doom.

To the east the sky was brightening, even the meager amount of sunlight that filtered through the building clouds was causing him pain.

Vool took one last look at the village before fading away into the shadows. Confident in the victory over the one being that threatened his existence.

CHAPTER THREE

Marcos stood within a circle of monolithic pillars. The graven rock towering fifteen feet above him. The twelve stones had been erected long ago upon the summit of Ga'ron. A broad hill that stood surrounded by dense forest in the land of El'radrien, upon the Isle of Eol.

The pillars were smoothly polished, reflecting the glittering light from the stars above. Marcos walked about the ring looking at each one in turn. Upon each, a crown bearing seven stars was carved. Beneath the crown intricate runes of brilliant silver had been skillfully inlaid. These markings glowed faintly in the darkness, bright swirling bands of sapphire light dancing within their depths.

A soft warm breeze blew across the hilltop stirring his mottled robe, bringing with it the smell of jasmine and wildflowers. Winter was coming to the world, but on Eol it could take no hold. The island had been perpetually blessed by the warmth of spring.

"Where are you now old friends?" he asked the quiescent stones. "Now that the season has turned, and you are needed most." He stepped forward, placing his slender hand upon the fiery runes.

The rock flared to life beneath his touch, the light within it intensifying. "So'san," he said aloud, reading the inscription. He looked up as if expecting some response from the rigid rock.

"In our youth we failed, and it was by your desperate act that this world was given another chance at freedom." His eyes wandered across the circle. His mind recalling memories he had long thought forgotten.

"But the cost of our desperation was high. A terrible price this world has paid, and now it may have all been for naught." He removed his hand, the light fading in response. "I alone must succeed now. Where we, at the height of our power could not."

Marcos walked across the carpet of soft grass to the center of the ring. Marked by a broad flat stone that rose slightly above the ground.

It was a sizable rock, dark gray with bands of sparkling quartz running through it. Countless rainfalls had worn the edges smooth over the ages. A circular shaft pierced its center, its bottom disappearing into darkness.

As he drew near the stone, the earth trembled. The sound of rushing water disturbed the stillness. Rising from the depths, the shaft quickly filled to within a few inches of it's top.

Marcos extended his hand over the water. Deep within its depths eight points of argent light flared to life. Spiraling about in the fluid they grew in size as they rose to the surface.

"Sa'ramir," he said softly. "Long have you guarded the tokens of our power. The time has come once more for you to release your icy hold, and free your charges."

The water roiled, overflowing onto the stone. The well glowed as if the water itself burned. Suddenly the surface burst, and eight brilliant rings of light rose into the air. Resembling the stars above, they shone with a clean pure light. They revolved slowly a few feet above the well's mouth.

Marcos reached out and one of the rings settled into the palm of his hand. The glow faded revealing a band of gleaming gold, fashioned from three separate strands tightly woven together. The ring's weight seemed to grow as he placed it on his finger.

The other rings dimmed and sank back down into the well, disappearing from view. The water's surface once more became tranquil as it slowly receded back down into the dark depths.

Marcos made a fist and a point of light flared upon the gold. "So simple a thing," he said softly lowering his hand. At one time long ago, the wearing of the band had filled him with excitement. He had felt that nothing was beyond him. The long years since had taught him the truth of it. The gleaming token was a fetter, one that could not be broken. The responsibility that came with it would make even the most courageous soul recoil from its touch.

Ravin Suni stood just outside the circle. He was scarcely discernible, a dark shape standing within the moon-cast shadows of the monoliths. He had heard little of what Marcos had said.

His attention was focused elsewhere. His eyes were constantly searching out the darkness. Alert for any threats to his charge. Almond shaped and dark they gave him the appearance of being half-asleep. A dangerous assumption many men had made in the past, often it would be the last mistake they would ever make.

He wore a simple linen tunic of light green, belted about his waist with a broad band of dark leather. Two iron staves were tucked through the belt. Their metal was dark and reflected no light. On his feet he wore sandals of soft leather, their thongs wrapping tightly about his calves.

Marcos left the ring of stones, his shoulders slumped with worry. He wore his dark hair short. The lightest touch of gray graced his temples. His face was narrow, with a thin nose above a well-trimmed goatee. He looked to be about forty but his eyes burned with wisdom beyond his apparent years. Their color shifted from gray to blue and green as he looked about.

He gave Suni a nod as he strode past, his ring-laden hand resting on the hilt of the long sword that hung from his waist. The scabbard swinging with each step he took.

Suni followed him in silence as they trod a seldom-traveled path down to the forest edge. He walked without making a sound, his gait smooth and graceful.

The mighty oaks of the Fa'lain Wood towered above them. The canopy rustled in the darkness, blocking out the moon and stars above. A deep gloom enveloped the thick boles. Broken only by soft patches of phosphorescent light, emitted by long sheets of hanging moss that swayed gently in the breeze.

A thin footpath led deep into the wood, coming to a collection of ruins. Thick roots had cracked the stone, pushing aside ancient walls, as the forest strove to reclaim its lost ground. Tall spires of stone had once touched the sky, but now all that remained were piles of rubble, and broken foundations. Thousands of years ago this had been a thriving city. Now it was nothing more than a sad testament to the people who had once lived here.

Through the tree and rubble strewn thoroughfares they walked in silence, with Marcos leading the way. They traveled less than a mile when they came to a circular building with a conical roof of tarnished bronze. It stood within a small plaza. The polished marble paving remained untouched by the encroaching forest. A low ivy covered wall enclosed the area, festooned with bright blossoms of red and yellow. The delicate flowers filled the air with a sweet fragrance.

An arched opening led into the plaza. Where a small fountain gurgled in the shadows. The flowing water spilling over into a shallow pool teeming with brightly colored fish.

A small garden grew here, in large planters of stone. It had long ago grown wild. Flowering vines spilled out onto the ground in a delicate carpet of vibrant colors.

Marcos lowered himself onto a stone bench, watching the water as it flowed down into the pool. The flashes of color as the fish struck at small insects on its surface always intrigued him. There was beauty here, both simple and elegant. He would often come to this place to relax. The sights and sounds soothing his troubled mind.

Suni stood a few paces off, allowing him his solitude. Marcos would speak when he was ready. Until he did Suni maintained his vigil. The Anghor Shok was a patient man; he had spent a lifetime perfecting the skill.

"The time for us to leave our seclusion has come Suni," Marcos said softly. "Our enemy is stirring and I have felt the echoes of his castings. His servants have openly used their power, Confident in their master's strength." Marcos looked to his stoic companion. "I only pray that he has not grown so powerful that we cannot stop him."

Suni inclined his head as he spoke, offering a rare piece of wisdom from his studies. "Victory is never certain, until it has been accomplished."

"The universe is rarely certain on many things," Marcos answered. "I will ask you once again old friend. Will you not take up the sword?"

Suni shook his head, "I cannot forsake my vow. It encompasses all that I am. No Anghor Shok can wield an edged weapon, and remain Anghor Shok." Suni rested his hands upon his staves, "The Kalmari are the weapons of my order."

"And yet you do know the way of the sword," Marcos said somewhat flustered by Suni's refusal. "Did you not wield one in training?"

Suni nodded sharply, "A blunt edged blade only. To know the weapon of your opponents gives you the advantage. Ignorance often guarantees defeat." Suni looked unflinchingly into Marcos's eyes. "What you ask would violate my very nature. Have you grown so desperate that you would make me akin to So'san?"

Anger flashed in Marcos's eyes, a faint aura of power surrounded him. He took a breath and calmed himself. Suni had only spoken the truth. Who was he to ask this man to toss aside the doctrines he had followed all his life? The nebulous glow around him faded, "Forgive me Suni." He asked knowing Suni had felt no insult, no Anghor Shok allowed his emotions to rule him. "What So'san did was an act of desperation, in his despair he had lashed out. His might was enhanced by his emotions, and for the briefest instant he had shone as the sun on that dark day.

"His mind pulled the creator's hammer down from the heavens, a burning mountain of stone and metal that smote the armies of Sur'kar, and the forces of freemen as well. Millions died in the inferno of fire and wind. The earth nearly cracked in twain from the force of the blow. Rivers of molten rock burst from the tortured ground, igniting the forests of the world. The heat was so intense that the oceans boiled in places and a thick blanket of dust darkened the sky.

"A deep winter seized the earth, lasting decades. Glaciers crept down out of the mountains, driving men out of their lands. A third of the world starved, and yet we persevered.

"Our powers were hard pressed to even save a few, but we managed. Sur'kar's tower, V'rag was gone, and the mountain in which it had been built was sundered in half. Of him we could find no sign, some of us thought him to be destroyed. But I knew better, something that evil and powerful is not so easily done away with."

"Did you not search him out?" Suni asked. He knew the lore, it was taught to those who entered the temple of Isembahl. There the old ways remained, preserved by the clerics.

Only a few young men were chosen to enter its halls of learning. There they are taught the skills needed to become a guardian. Few ever finish the training; many die during the trials of blood. Suni was one of the few; he had mastered all that the war masters could teach.

"His body was vaporized," Marcos said. "He was little more than a spirit, a shadow of what he once was. It would have been easier to find a child's breath in a gale. Besides we were far too busy trying to save this world.

"Much of this world's beauty has been lost forever. My people could no longer remain, haunted by the knowledge of what we had brought here with us. It was in grief that they boarded the great ships and left. Returning once more to the Darkling Sea. I alone of the Tal'shear remained, convinced that Sur'kar would once more come to power, and fulfill his malign ambitions."

"What course do we take now?" Suni asked.

"We must seek out a man, one of honor. Who is a skillful swordsman with the fortitude required for the task before us."

CHAPTER FOUR

Casius awoke gagging. He lay face down on the dirt floor in a pool of vomit. He tried to move and found that his hands had been tightly bound behind his back. His wrists burned from the rough cord cutting into his flesh. Rolling onto his side he heaved violently as another intense feeling of nausea washed over him.

Casius's head pounded as if at any moment it would split open. His whole body ached with the effort of trying to empty an already vacant stomach. Once the heaving subsided, he lay very still. The bitter stench of bile assaulted his nose, threatening to start the whole affair over again.

Opening his eyes he took note of his surroundings. He lay on the floor of the Long House, near Baln's table. How on earth had he gotten here, he wondered? The last memory he had was of being in his own bed. He still wore the long nightshirt that he had slept in.

Now he had awakened, to find himself in the midst of a small number of women and children. They were in various states of wakefulness as well. They too were bound tightly. Many of them were just as sick as he. The air of the Hall was repugnant, reeking of vomit and spilt blood.

A light metallic clinking sound drew his attention away from his fellow prisoners. Seated in Baln's very chair was G'relg. The Raider was a horror to behold. A nightmarish figure covered with blood from head to toe. From his relaxed manner Casius knew that none of the blood was his own.

He was counting a small number of coins that lay piled before him. The soft clinking was the sound of them dropping from his gore-covered fingers into a leather bag. Leaning against the chair at his right hand was Lord Baln's battle-ax.

Casius's hopes died when he saw the weapon. He knew what it signified. There would be no rescue. Lord Baln and his men were surely dead. His father would be among that number as well.

He closed his eyes and swallowed his grief; there would be time for it later. He heard the sounds of footsteps. Opening his eyes he watched as the remainder of the sailors crossed the halls earthen floor. Like G'relg they too were covered in blood. Casius wondered at what could have happened. It looked to him as if every one of the sailors was present and not a single man bore a wound. Even those who had arrived bandaged were hale without a mark. How could New Hope have fallen without the death of at least some, if not most of these men? He wondered silently not daring to speak.

G'relg finished his silent count and tied the sack tightly shut. He was not pleased by the amount. Casius could tell by the way he held his jaw clenched in anger. He stood and shouldered Baln's axe, grunting with the effort of lifting the massive weapon.

"Let's get this offal aboard the ship," He ordered.

Casius was roughly jerked to his feet by the neck of his sleep shirt. The man held him firmly until he was steady. He nearly collapsed under a wave of nausea that struck him at the sudden movement.

Dulrich shook his head; "We should wait out the storm." He suggested.

Outside the Long House the wind moaned mournfully. The door to the Hall was open and the freezing wind slammed into them, bringing into the Hall the smell of burning lumber and wafts of irritating smoke.

G'relg stood in the doorway looking up at the sky. "Scared of a small rainstorm?" he asked smiling. He waited but Dulrich offered no answer. "Let us go then, the tide waits for no man." He said as he strode out into pre-dawn gloom.

Casius was shoved forward by one of the men. He turned to look at him and was struck over the eye by the pommel of the man's sword. Blinded by pain, he staggered. The man grabbed his arm and thrust him roughly through the doorway. The sword's pommel had cut him deeply and blood was flowing down his face.

The man followed him outside and threw him to the ground. "Look at me again boy," he hissed. "And I will cut your eyes out."

Casius climbed to his feet. He kept his head down not wishing to provoke the violent man further. He was led with the others down to the shore. The sounds of crackling wood drowned out the noise from the sea. The raiders had set New Hope ablaze, and in a few hours there will be nothing left but burned out ruins.

Heat and smoke assailed them as they staggered down the lane. Even the boats along the shore had been torched and were burning brightly. Bodies lay along the shore. He could not tell to whom they belonged. They had been covered in oil and now burned as brightly as the surrounding buildings.

He was thrown against the hull and rough hands reached down grabbing his clothing. They were none too gentle as they pulled him over the railing. The wood scraped his back raw; he nearly blacked out as his head hit a rowing bench. With great effort he managed to sit upright. Bodies lay against him, pressing him against the rough wood. The captives sat frozen with fear, their eyes numbly reflecting the flames devouring their homes.

The fire raced through the town. Towering flames leapt from roof to roof, the thatch exploding into flame. Even the Long House was engulfed. Writhing about as if it was alive, the fires hungrily devouring the large logs of its construction.

Casius watched in mute horror. He had never seen anything like this in his life. He yelped as he was yanked harshly to his feet by his hair.

"No need to sit with the women, boy." G'relg said throwing him over one of the rowing benches. "There's work to be done and you look strong enough to pull an oar." He sliced Casius's bonds with his knife. Taking little care as he did so, the blade cutting deeply into Casius's left palm.

Casius winced at the sudden pain but he kept his mouth shut. Ignoring the wound, he sat down and took up an oar. Hot blood flowed from his palm making the wood slippery. He kept his discomfort to himself. He knew that one should never show these animals any sign of weakness.

G'relg laughed at his attempt at bravado. "Pray you row well, If not I'll flay the skin from your back. He lifted a cat-o'-nine-tails from the deck. Cracking it loudly in the air. "Pull hard when I give the order," G'relg reminded him. He lashed his back with the whip as he walked back to the vessel's stern.

Casius risked a glance over his shoulder. He saw that all the captives had been set to benches. Even the smallest of children sat beside the adults. Their faces wet with tears.

The ship began to lift from the bottom as the tide advanced. G'relg stood with his hands on the tiller. "Cut the lines!" he shouted. "Row!" he barked once the lines had been severed. "Row...Row...Row!" He shouted the cadence as the boat slowly inched back from the shore. Out into the choppy water they sailed. When they had gone a hundred yards he ordered them to shift positions.

Casius ducked under the oar and swung around on the seat. His back now faced the prow and he looked directly aft.

G'relg cursed and with his whip he soon had the others facing correctly. Once more the oars bit into the water. They cleared the breakwater and entered the open sea. Large rolling waves lifted the vessel high into the air.

From where Casius sat he could see the conflagration upon the shore that had once been his home. He thought of his father and tears came unbidden to his eyes. He fought to hold them back, but there was little he could do.

The wind was blowing steadily at their backs and G'relg had the sail raised. A much-mended square of white canvas, dirty and mildew stained. It flapped loudly as it filled. The rigging thrummed and the boat fairly leapt forward. On G'relg's order the oars were pulled in. The captives sat hunched in their seats exhausted from the unfamiliar labor.

G'relg kept a tight grip on the tiller as they swung out to the southwest. He was studying the horizon with concern. Perhaps Dulrich had been right, this appeared to be more than a small squall.

The sun was up but very little of its light was piercing the thick veil of clouds above them. He wanted to go north back to Cythera, but the storm stood in their path. He decided to ride the storm's wind and eventually circle around it. Bright flashes of light shone along the front, a testament to the storm's fury.

It was nearing noon and the weather had progressively gotten worse. The boat was being tossed about on waves as high as thirty feet. The wind was threatening to tear away the sail at any moment, and a freezing rain lashed down at them stinging their faces. Lightening flashed through the clouds accompanied by deafening peals of thunder.

The men were getting angry with G'relg. It was his order that had them put to sea in the path of this storm. A massive foam capped wave washed over the vessel drenching them all with freezing water.

One of the men had had enough, "Don't be a fool G'relg!" He shouted over the roaring wind. "Turn back now and we may yet live to reach the shore."

G'relg's hand shot to his dagger, "Mind your tongue Shoffal, lest I cut it out." He shouted back.

"Damn it G'relg!" Shoffal cursed. "It will profit us nothing if we drown!"

Dulrich stood using the ship's mast to steady himself against the pitching deck. "He is not alone," he said glaring into G'relg's eyes.

"A bit of bad weather and the lot of you turn tail and run, little more than a pack of beaten dogs." He grumbled, his voice betraying a hint of fear as well. This storm was the kind that would frighten even the most seasoned sailor.

"Turn the ship back," Dulrich yelled.

"That way leads to the very heart of this blow!" G'relg shouted.

"Aye," Dulrich nodded. "And the nearest land for miles. Turn her back, or we turn her ourselves."

G'relg was no fool he could see that the men had their knives drawn, and murder burned in their eyes. "Very well," He conceded. "How many of you wish to spend an evening on an island full of revenants?" He asked seeking to play on their fears.

"The vengeful spirits of the men we murdered are sure to be out for our hides. We are safe enough on the water but once we touch their land we're doomed." He could see his words were having an effect. Knives were returning to their sheaths. There wasn't a man here who wanted to face the undead. He had gambled, playing on their fears and won.

Dulrich looked at the men in disgust, "Are you men, or children to be frightened by such talk?" The sheepish looks he got in response set aside any hopes he had of wresting power from G'relg. He sat down his hand upon his knife, he knew it was only a matter of time until G'relg would try and kill him.

The ship sped before the wind, the rigging threatening to break under the strain. The wind grew fierce its direction no longer steady. Waves washed over the sides frequently. Two men were lost when a large wave crashed down onto the deck. Sweeping them over the side into the dark water.

It had grown so dark Casius could no longer tell where the sea ended and the sky began. The temperature plummeted and ice began to form on the lines.

Casius clung to the rowing bench for all he was worth. The water threatening to drag him over the side with each crashing wave. His arms were growing numb with cold. His thin nightshirt offering scant protection as it had been soaked completely through.

One of the sailors tossed a leather cloak to him. It was old and filthy, smelling of urine. Casius was thankful nonetheless. He tried to thank the man, but the sailor smacked him across the mouth.

"Keep your gratitude to yourself," The man said in disgust. "You're worth nothing dead."

Casius wrapped the offending garment about himself. Trying not to think about the fleas and lice that must be teeming within it.

With the coming of night the storm continued to grow stronger, becoming more violent by the hour. Its waves reached epic proportions; becoming rolling mountains of foam capped death.

The tiller was suddenly torn free of its mountings, nearly pulling G'relg over the side with it. Without a rudder the vessel was now completely at the storm's mercy.

They tried to use the oars, but they were wrenched from their hands by the violent water. The sail finally gave in with a sharp ripping sound. It was shredded, flying from the spar in tatters, the canvas popping loudly.

For two days the sea tossed the boat about mercilessly. The crew could do nothing but hang on for life. Exhausted and half-frozen they prayed to whatever gods they believed in to spare their lives.

On the morning of the third day the boat's mast split in two. The broken end kicked out striking one of the raider's in the face, removing his head in a spray of bloody pulp. The thick timber fell overboard, tearing a gaping hole in the boat's side. Water began pouring into the craft, faster than they could bail.

The boat was struck violently on its side by a powerful wave. The vessel rolled over and for a moment it looked as if it would capsize.

Casius clung to the bench, his grip reopening the gash on his palm. He ignored the pain and watched with morbid fascination as the dark blood washed down over the wooden seat.

G'relg was terrified. It appeared that the gods had forsaken them. The mighty Aikinor, god of the oceans, was throwing his wrath at the helpless craft. He knew what he had to do. A sacrifice was needed to appease him. He drew his knife and his eyes locked with Casius's. He saw hatred burning there. The boy actually had the nerve to hold his gaze.

Casius tensed as G'relg pulled him to his feet by his collar. Standing with his legs braced against the rolling deck G'relg laid the knife across Casius's throat.

"Aikinor hear me!" G'relg shouted at the storm. "With this life let your fury abate."

Casius knew he was about to die; He threw his head back with all the strength he could muster. His head struck G'relg soundly. He felt the man's teeth crumble with force of the blow. G'relg's grip eased slightly and Casius threw the man aside. G'relg fell across the rowing seats, blood streaming from his broken nose. He spat out shards of teeth and tried to regain his feet.

Casius leapt over the side. It would be better to drown than give the raider the satisfaction of killing him. He hit the water and was shocked by how cold it was. The salt burned in his wounds, and stung his eyes. Sputtering for air he reached the surface, and with powerful strokes he swam away from the floundering boat. It was only a few moments until he could no longer see the ship in the gloom.

The waves carried him along. He gave up fighting their pull. Instead he focused his attention on staying above the churning froth. As he fought to stay alive a soft booming sound reached his ears over the roar of the wind.

Casius's heart leapt, a ray of hope giving him strength. It was a familiar sound, the call of waves breaking upon a shore. He swam with renewed vigor letting the rumbling lead him.

He tumbled down the face of a breaking wave and was violently slammed into the sandy bottom. As he clawed his way to the surface another breaker drove him back down.

Battered and exhausted he staggered out of the crashing surf. He was on a small beach littered with debris. In the darkness to the northwest he could see the faint golden glow of lamplight.

Casius wrapped his arms about himself, the cold seeping deep into his weary muscles. The rain stung his flesh, numbing his face. He needed to find shelter, and soon. Up the dunes he scrambled, the long sea oats entangling his legs making him fall several times.

Beyond the dunes he came upon a deeply rutted cart path. He sloughed through the muddy track towards the faint light. It brightened and faded as the rain fell in wind blown sheets.

He passed several small buildings in the dark, from the smell he could tell that they were used to house livestock. The light that drew his attention was coming from a window in a small wooden cottage. A crude fence constructed of driftwood surrounded it. Casius could see no gate in the darkness. He ducked between the rails and crossed a muddy yard to the rickety porch.

The windows of the cottage were shuttered against the storm. The wood was old and warped, through the cracks seeped the warm golden light that flooded out onto the yard.

Casius leaned against the doorjamb his ear pressed to the wood. From inside the cote he could hear the muted sounds of people speaking. An inviting smell of roasting pork drifted out from beneath the door. His stomach grumbled in protest, it had been a long time since he had last eaten.

Desperation overcame his fear; he pounded on the door with his uninjured hand. The voices stopped and a shadow moved past the window, dimming the light coming through the shutters.

Casius waited but the door did not open. He pounded all the harder, shaking the door in its frame, and yet no answer came. He could no longer feel his feet and his cheeks burned hotly. He needed to get near a fire and soon. The only thing between him and warmth was the sturdy door.

Trying the latch he found it locked. He wiggled it several times to no avail. "I need help!" He shouted, doubting anyone inside heard his call over the roaring wind. Stepping back he threw his full weight against the door. The lock snapped and he staggered into the bright light and warmth of the home.

An elderly couple stood at the far side of the room. Their eyes were wide with fright. The heavyset man held a pitchfork before him. From the look in his eyes there would be little doubt that he would use it.

"Be gone from my home, spirit!" He shouted waving the sharpened tines threateningly.

The woman's face relaxed and she looked at her husband with disapproval. "Carl," She said sharply. "No spirit has come across our doorstep. It is only an injured boy." She stepped out in front of her husband. "I am Winowa," She said reassuringly. "And this oaf is my husband Carl. We will not harm you."

"Woman!" Carl snapped. "Step aside this instant!"

"Carl, in the fifty years we have lived here, you have never spoken to me in such a manner." She gave him a look that made him flinch. "I will not have you start doing so now."

"You've never consorted with storm wrought spirits in that time." Carl replied in a more congenial tone.

"Carl Dunburrow, put that fork down this instant." She grabbed the haft and pushed it aside, cutting him off as he started to reply; "No buts mind you. Unless you believe a spirit would stand there seeping blood onto my floor."

Carl lowered the weapon as he saw the blood dripping from Casius's hand onto the polished wood. The boy was a mess his dark hair filled with sand and bits of sea grass. He wore a filthy leather cloak over a thin linen shirt that was stained with dried blood. A dark bruise surrounded a half-healed gash over his gray eyes. He was pale and frightened holding his left hand cupped in an effort to catch the flowing blood.

"You're damn lucky you picked our place, boy." He said leaning the fork against the fireplace. "Most in these parts would have killed you, bursting in here like you did." He smiled revealing a mouth with few teeth. "Don't just stand there dripping, come sit by the fire, while I see to that door."

Winowa took Casius by the arm and led him to hearth. He sat down heavily before the flames on a thick rug of woven wool. Casius could not remember a time when a fire had ever looked so inviting.

Winowa placed a cup of hot tea into his shaking hands. "There now, you're safe here. Carl is a good man and will do you no harm."

Casius sipped from the cup, "Thank you." He stammered through shivering lips.

"Have you a name?" She asked.

He nodded, "Casius." His voice was cracked and hoarse. "Casius Rhaine of Kale."

"Kale," Carl said, tying the door closed. "You've done a fair bit of traveling from Baln's holdings." Carl stopped, he had turned and as Casius removed the soiled cloak he could see the angry red welts and torn cloth from G'relg's lash. "What the devil has happened to you?" he asked pulling a stool over to the fire.

Casius looked into the dancing flames, his eyes growing moist as the all too traumatic memories came to mind. When he spoke it was in a voice torn by grief. "Raiders," He said the word as if it were a poison. "They killed most of my people. Only a few of us were spared and taken aboard their ship, fated to become slaves upon Cythera.

"A scarred man named G'relg led the raid. When the ship became damaged in the gale he sought to sacrifice me to Aikinor. I jumped ship and the sea drove me up onto the shore. From there I simply followed the light from your window."

Carl shook his head in amazement. "You're damn lucky, Casius. The waters here are treacherous and filled with jagged rocks. The fact that you are alive at all is a miracle." He patted Casius's arm, "Though you may think differently now, one of the Gods was watching out for you."

Winowa set a bowl of water near the fire, "We need to get you some dry clothing and tend to those wounds. They will run with pus if we do nothing."

Carl nodded and went to the open doorway leading to a separate room. "I'll see what I can find that will fit him." he said over his shoulder. "He may want to eat a bit as well I'd wager."

Casius shook his head, "Warm and dry for now." His stomach rumbled at the thought of food.

Carl grunted at the sound. "Can't say as I would have much of an appetite after going through what you have." He stepped through the doorway disappearing into the room beyond.

Casius handed Winowa the empty cup. "Where am I?" He asked.

"You are in Lakarra," Winowa answered refilling his cup. "Near the village of Ansell at the edge of the Copper Hills." She handed Casius the cup and examined the cut over his eye. "You can not remain here long I'm afraid. The Cytherans come here often, and they will come looking for you." She bound the wound on his hand with a clean cloth. "They never allow anyone to escape, this G'relg will hunt you down."

"Lakarra allows these raiders on her shores?" Casius asked in disbelief.

"Sadly yes," Winowa nodded. "Our king is cast from the same mold as their leader. He sees only profit and power from their relationship. The glitter of gold blinds him to the suffering of his people. They bring in their poison, Black Trumpet. Selling it to any who have the coin for it."

"My being here places you in danger." Casius began to stand "I must leave."

"Not tonight nor tomorrow. This storm will last that long at the least." Carl said from the doorway. "Any raider ships out there," He nods towards the ocean. "Will remain far off shore, and hopefully they wont survive this tempest."

Winowa helped him remove his shirt and gasps at the long cuts. "These will scar," She said gently applying an ointment to his back.

Casius nods, "Those are the least of the scars I shall bear the rest of my days."

Winowa smiles sadly, "For you to say such a thing shows that there is yet hope. I see no hate or anger within you, only sorrow."

"My father once told me that a man is that which he chooses to be. It is the choices that we make today, that shapes who we are yet to become." Casius looked away uncomfortable beneath her probing gaze. "Should I feel hatred and seek revenge." He shuddered at the thought. "I will not become akin to the men on that boat. G'relg's lash will not make me change who I am."

Winowa smiled, her eyes moist with compassion. "That is good Casius, your father was a wise man." Winowa patted his forearm in sympathy. "We had a son Casius, Peyetor was his name. When he was twenty, a group of raiders landed on our shore. They demanded our horse and cart, when he refused, they slew him." She wiped the hint of tears from her eyes. "No one will dare resist them and there are a few here in Ansell who would gladly turn you over to them for a pitiful handful of coins."

Carl handed Casius a small bundle of clothing. They were simple in design and smelled of cedar. Casius dressed while Winowa ladled out a bowl of steaming stew. The clothing was slightly big but they were clean and warm.

Carl returned to his stool and stuffed a long stem pipe with tobacco. "Your safest bet will be to leave the coast and head inland." He said lighting the pipe with a thin taper he had held into the fire. Puffs of rich smoke surrounded his head as he spoke. "You can move into one of the larger cities. There's always work to be had, and one more foreigner will draw no attention."

Casius nodded, he had not thought that far ahead. He had few options left, and Carl's suggestion at least offered him some hope for the future.

"That's it then," Carl smiled exhaling a long stream of smoke. "When the storm passes I'll take you to Graystone. It is a trek of three days, across the Copper Hills. I have a nephew who lives there; he will see that you get off on the right foot.

"Graystone is a large city, lying on the old trade road. It is far removed from any seaport and raiders will not likely venture there. As safe a place as any I'd say." Carl blew out a thick ring of smoke. "Do you have any skills?"

"My father was Lord Baln's Ship Thane and he taught me much of his craft." Casius answered around a mouthful of steaming stew.

Carl frowned in thought. "Not much need for boat builders in Graystone," he mused aloud. Then his eyes lit up as he had an idea, "Carpenter!" He nearly shouted, pleased with himself for thinking of it. "Woodworking you know, how much different can it be, building a ship or a home."

Casius was less than enthusiastic. Boats, he knew but that was a far cry from what Carl was suggesting. "Your cousin, is he a carpenter?"

Carl laughed, "No not him, he's a merchant and a scribe. Makes his living selling rare books to the nobles and writing up contracts and such."

Casius finished off the stew and handed the bowl to Winowa. "Thank you," He said his stomach no longer aching. he was warm and full, and could not help yawning.

Winowa handed him a thick blanket and a pillow of goose down. "Here," she smiled. "You're exhausted and need to rest." She pointed to the back room. "Take the bed tonight."

Casius shook his head, "I can't do that, and I'll rest here instead, before the fire. You have done enough for me, I'll not take your bed as well."

Carl smiled, "Have it your way. Though I have to admit, at my age sleeping on the floor is none too good for my back."

Casius smiled at the man's honesty, "I can not thank you enough for what you have done." Casius wrapped the blanket across his shoulders and stretched out on the floor.

Carl smiled, "Tis nothing, any decent folk would do the same."

"Peyetor was a lucky man to have parents such as you." He did not hear them leave the room, falling into a deep sleep as his head touched the pillow.

Winowa crept through the room and extinguished the oil lamp. A soft darkness settled within the cote, broken by the flickering light of the low fire burning within the hearth. Outside the wind howled in fury, shaking the stout walls of the Dunburrows' home.

Carl stood in the doorway for a short while. He watched the shadows play across the walls as he smoked his pipe. The memory of his son's death, sent tears streaming down his cheeks. "I could not save Peyetor," he whispered in the darkness. "But I will not fail again." He tapped the contents of his pipe into the fire; setting it upon the mantel he quietly went to bed.

The storm lingered for three days, hammering against the slopes of the Copper hills. On the third day the rain lessened and eventually stopped. The wind died down as well. It remained a strong breeze, but no longer threatening to rip the roof from the cottage.

They stepped out onto the porch. Watching the dark fragmentary clouds drifting southward in a sky of burnished gold.

Carl set to work immediately, righting rain barrels and seeing to his livestock. Casius pitched in and helped where he was able. They accomplished much in the few hours of sunlight they had. Exhausted from their rushed labor they trod through the thick mud back to the cottage where Winowa had prepared a hearty meal.

CHAPTER FIVE

On the morning of his fourth day since coming ashore in Lakarra, Casius and Carl prepared to leave. Carl hitched his small two-wheeled cart to the largest horse Casius had ever seen in his life. It was a powerful beast bred for pulling plows and overloaded wagons, light tan in color with a mane of dark russet.

"Tis no nobleman's buggy but she'll get us to Graystone safely enough." Carl reached into the wagon and tossed him a worn leather belt. Attached to it was a scabbard holding an old short sword. "Wear this," he said fastening another about his own waist.

Casius drew the blade; it was a poor-man's weapon, crudely fashioned with an edge that had been sharpened many times. "I do not know how to use this." He said sheathing the blade. He attempted to hand it back, but Carl refused to take it.

Carl looked at him strangely, "You are close to sixteen. Did your father teach you to defend yourself? There are brigands in these mountains, to go unarmed is to invite attack."

My father taught me to wield an axe," Casius answered strapping the belt around his waist. "We had no brigands on Kale."

Carl shrugged, "There's a wood pile round the back. Take the axe if you wish."

Casius retrieved the axe and swung it a few times. The balance was off but it was a stout tool with a sharp edge. He placed it in the back of the cart within easy reach of the wooden seat.

Winowa came down out of the cottage and handed Carl a linen wrapped bundle that smelled of freshly baked bread.

Carl hugged her close; "I'll be back in a week if the weather holds." He smiled, "Don't you worry none, I know the way as well as I know the back of my hand."

"I know Carl," she smiled softly. "But I shall fret just the same." She turned and gave Casius a hug as well. "Listen to Carl," She told him. "He's a good man who will not lead you astray."

Casius nodded, "Thank you Winowa," he said.

Carl climbed up onto the riding seat and took the reins in hand. "Come on Casius," he motioned to the seat next to him. "The days this time of year are short and there is little light we can afford to waste."

Casius climbed up and once he was seated Carl clicked his tongue. The horse responded setting off at a brisk walk. Casius was nearly thrown backwards by the sudden jolt. Up the rutted trail they went, the wagon lurching with each bump in the road.

Casius took one last look over his shoulder at the weathered old cottage. Winowa stood upon the porch her gray hair touched with gold, reflecting the light of the rising sun. She waved and went indoors; not found of long good-byes she preferred not to watch them go.

The countryside about the farm was colored in the soft hues of autumn. Trees of gold and burgundy stood amid fields of rich brown earth. The pools of standing water left by the storm glinted brightly, mirroring the colors of the sky.

The air was brisk, but tolerable. Thanks to the heavy coats and gloves that they wore. Before them out of the morning mist emerged the Copper Hills. Although named hills, they were in truth a range of snow-clad mountains with deep valleys and soaring peaks. The upper reaches of naked stone rising high above a dense forest of evergreens.

The trail they followed skirted the lower reaches of the foothills, following the contour of the land it clung to the edge of the wood. They passed by old farmsteads whose buildings had collapsed into disrepair. The once tended fields about them now sporting scattered groves of young trees.

Carl guided the horse little; the beast knew the way and stayed the course. As they climbed higher into the hills Casius could see in the distance where the mountains reached down to the sea.

The snow-clad peaks spellbound Casius. He had never seen a mountain in his life. He had thought the eastern crags on Kale were tall, they hardly compared to the foothills through which they were now traveling.

Now and then the road would enter the wood. The lofty pines whispered in the wind above them as they passed. The aroma of their needles added a pleasant touch to the gentle breeze.

They crested a rise, and came to a fork in the road. The right branch led down a steep slope into a low valley that was bordered on one side by the sea. Clustered tightly together along the shore stood a sizable town, the whitewashed buildings glowing with the morning sun. Ribbons of smoke snaked up into the air above their roofs of slate, leaving the only marks in an otherwise perfect sky.

"That be Ansell," Carl said taking the left-hand way. "To the north there are miles of good bottom land. Rich soil worked by many farms."

Casius strained to see but the mist blowing in from the ocean obscured the landscape just beyond the town.

"We've gotten here early enough," Carl said around the stem of his unlit pipe. "Not a soul will see us, and once beyond the next ridge they never will."

"Surely," Casius said turning to face the old farmer. "These people can't be all bad."

"Good or bad has nothing to do with it," He said. "Those people are scared, and a frightened man can be just as dangerous as one of them raiders. That's why I choose to live away from the town. It's a sad thing when a neighbor cannot trust another.

"Ever since Ganeth seized the crown and founded the Senatum, Lakarra has become a den of thieves and frightened informants." Carl spat loudly as if the words left a foul taste in his mouth.

"Senatum?" Casius repeated.

"Aye," Carl replied. "Little more than thugs and hoodlums who wear the king's colors. They supposedly uphold the law, but it is they who break it more often as not. Lakarra is going through dark times, Casius. If we see any of the Senatum we will be sure to make ourselves scarce."

Casius nodded, he was overwhelmed by the strangeness of this land, and by the chaos that his life had become.

They rode on mostly in silence throughout the day, following the winding path higher into the mountains. The thick forest blocked out most of the sun's light and it was within their shadows that they rode. Overhead a blanket of clouds drifted down from the north covering the sky.

Casius marveled at the beauty of the mountains and it's surrounding forest. Carl seemed to be enjoying the ride himself. It was not often that he got to venture far from his homestead.

As the sun began to set they were traveling along a narrow ridge. There were few trees this high, only an occasional stunted pine that stubbornly clung to life amid gray stone. Carl stopped the cart and lit two oil lanterns that hung from poles on either side of the wagon.

The road was narrow here with steep slopes on each side. The way ahead snaked along the ridge top. The lanterns gave off enough light that they could see a few feet ahead of the horse. Carl kept his eyes on the path. It would be far too easy for them to lose their way and inadvertently roll off the ridge.

"There's an old toll house less than an hour away," Carl said, his eyes never leaving the torturous path. "We will camp the night there and cross over in the morning."

It was the longest hour of Casius's life. Dark shapes loomed in the darkness, massive boulders that had fallen from the heights long ago. The darkness on either side of them at times echoed with the sounds of the horses hoof falls. Vast yawning chasms of black that threatened to swallow them should they stray from their way.

Carl's estimate was accurate, and within the hour the trail opened up onto a wide plateau that sloped gently upward disappearing into the gloom. A small cote of rough stone stood nearby. The roof was in poor condition. More than a few of its slate tiles were missing, exposing the wooden beams beneath. An empty doorway faced the road its opening looming darker than the surrounding night.

"Here it is," Carl announced. "Not much to look at but it will keep the wind off our backs." He took one of the lanterns down and handed it to Casius. "Don't wander far," He warned him. "You wouldn't enjoy falling off a cliff in the dark." He looked up into the looming darkness overhead. Only two stars were visible, burning weakly through the veil of clouds.

Casius went to the back of the building and relieved his bladder. He looked around but could find nothing but barren earth and stone.

"Not much wood to be had," He told Carl returning to the cart.

Carl looked up, from where he was busy tending to the horse. "What do you think happened to the door?" He asked patting the horse's flank as he walked to the back of the cart and lifted a tarp exposing a neat stack of wood.

Casius grinned, "I take it you've been this way many times." He lifted an armload of wood and entered the ruined building.

"A few," Carl answered following him into the room carrying the lanterns.

The swinging lantern light revealed a simple square chamber with an earthen floor. It was sparse but dry, in the shadows it's sole occupant a large rat scurried along the wall, escaping through a chink in the stone. In the room's center a shallow pit had been dug. It's bottom littered with the blackened debris of many fires.

Casius started a small fire, the dancing flames spreading heat throughout the room. Carl covered the doorway with the tarp sealing off the cold mountain breeze.

Carl sat across from Casius, the fire burning between them. "By tomorrow night we will be through the mountains and on the upland plains." He opened the bundle Winowa had given them. It contained a loaf of bread and a wheel of cheese. He cut these in half and passed them to Casius.

Casius took his share and began eating, watching the wood pop and sizzle.

"We will leave at daybreak," he said around a mouthful of bread. "Winter's bite is soft here but once beyond these mountains the warmth of the sea fails and the plains will be in winter's grasp."

"What's your nephew like?"

"Nice fellow," Carl said prodding the flames. "In his thirties with a wife but no children as of yet." Carl lit his pipe adding the pungent aroma of tobacco to the smoke from the fire. "He's a shrewd businessman as I hear it. Always seems to come out on the best end of a deal, very much like his father." Carl leaned back against the wall and smoked his pipe.

Casius wrapped his blanket around his shoulders and lay down. Closing his eyes he tried not to think about the rat that he was sure was skulking nearby.

Carl finished his pipe and lay down as well. "Get some rest, we have a long day ahead of us and dawn comes early in these parts."

Casius awakened several hours later, the fire had burned low and the cold was creeping back into the building. As he put a few logs onto the fire. He thought he had heard something outside but now was not so sure. It could have been anything. Carl lay on his side oblivious to the world and snoring loudly. Casius thought about waking him but decided to let the man sleep.

Casius lay back down; he was about to drift off when an eerie cry broke the silence. A dreadful wail that echoed softly from the surrounding rock. Casius cringed, that is what a spirit must sound like he thought.

Three times the piercing wail sounded, each time growing father away. Casius gripped the axe protectively and sat against the wall, his eyes on the gently swaying tarp covering the doorway.

Eventually the call subsided and only the sighing of the wind competed with Carl's thundering snores. The hour grew late and Casius inevitably fell asleep once more.

The light of dawn filtered through the tarp covering the doorway. Where it shone brightly, a multitude of dust motes drifted lazily about. Carl sat up and stretched, smacking his lips loudly. He looked well rested and ready to take on the day.

Casius groaned and rolled over putting his back to the light. "How could you sleep with all that wailing and screaming going on?"

Carl looked puzzled for a moment. "I should have warned you," he said laughing. "Those were the calls of the Nightsinger, a small bird with a very large voice."

"Bird?" Casius laughed pulling on his coat. "I spent half the night frightened by a bird? It sounded more like a demented spirit wandering these hills."

Carl chuckled packing up their supplies. "Just a bird, nothing more. There are many strange tales surrounding it though."

Casius grinned. "Anything that sounds like that is bound to have started a few stories."

"Aye," Carl agreed. "Spun by drunken travelers, and told for a spot of ale in many an inn."

Casius helped him load the cart. They left the wood stacked neatly against the wall inside the building. Carl said it had been a common practice at one time, which was rarely followed anymore.

"Always leave a little for those that have none." Carl had said. "The next man to come this way may be half frozen and without supplies. A lost hunter, or a waylaid merchant." Carl shrugged, "It costs us little and may actually save a life."

Casius climbed up onto the cart dreading another day of bone jarring jolts and bumps.

The small building stood at the edge of a shallow slope that led up between two peaks. The pass itself was a broad saddle of barren rock littered with scree. The way ahead had been cleared of debris long ago. The discarded stone lay piled in mounds along the way.

The air grew cooler as they climbed the winding trail. The horse's hoof falls echoing from the gray rock walls became a monotonous cadence marking the slow passage of time. The pass was shrouded in gloom. The sun's rays would not reach into the break until late in the afternoon.

Cold air flowed down from the snow-clad peaks above. Thin tendrils of fog, coiled and drifted down the face of the rock. Through the gloom they passed coming out into the daylight.

The land beyond the mountains spread out below them. A vast low plain dotted with dense woods and gleaming rivers.

Down the western face the road took them, disappearing into a dense wood that spread out over the foothills. They were well within the wood as the sun slipped below the horizon, as the light faded Carl stopped the cart.

"We'll go no further tonight." Carl said stepping down from the cart. "This is the Braelin Wood, we will be within its borders until we come to Graystone."

Using the tarp they improvised a shelter and lit a small fire.

"Keep your sword handy tonight." The old farmer suggested. "This wood is safe enough, safer than most. But trouble has a way of showing up when you least expect it. There is always the occasional brigand wandering about."

They spent the night huddled beneath the tarp. Carl told Casius many entertaining stories of his youth. How he had met Winowa while serving in the king's army. They talked late into the night, while the fire crackled.

They were on the move once more with daybreak. Down through the tree shrouded hills they rode, the dense pines giving way to tall stately oaks. Their leaves a riot of fall colors from brilliant red to gold.

It was late in the afternoon when they crossed a fast flowing rill spanned by a well built wooden bridge. The forest ended here rather abruptly, only a few trees grew across the stream.

The sky was overcast and gloomy, with scattered openings that allowed rays of golden light to fall onto a vast expanse of wavering grass turned golden by the first touch of winter.

Graystone stood in the distance, a massive wall of stone that stretched a mile across. Forty towers were spaced along its length, rising fifty feet; each twice as high as the wall itself. Beyond the wall rose the high peaked roofs of various buildings, many of them clad in tarnished copper. From poles on their tops flew pennants of many colors.

Two large gates led through the wall. The city was better than a mile away, but even at this distance they could see the throng of people milling about the entrance.

Carl reined the horse in, allowing Casius a good look. "Imposing isn't it?" He nodded to the wall. "Well that's just for show, only the wealthy live within those walls. The real city lies on the other side, along the banks of the Taelus River."

Casius watched in awe as they neared the city. Along the battlements atop the wall and in the towers he could see men moving behind the crenels. The sunlight reflecting from their polished armor, glinting as they passed between the merlons.

"That's where the money is made," Carl said looking at the rooftops beyond the wall. "Ore from the mines is loaded onto barges and sent to markets in the south. If it weren't for the river, Graystone would not exist."

"Does your nephew live within the walls?" Casius asked eager to see what lay behind the protective stone edifice.

Carl grinned and shook his head, "No, he is not so wealthy a man. He does have aspirations of being so one day though. He lives in a modest area away from the waterfront."

Casius nodded, "Still I would like to see what lays beyond those walls."

"It's not likely you ever will," Carl said. "You need an invite to get through the gate. You and I are not the kind of people who are willingly allowed entry. Besides the Senatum guards those gates and we do not want to come under their scrutiny."

Casius agreed with Carl, he had had enough dealings with thugs and did not wish to tempt fate.

The road improved as they came within the wall's shadow. It was no longer a simple dirt track; the way ahead was paved with smooth stones tightly fitted together. Carl guided the horse around the edges of the crowd before the gate. He followed the road, riding along side the wall.

The wall curved in a broad arc until they rode southward. The land ahead sloped downward towards the river. Buildings of all sizes crowded the banks. Narrow streets formed a veritable maze up the slope. The buildings ended a few hundred feet from the wall. The land between was barren, devoid of both grass and trees.

"They hold tournaments there during the spring," Carl said answering Casius's unspoken question.

The small cart entered the narrow streets, winding about the buildings. Carl took turn after turn until Casius became lost. There was no plan to the city's streets. It was a maze of alleyways and cobbled lanes. People by the hundreds moved along them. The cries of merchants hawking their wares competed with the boisterous music coming from the many tavern windows.

The din of noise and the powerful aromas of the city threatened to overwhelm his senses. Casius quickly learned not to breath too deeply through his nose. The smell of human waste and rotted food permeated everything, a noxious undertone to the boisterous excitement of the city.

Through this chaos Carl expertly guided the wagon. Weaving around carts and pedestrians alike, he often grumbled to himself displeased by the slow progress they were making.

Casius hardly noticed the delay, never before had he believed there could be so many people in one place. Unlike the small houses he was used to, many of these buildings stood three stories above the crowded streets.

He saw people on the balconies, hanging the wash out to dry. On one balcony near the waterfront he saw three scantily dressed women. They smiled and waved to him as he passed.

"Stay clear of them and their ilk," Carl laughed. "Nothing but trouble for an honest man."

Casius blushed and looked away, the whole scene reminded him of the grand parades he had read about. He could imagine himself at the head of some victorious army marching through the streets. The cheers of the populace blending into one joyous roar that shattered the autumn air.

The rancid odors of civilization thickened as they neared the water. Casius placed his hand over his face in a futile attempt to lessen his exposure.

If Carl noticed the offending smells he gave no sign. He took a turn and the cart slowly wound up a broad thoroughfare that led uphill away from the water.

The buildings improved, becoming well kept with stained glass windows. The smells lessened considerably remaining only the faintest shadow of what they were near the river. The alleys here were few; those that did exist were clean. The people who lived here refused to allow the rubbish to accumulate.

Both sides of the street held multi-storied homes, their lower floors given over to various storefronts. Carl turned into an alley between two modest buildings of whitewashed wood. Behind the houses lay a small yard with a sturdy barn.

Carl stopped the wagon and stretched. "Here we are," He said wincing as his neck popped. He climbed down and unhitched the horse leading it into the barn. He returned after a few minutes, retrieving a small bundle from the cart he walked down the alley and up onto the porch. With a reassuring nod to Casius he opened the door and stepped into the shop.

A small bell rang as Casius closed the door behind him. He looked about the shop in amazement. Books by the hundreds lined the walls. They filled the shelves to capacity, overflowing into neat stacks on the wooden floor. Casius had never imagined such a sight, until now he had only seen perhaps a dozen books in his life.

The musty smell of old leather and parchment hung in the air. Casius found it to his liking, he ran his hand along the spines yearning to pull one down and leaf through its pages. What secrets must lay hidden here, stories by the thousands waiting to be discovered.

His eyes roamed from title to title, most of the books were written in the king's tongue, an ancient language that was rarely used. At one time it had been the unifying language of the world, used widely by the eastern kingdoms.

A few of them were written in a flowery script that he could not recognize. The swirling letters held his eye and tickled his imagination.

A boyish looking man in his mid thirties rushed out of the back room. He was heavy set and kept his hair cut short. It lay flat against his head; light brown in color with the barest touch of gray at his temples. A broad smile spread across his cherubic face when he recognized Carl.

"Well I'll be damned!" He exclaimed wiping his hands on his ink stained apron as he crossed the room. He grasped Carl's hand in a firm grip, "Never thought you'd make the trip this late in the year." He looked about the shop, "Where's Winowa?" he asked with a touch of concern in his voice.

"Back home and in good health," Carl answered reassuringly. "There's only room for two in my cart," he placed his hand on Casius's shoulder. "I want you to meet Casius," he said introducing him. "Casius, this is my nephew Gayn."

Gayn reached out and shook Casius's hand; his fingers were dark, stained with ink of various hues. "Welcome to my home," he said with a polite smile.

Carl cleared his throat, "Gayn could we go in the back, I need to speak with you in private."

Gayn nodded. "Of course," he looked at his uncle with a slightly puzzled expression.

"Stay put," Carl told Casius. "We wont be long." He led Gayn across the shop speaking softly as they went.

Casius knew they were talking about him, ignoring the voices coming from the other room he browsed through the shop. He found one large tome, bound in dark leather with gilded letters along the spine. It was the early works of Lenar, bard of Ril'Gambor. Casius sat on the floor and carefully opened the book.

He found it difficult to concentrate on the small handwritten letters. The muffled voices from the backroom had risen as if they were arguing. He could not make out the words they were saying. Suddenly he felt very uncomfortable, he did not wish to bring any trouble to Carl and his family.

He stood looking to the door, Graystone was a big city perhaps he could make a life of his own here without imposing on others.

"Do not force the bend," His father had told him once while he watched him work a wooden plank into place on a boat's hull. "Do it one step at a time, ease it into place lest the wood split and become useless. Life is handled in the same way, one step at a time. If you try and hurry it, all you will have to show is ruin."

Casius's eyes misted over at the thought of his father. He wiped them dry with the back of his hand and took a step towards the door. As he took hold of the latch the door to the back room opened behind him.

Gayn looked at the book he held and frowned, "Young man that book is worth more gold than you will see in a lifetime. Put it back carefully. It is one of the oldest works I own."

Casius carefully returned the book to the shelf. "I am sorry Gayn," He said embarrassed at having had taken liberties with someone else's property. "I saw that it was written by Lenar and could not resist looking at it. My mother had taught me to read using one of his books. It was much smaller with fewer tales but I have read it a hundred times over."

"Your mother was educated then?" Gayn asked somewhat surprised.

"Very," Casius answered. "I was reading and writing in king's tongue before my fourth birthday."

Carl smiled and slapped Gayn on the back.

Gayn snatched a book from the shelf and tossed it to Casius. "Who wrote this?" he asked.

The small book was worn its leather cover faded and scratched. Casius carefully opened it to the first page. The ink was faded and the vellum yellowed with age. It was an older form of King's tongue and took a few moments to read some of the highly stylized letters. "The use of herbs in the care of livestock." Casius read aloud, " by Oref Moind." He finished closing the book. "There is a date as well but the ink is too faded for me to make it out."

Gayn took the book and returned it to its place. "I'll be honest with you Casius," He said smiling. "I was more than a little angry with Carl for bringing you here. I thought you to be a liability, a homeless thief who had conned my Uncle for a meal and shelter."

Carl grunted but remained silent allowing Gayn to finish.

"I run a profitable business here and have been in need of help for some time now. Forget the carpentry Casius, work here with me. I have a spare room that you can use for as long as you like."

Casius was pleased with the offer, "I don't know what I can do to help you?"

"You can read and write," Gayn answered. "That's a good start, I'll teach you the rest." He turned to Carl, "With that settled will you be staying with us for a bit Uncle?"

Carl shook his head, "I wish that I could, but I best be on my way come morning. I hate leaving Winowa alone for long, she might get it in her head to throw out my pipes."

Gayn laughed, "She just might, you know she hates that habit of yours. At least you'll have supper with us, Elain will be happy to see you."

"Speaking of Elain, Where is your wife now?" Carl asked toying with the pipe in his pocket.

"At the market," Gayn answered.

Carl opened the door to shop, "Come on Gayn, close up for the day. I don't get to the city often and I want to have a look around."

Casius stopped Gayn as they left, "I don't know what to say other than thank you."

"This isn't charity Casius, you'll earn your keep and a modest wage as well." Gayn ushered them out onto the porch and locked the door with a large bronze key. "Let's have a walk then," He smiled tossing his ink-stained apron over the railing.

Casius followed him down the stairs eager to explore the city.

"The words of a traitor cut deeper than any blade, forged by the hand of man."

Lenar, Bard of Ril'Gambor

CHAPTER SIX

The sun was setting when G'relg spotted the isle of Cythera low on the horizon. The sky had become a roaring fire of red and orange. The brilliant colors gleaming on the snow-clad peaks of the Lycian Mountains that lay within the island's heart.

The knot of fear that was slowly growing within him quickly overshadowed his relief at finally seeing the island. His ship was in shambles and would likely never sail the open sea again. The storm had nearly sent them down into the abyss.

It was only by good luck that they had survived. For three weeks they had worked the oars, with little food or water. Half his crew was dead, either lost over the side during the tempest or from exposure. Of the captives from Kale, only a pitiful few remained and most of them would not survive long within the slave pits.

He idly fingered the small sack of coins on his hip, it was a paltry sum and would not pay a tenth of what this proud vessel would cost to replace.

The storm was beyond his control, and he had done his best given the circumstances. How would Bjorn handle the loss of so many men and the crippling of his ship? G'relg wondered if he would survive to see the morning. Bjorn's sense of justice was brutal at best. After all, the man had become the leader of the raiders by killing any who had dared oppose him.

He ran his tongue over the aching stumps of his front teeth. The damned boy had ruined his mouth, and broken his nose in his escape. The sea had him now, there was no way he could have survived long in that tumultuous water.

He could feel Dulrich's eyes upon his back. Turning his head he locked eyes with the grinning man. He stared in challenge but both men were too weak to do anything about it. In a few days time he knew he would have to kill him.

He turned away, "Gloat now," He mumbled. "Soon you will be dead." G'relg promised toying with the hilt of his dagger.

It was one hour after midnight when the stricken vessel reached the harbor's mouth. The moon was a thin sliver of argent hanging low in a sky ablaze with stars. The soft light outlined the tall cliffs of the shoreline, the sea at their feet was alive with glimmers of reflected light dancing on the rolling waves.

A narrow channel lay between two outward jutting cliffs. The towers of Torinth guarded the opening, each tower rising on either side of the channels mouth. The massive square constructs were illuminated by the glow of hundreds of torches. Men moved along the battlements keeping a watchful eye turned towards the sea, Bjorn had made many enemies, and the raiders were a wary lot.

The channel between the towers was scarcely wider than sixty feet, the waves rumbled as they raced through the narrows. A bridge of stone spanned the gap connecting the two Tower's at their mid point, fifty feet above the waves. Merlons crowned the span, ample cover for defenders attacking any ship that sought to pass through the channel.

A heavy chain blocked the entry; it was visible in the troughs between waves. It was lowered into the depths by winches in both towers when a ship was granted passage.

G'relg blew four sharp notes on a silver whistle he wore about his neck. An answering call rang out from the battlement. In the gloom he could here the rattling of the chain as the winches were turned within the towers.

Men lined the span as they passed into the darkness of the channel. Hard faced men who held their weapons ready, always eager for combat.

G'relg stood on at the prow defiantly meeting the gaze of the men above. He was one of Bjorn's captains and would not be cowed by anyone. Strength earned a man respect on Cythera, by the sword was his fortune made.

Beyond the Towers the channel emptied into a shallow bay. Stone quays lined the western shore. The shadows of a thousand masts darkened the sky. The town beyond was dark with only a few oil lamps burning along the waterfront.

Further inland the palace of Bjorn stood above all, built on the edge of a cliff it commanded a breathtaking view of the harbor. Lamps flickered along its many balconies, reflecting brightly from the polished marble of its walls.

As they neared the docks a deep voiced man shouted from the darkness. "Who goes there?" He asked holding a weakly burning lantern high.

"G'relg Halmfist and what remains of crew and ship."

The harbormaster squinted in the darkness, trying to force his weak eyes to focus. "So it is," He said recognizing them. "Tie her up here," He motioned to the quay upon which he stood with a wave of his lantern. "Thought the storm had taken you lads."

"It damn near did," G'relg replied tossing the man a line.

The old sailor looked the vessel over with an experienced eye as he tied the mooring line in place. The he shook his head in amazement. "A wonder you made it at all."

G'relg stepped up onto the pier as a crowd was forming. It was not often that a boat dared the narrows in the dark. A ship that was presumed lost was sure to draw the curious.

The harbormaster hobbled over and held his lantern high to light G'relg's face. "Glad to see you back, now that damned warlock will stop coming around every night."

G'relg's heart lurched, "Vool has been waiting for us?"

"Like a vulture," the man replied. "Always lurking in the shadows looking like death herself."

The harbormaster's rheumy eyes opened wide in surprise. "I have…" He stammered. "Other pressing needs." He scuttled away as fast as his crooked legs could carry him.

G'relg need not turn around to know that Vool was behind him. He could feel the aura of fear that surrounded the enchanter clutching at his heart. The hair on his neck rose as he turned to face the black robed figure.

G'relg's heart skipped a beat when he turned and looked into the malevolent stare of Vool. Twin coals of emerald light burned sickly within the inky blackness of the enchanter's hood. Tongues of green flame flowed up out of the sockets casting no light on their surroundings. He swallowed back his fear and inclined his head in respect.

"Is it done?" Vool's menacing voice whispered, he had spoken softly but his words traveled far in the night air.

G'relg nodded, "New Hope is no more, save those few we have taken captive."

Vool's gaze drifted over the few women who survived the trip. The brightness of his gaze dimmed. "All female?" He asked turning to face G'relg once more.

"All of the men were slain as you instructed Lord Vool."

"Perhaps not all, Lord Vool," a voice said from behind G'relg.

G'relg spun on his heel and faced Dulrich's smiling face. "Be silent!" He snapped at the man drawing his dagger. He was fully intent on killing the man here and now.

A wave of dread slammed into his back forcing him to stagger forward. Dulrich felt the blow as well; both men stumbled and nearly fell.

"Sheath your blade and hold your tongue!" Vool's voice commanded with a serpent like hiss. Stepping forward Vool brushed G'relg aside with a glance. He ignored the raider as he was thrown to the hard stone of the quay.

Dulrich was having second thoughts about the wisdom of trying to use Vool to rid him of G'relg. The enchanter stood glaring down at him, those burning eyes threatening to sear his soul.

"Speak," Vool hissed threateningly, the awful glow within his hood flared anew.

Dulrich's knees shook and his voice cracked with fear as he spoke. He could not look away, Vool's eyes held him captive. "One young man was taken aboard by, G'relg. During the storm that overtook us he managed to escape."

"Is what he say's the truth G'relg?" Vool asked turning his withering gaze onto the raider captain.

"He was a boy," G'relg replied defensively. "Barely fourteen summers old," He eyed Dulrich murderously. "he was a threat to no one."

Vool's anger could be felt in the air, people began to leave the quay. Instincts of self-preservation suddenly overrode, morbid curiosity, urging them to flee for their very lives. "Where was he lost?" He asked in a voice that shook the stones beneath their feet.

"During one of the worst storms I have ever lived through. It damned near destroyed this boat and all aboard it. No-one could have survived long in that tempest's clutches."

The glowing embers narrowed further, "I asked where he was lost, not for your speculation."

"Near Lakarra's eastern shore." He replied quickly, the cold knot of fear growing within his chest.

Vool exploded into rage at the mention of Lakarra. A bone white hand shot outward clutching G'relg's throat. A long sinister hiss escaped the enchanter's lips.

G'relg pried at the vise like grip, He was a strong man but compared to Vool he was little more than a child. Slowly the world began to fade into darkness as Vool lifted him from his feet.

The few people who had remained on the pier fled in horror as the force of Vool's anger hit them as if it were a physical blow.

Dulrich looked on in horror, he was unable to move Vool's aura overwhelmed him with terror.

The enchanter's robe had fallen to the ground, Vool stood wrapped in gossamer flames of emerald light. His face was pale and thin; his eyes were empty sockets that smoldered as if hot coals had been placed within them.

He wore armor constructed of hundreds of overlapping silver scales. It flowed freely with his movements, glittering in the light of his power. A dark circlet of iron rested upon his brow keeping his flaxen hair out of his face.

With his free hand he drew a long sword and held the blade up for G'relg to see. The three feet of bronze writhed in his grip as if it were alive.

His vacant sockets narrowed as he considered running the man through. With a look of disgust he tossed G'relg aside as if he were a rag doll. "That death would be too easy for one such as you G'relg." He said sheathing his strange blade. "There are many slower ways for a man to die."

The fear that had held Dulrich paralyzed subsided as Vool's temper eased. Dulrich shook himself free of its grasp and decided it was time for him to leave. He came to his feet slowly and took a step backwards. Vool's head snapped in his direction, the empty sockets of his eyes radiating evil.

"One more step and you shall share his fate." Vool hissed, his voice the thin rasp of a serpent's scales.

Dulrich froze, his knees shook with fear and his heart was hammering so hard that at any moment he believed it would break free of its prison of bone and flesh.

G'relg was on his hands and knees gasping for breath, and was unprepared when Vool struck him with the back of his hand. The raider cried out, the force of the blow lifted him several feet into the air and hurled him fifteen feet down the quay.

"Fool!" Vool snarled exposing his teeth. "A simple task was given to you and yet you failed. You may have succeeded in bringing about the very thing we sought to prevent!"

G'relg somehow had managed to get to his feet. Blood flowed from his right ear and his neck was turning dark purple where Vool had held him. His eyes burned and his sense of balance was slowly returning, though his ear rang with a steady high-pitched tone. Vool was drawing near; with each step the enchanter took the mind numbing fear that assailed his senses grew.

"Prove your worth," Vool grinned malevolently. "I may spare your life."

"Then let him do so with his deeds!" A voice shouted from the darkness.

Vool spun and fixed his gaze on Dulrich.

Dulrich flinched under his scrutiny, he had not spoken, but he feared he would be struck down because of it.

"Enough Vool!" The voice repeated. Bjorn Ironfist stepped out of the shadows. He wore only his breeches and his broad chest heaved as he controlled his own anger. At his back stood a large number of heavily armed men. He had brought his household guard. "These are my men, not yours for the taking."

Vool glared at the raider chieftain. "Careful Bjorn," He said coldly. "Do not forget who my master is."

"I am the master of this Isle Vool, and the men who live upon it." Bjorn raised his heavy crossbow and held it level with Vool's chest. "It is I, and I alone who casts judgment on those who serve me."

Vool looked on the men with contempt, a part of him wished they would attack. He would savor their deaths but his master had been quite firm, he was forbidden to destroy these petty mortals. He allowed his power to ebb; the time of their deaths would come soon enough.

"These men accomplished the task set before them, what is one boy lost in a storm tossed sea?" Bjorn said not knowing how close he had come to dying.

Vool's robe slid up from the ground on its own. Enfolding him within its black layers. "That boy may bring ruin to us all in time." He answered his face once more lost within the dark shadows of his hood.

The men raised their weapons as the cloth moved. Bjorn stilled them with a sharp look. He too was unnerved by what he saw and he knew that should Vool desire it, he had within him the power to slay them all.

Bjorn motioned to G'relg with his crossbow. "They alone have seen this child, who better to search him out?"

Vool paused briefly considering Bjorn's statement, "Very well, let them go and find this boy. Whether he lives or not, I want his corpse brought back here."

"Done," Bjorn said with much relief. "G'relg and his men will leave for Lakarra this night." Bjorn turned his back to the enchanter and headed back to his estate.

"Bjorn," Vool hissed. "Do not ever think to pull a weapon on me again..." Vool let the threat hang unfinished in the air.

Bjorn's back stiffened as he replied without turning to face Vool. "If I ever do so again, it will be to remove your frozen heart." He had spoken rashly, and regretted it immediately.

Vool laughed, a hollow sound filled with promised torment and agony. He melted away into the shadows his voice lingering a few heart beats after he had disappeared.

G'relg fixed his gaze upon Dulrich as if his anger alone could slay the man.

Dulrich was wary; despite G'relg's battered appearance he knew the man was dangerous. G'relg had a well-earned reputation as a formidable fighter. His skills with the knife were second to none.

Dulrich had run his gambit and in doing so had nearly gotten them both killed. He had betrayed G'relg, and now it was only a matter of time until G'relg would kill him.

G'relg drew his knife and before Dulrich could react he buried the blade to the hilt through his throat. G'relg smiled coldly as Dulrich's hot blood splattered onto his cheek.

Dulrich clutched the wound seeking to stem the flow of blood. His windpipe was severed, and as he fell he cursed G'relg's name. The only sound that passed his lips was a long drawn out wet gurgle.

G'relg wrenched his knife free, opening the wound further as Dulrich fell to the ground. He wiped the blade clean on the dying man's shirt. With his boot he rolled Dulrich over so he could watch the light of the man's spirit fade from his eyes.

Bjorn stood on the balcony that over looked the harbor below. The sun was rising, coloring the sky with a pallet of brilliant gold and fiery orange. Down in the harbor he knew G'relg and his surviving crewmembers were readying their ship with hasty repairs.

His confrontation with Vool had ended several hours ago and yet his hands still shook. The sheer terror of standing before that demon had nearly undone him; no amount of power could be worth the price he feared he was yet to pay.

War was coming and Bjorn had sided with the only force that would accept him. By his deeds he had damned himself and those that followed him to serve Vool's master. Suddenly the thought of ruling his own people under that dark yoke frightened him to the very core of his being.

Looking to the ships below he felt the sudden urge to join G'relg and flee his predicament. He knew it was folly to think he could escape. His die had been cast, and all he could do was hope to survive the outcome of the roll.

CHAPTER SEVEN

With the coming of his fourth spring in Lakarra, Casius had become a close member of Gayn's family. He worked hard and delighted the scribe by his ability to quickly master the nuances of creating artful manuscripts.

In two short years his penmanship had surpassed Gayn's, and his knowledge of the many languages of the world grew in bounds. He read voraciously, his craving for knowledge never fading. He had even mastered the guttural Hyyari, a difficult tongue spoken only in the northern wilds.

Gayn's wife, Elain grew heavy with child and their many trips to the nearby settlements came to an end. Gayn could not bear to part with her as she came to term.

A merchant from Aenos, a small city to the south, commissioned a deed to be drawn up to several of his mines in the Carec Mountains. He was a wealthy man and offered a handsome sum once the documents were delivered to the buyer in far off Elkrun.

Gayn could use the money, and after much persuading on Casius's part he gave in and accepted the commission. Casius was after all a man in his own right, and if he choose to travel the two hundred miles to the city of Elkrun on the shores of the Darkwater River. It was not Gayn's place to stop him.

He did insist however, that Casius journey with a spice caravan. The open plains are a wild place where the safety of numbers is needed.

Casius was excited; he purchased a stout horse, and supplies the day before he was to leave.

Elain prepared a veritable feast for them that night. After she had gone to sleep Casius and Gayn spent several hours sitting on the porch enjoying the night air.

An hour after dawn Casius left Gayn's house, and trotted the horse through the newly stirring streets. He found the Caravan yards by following his nose. The heady scent of so many animals packed close together could be smelled across much of the city.

The March air was brisk and the sun's rays warmed him as he rode out of the shadows of the buildings. This time of year the nights were cold and the days hot. It was as if winter's icy fingers refused to release their final hold on the world.

Urbas Ugei, the caravan's master met him as he arrived. He took one look at Casius and snorted in disgust. He believed Casius was nothing more than some rich merchant's son who was being sent away because of some minor offense.

"You travel with us," he said with such a heavy accent that it took Casius several moments to understand him. "You listen to me good and we have no trouble." Urbas looked to the short sword Casius wore about his waist. "You know how to use?" He asked shaking the scabbard.

"Some," Casius lied, He could swing it but that was about all. He had never gotten around to learning the fine art of sword fighting.

"Good," Urbas grinned revealing teeth stained a dark yellow from years of Guall chewing. "Keep it sheathed unless I tell you otherwise." The dark skin of his brow wrinkled as he caught a glimpse of the thick leather tube tied across Casius's saddlebags. He poked it with the switch he carried. "What are you carrying there?"

"A deed to two mines," Casius answered. "Worthless except to the man for whom it was written," He added quickly, as he opened the weatherproof tube. He unrolled the heavy parchment slowly for Urbas to see.

"Your master has great skill with letters." He said appreciating the flowing script of the deed.

Casius grinned, "Thank you, but it was I who wrote this." He carefully returned the document to its case.

Urbas laughed, "Well then, we have a scribe among us." From within the folds of his stained traveling robe he produced a small leather bound book. Its cover was faded and the pages ragged and yellow. He handed it to Casius, "A Talen of gold if you would keep a record of our journey."

Casius tucked the book into his saddlebag. " You have hired yourself a scribe," he said in fluent Te'Caleph, the language of Urbas's homeland.

Urbas's eyebrows rose in surprise, "You have been to Caleph?"

Casius shook his head. No one ventured far into that realm, unless he was born there or traveled with a host of armed men. The people of Caleph distrusted strangers, often slaying them. Since the armies of Lakarra had conquered their lands, all strangers were treated as spies.

"No, but I have learned many of the languages of this land from my employer."

"He taught you well Casius," Urbas looked to the assembled wagons and pack-laden mules. "We will talk later, it does my heart good to hear the words of my home."

Urbas swung up onto his horse and with the switch he carried he motioned the caravan forward. The drivers expertly led the pack animals across the narrow stone bridge that spanned the Taelus River. As they crossed the slow moving water they began to sing.

They followed a well worn road leading southwest, as the day passed the road gradually grew rougher becoming nothing more than a muddy track. The villages they passed grew smaller and further apart.

After three uneventful days they reached the small city of Aenos. The city had been built upon a low tor that stood on the edge of the Braelin Wood.

Fields of rich earth surrounded the city, home to a multitude of scattered farms. The orderly rows of vibrant green growth resembled a vast quilt spread out beneath a stunningly blue sky.

For two days the caravan camped outside the city walls. Each morning as the sun rose, Urbas would take his place in the open market.

Casius had been to many markets before, but he had never heard a hawker as proficient as Urbas. By the end of the first day Casius was convinced this man could sell a dairy farmer his own cattle.

Urbas's thick accent only added to the allure of the strange and mystical herbs and spices he sold. Many of which could only be found in the land of Caleph. Hounds tongue for aches, the golden mint Mea'real for colds. He even offered the sap of Fire thorn, a legendary remedy to cure the worst of infections.

Casius kept an accurate count of the caravan's wares, much to Urbas's delight. For once he was able to enjoy his work without the tedious task of keeping track of his stock.

On the second night outside of Aenos, Casius wandered through their encampment. The hour was late but he could not sleep. He found Urbas sitting about a fire with several of his drivers.

The Merchant was skillfully juggling three small knives. The leaf shaped blades flashed in the firelight, going faster and faster until they became nothing more than a blur. With a mere flick of his wrist two of the blades flashed through the flames and embedded themselves in a log twenty feet away. The blades sank deep into the wood, with scarcely a fingers width between them. The drivers cheered, and shared a drink from a goatskin bladder. From the smell, Casius could tell it was a very strong liquor that they were drinking.

"So Casius," Urbas said catching his remaining blade by its leather wrapped handle. "How is our scribe this evening?" He asked motioning to an empty spot near the fire.

Casius lowered himself to the ground next to Urbas, nodding in greeting to the drivers. "Well enough thank you." He replied watching as Urbas idly twirled the small knife through his fingers. "You do that well."

Urbas looked puzzled for a brief moment before realizing that he was referring to the knife. "This," he said handing the small blade to him. "Is called a Ka'rich, in Caleph every child is given a set at the age of five. Most children master them before their seventh summer."

The blade was six inches long, fashioned to resemble a broad leaf. Two razor sharp edges ran down two thirds of its length. From the tip to the leather wrapped grip. It was finely crafted and remarkably well balanced for throwing.

Urbas nudged him with his elbow, "Go ahead throw it."

Casius gripped the hilt and tossed the blade, it struck the log on its side, ringing loudly. The blade bounced back into the crowd of drivers causing them to scurry out of its way. The small knife ended its errant flight, landing near the fire its tip embedded in the earth.

Urbas laughed as he retrieved the knife, "No harm done," He said returning to his seat. "You'll need to practice that throw of yours." He handed Casius one of the blades. "Keep this and learn it."

Casius attempted to hand the blade back to the caravan master. "I cannot keep this," He protested. "It is too valuable."

Urbas held his hand up to deter any further protest, "I have others, and in Caleph it is a great insult to turn aside a gift freely given. Besides I cannot bear seeing a young man without a Ka'rich in his belt."

Casius lowered his head in acceptance, "Thank you Urbas."

"Just be careful," Urbas quipped. "Try not to cut one of my drivers with it."

The men around the fire laughed and passed the skin about for another round.

"Tonight we rest," Urbas proclaimed loudly. " Tomorrow we begin our trek in earnest."

Several of the men made a show of groaning in protest, drawing laughter from their leader. Despite the protests, the men lingered about the fire until well past midnight. By that time Casius had actually managed to sink the blade into the log several times. On each occasion the men would cheer, and the skin was passed about in celebration.

Dawn came far too early for Casius's liking, his head pounded fiercely as he packed away his gear. He moved through the camp in a fog of pain, Casius was experiencing his first hangover, and within an hour he had sworn off hard drink forever.

By the time the blazing orb of the sun had cleared the horizon the caravan was on the move. For all the drink that was passed about the fire last night, it was Casius alone who looked the worse for wear.

Urbas led them southward keeping the dark wall of the Braelin Wood on their left. The road swung to the west, a thin line in the sea of grass running to the distant horizon. The caravan continued south out onto the vast plain.

The grass grew tall, waist high to a man. It was vibrant green swaying with the gentle breeze that blew in from the east. The verdant waves often crested in places by dense patches of wild flowers, their petals every color imaginable.

On their second day out from Aenos they spotted a distant herd of plains deer bounding away from the slow moving intruders. The bucks tore at the grass with antlers that spanned easily eight feet across.

Urbas was riding next to Casius when they had spotted the deer. "Magnificent creatures," Urbas commented as the deer raced away.

"That they are," Casius replied watching in awe at the sheer grace and power they projected. "Dangerous as well, I'd say judging by the look of them."

Urbas shook his head, "Not really, the deer always give ground, and rarely do you see one close by, unless it's wounded. Then again any wounded animal can be a fell beast to contend with." Urbas spat a cheek full of quall onto the ground.

"Now the Greensward bison is another thing altogether, a great black beast with massive horns. Some bulls weigh as much as three horses put together. They stand seven feet at the shoulder and can run a horse to ground over a short distance.

"They are known to attack any who stray too close to the herd. The bison will often charge in mass, led by the biggest bull. Once their ire is raised, they are relentless until their bloodlust is satisfied. Whole caravans have been lost due to carelessness."

"Have you ever run into one?" Casius asked, trying to imagine a bull of such size.

Urbas laughed, "Anyone who is worth their salt in this business has. I was a driver in my youth, one day we strayed near an old bull who had lost his herd to a younger male. He had grown quite mad in his solitude.

"He stalked us for days, late one night he charged into our encampment killing men and horses with abandon. Four drivers and twenty one horses died that bloody night, until we brought that cloven hoofed devil down with a well placed arrow."

Casius shook his head, for all he had read he was amazed at his ignorance of the real world. "I hope we don't run into any of them."

"Not likely," Urbas replied. "Where you see plains deer, the bison are scarce. Then again on the Greensward anything is possible, we still have six days until we reach the Carec Mountains, that's a fair piece of travel yet."

One day led into another, mile after mile the long train of pack animals slowly plodded southward. The scenery hardly changed, the wide-open grasslands brimming with the colors of spring surrounded them on three sides. The dark forbidding wall of the old forest lay but a mile distant on their left.

Casius quickly fell into the routine of the merchant train. He began to get to know the drivers that followed Urbas across the trackless plains. They were tough men, hardened by a life spent in the wilds.

Urbas was very particular about the character of those he traveled with. Not one of his men could be considered anything less than honest. They were trustworthy companions, who would defend one another against any threat, either large or small.

Casius was soon welcomed among their number. He spent the long nights sitting about the various fires listening to their exaggerated adventures while he practiced with his Ka'rich.

On the fourth day, a line of distant mountains crossed their path far to the south. Old and worn by countless eons of howling wind and rain, they offered a gauge for Casius to judge the caravan's slow progress by.

That evening, just after the last of the sun's light had faded, a brightly painted minstrel's wagon rolled up to the camp's edge.

Urbas welcomed the performer gladly; the old bard did not offer his name, and it was not requested. Traveling bards simply plied their trade for the love of music. They rarely sought wealth or fame and out of respect for this tradition a minstrel was never asked to identify himself.

The man wore a crown of wild hair the color of new fallen snow. His eyes burned brightly, set deep within a maze of wrinkles. He played a battered old lute that had seen better days. The instrument sounded far better than it looked, his skill a pleasant surprise to all who heard.

After an hour of nonstop playing Urbas passed him a steeping cup of tea. "What news do you carry from afar?" The caravan master asked seating himself next to the Bard.

The old man frowned, deep furrows crossing his wrinkled brow. "Nothing good I'm afraid," he replied sipping at the tea. "My travels have carried me far this last year, from the rocky shores of Ao'dan to the deep bay of Ship Haven in the south.

"Strange things are afoot in the north," the man said softly with the exaggerated facial expressions of a long practiced storyteller. "Men tell of mysterious riders in the dark, passing through the less settled lands. With great hounds as big as bears loping along at their sides. Many believe the Morne are stirring once more."

At the mention of the dreaded Morne the idle banter nearby ceased as the men waited for the bard's next words.

The minstrel paused allowing the tension to build, "They also claim that the Ice Trolls have left the northern wastes and rove the deep woods, slaughtering careless travelers."

Urbas laughed breaking the minstrels spell, "Morne and Trolls!" He slapped his leg, "You are a master of your craft," he said as his laughter subsided.

The Bard smiled at the compliment. "I only repeat what I have heard whispered in the taverns during the still hours of the night."

"Ah…" Urbas quipped. "The yarns spun by drunkards and brigands."

The bard shrugged and drained his cup. He wiped his long mustache with the back of his sleeve. "Take care in the hills good sir," He said seriously. "I passed through a camp two nights past, never have I seen such roguish men in these parts before. They knew me for what I am, and assumed I was without coin and left me well enough alone."

The smile on Urbas's face faded, "How many?"

"Ten perhaps more," The Bard guessed. "Not enough to try your swords."

Urbas spat, "Cowards," he exclaimed. "Should they get brave enough to test our mettle, they are in for a rude awakening. My drivers are all veteran soldiers from the king's army. There are a few of them here that I would swear were born with a blade clenched in their fists."

A gentle rain fell that night dowsing the flames of their fires. Casius spent the remainder of the evening huddled beneath a canvas tarp that kept most of the water out. Many of the men simply lay out in the open, wrapped in blankets with cloaks propped on sticks covering their heads.

The rain lasted most of the night, ending sometime before dawn. Casius awoke to the sounds of the camp stirring. The smell of bacon and coffee drew him out of his shelter, as a moth is drawn to a flame.

He joined the men about the fire, as he ate he noticed a subtle change had come over them. Their banter was subdued, eating quietly their eyes constantly watching the forest's edge. The bard's warning was not being taken lightly. Casius noticed that nearly all of the men were now wearing swords about their waists.

The camp was a nightmare of mud; pools of standing water were everywhere. The wet grass soaking their legs as the men broke camp.

It was in all a miserable morning; the heavy clouds above only promising more rain yet to come. Even the distant forest appeared all the more forbidding beneath a steel gray sky.

It rained off and on throughout the day. The men's mood turned as bleak as their surroundings. The land began to rise in rolling hills, many of which were crowned with small groves of pine and birch. They had left the plain and now were entering the lower reaches of the Carec Mountains.

That night the rain returned in force. The sky was ablaze with dazzling bolts of lightning, and rumbling peals of thunder shook the ground. Causing even the bravest among them to flinch. No one slept much that night; they sat together beneath hastily erected shelters of canvas and stout poles.

The morning came in a blazing sky of orange and red. Only a few dark clouds remained above, thin remnants of the night's storm.

Casius emerged from his shelter stiff and sore. He stretched his arms, inhaling deeply. Savoring the smells of wet grass and fresh coffee.

They must have made good progress yesterday; the mountains appeared much closer, looming over their encampment. The bare peaks caught the morning sun, the stone blazing with reflected light above their shadow cloaked lower reaches.

Casius stood holding his horse's bridle, admiring the scenic beauty of this wild land. He could understand the lure of the long road. These men who followed Urbas enjoyed a freedom that few men would ever know. For twelve days he has traveled with them. He now felt a part of the company, no longer a stranger.

Only after Urbas had called his name for the third time, did he come to realize that he was holding up the caravan. With a mumbled apology, he mounted his steed and took his place at Urbas's side as the caravan surged forward.

"We'll have fair weather today," Urbas said looking to the sky. "By evening we'll be well into the foothills. The pass itself is an easy trek, it lies low and is usually open the year round." He frowned in thought, "With all this damn rain it's going to be slow going. The pass is likely to be knee deep with mud."

"What of these men the Bard spoke of?" Casius asked still concerned about what lay ahead.

"The pass has places that are well suited for ambush," Urbas replied with a smile. "These men are among the best, we will not be caught unaware Casius."

"You would think the king would use the Senatum to keep the passes clear." To Casius the mountains appeared more menacing than they had in the morning.

"Ha!" Urbas guffawed, "Coming from someone as learned as you, true naiveté is somewhat surprising."

"I am learning that books are a poor substitute to actually living in the world."

"Wise words," Urbas said approvingly. "The Senatum are not concerned with the likes of us, often they are the brigands themselves."

Casius scowled, "The more I learn of them, the more I dislike all that they represent."

Urbas nodded in agreement, "Just keep your opinions to yourself in public. Those words you have uttered would buy you a visit from the headsman and his axe." Urbas leaned forward in his saddle, his dark eyes fixing on Casius. "You truly have lived far off the beaten track Casius."

"About as far as one could get before falling off the world's edge."

"And here I had thought Caleph was about as far as one could go."

"I am sure there are places far more isolated than our homes." Casius said with a smile.

"Aye," Urbas shrugged. "And they're all the better for it."

Casius agreed with the caravan master, "The more I learn of the world, the deeper my heart yearns for the days when I lived in ignorance of the evil that men are capable of doing."

"By the gods!" Urbas exclaimed in astonishment. "You are far to young to speak such things." Urbas's eyes narrowed as he studied the young man. "Are you truly what you claim to be? Or are you a wizard traveling in disguise?"

"I should think a wizard would shun the company of your smelly pack animals, and travel abroad in a gilded chariot at the head of some grand procession."

Urbas feigned insult, "Smelly animals indeed! That my boy is the sweet aroma of honest profit."

"I'll remember that the next time I step in one of your steaming piles of dropped profits!" One of the men shouted from the line. Drawing good-natured laughter from the drivers.

The Caravan came to a well-worn track that led up the face of a steep tree covered slope. It zigzagged among the moss-covered trunks, disappearing beneath the thick canopy of leaves.

The day had grown hot, and the relentless sun beat down on their backs without mercy. Up the steep hillside the Caravan wound. It was cool within the shade provided by the overhanging bowers, a welcome relief for the men.

They crested the hill and Urbas halted the Caravan allowing the animals to rest.

They looked down into a shallow valley that held a deep lake of still water that reflected the sky and surrounding mountains clearly. On the southern side less than a mile away a narrow gorge ran up between two peaks, through this flowed a narrow stream.

Urbas pointed up the gorge. "There lays the pass," he said. "We will camp at the opening in a small clearing."

They lingered on the hill's crown for only a short while; once the animals had been tended Urbas led them down into the vale. They followed the narrow shoreline around the lake's eastern side. Coming to a small circular clearing that bordered on the water's edge.

The men quickly set up camp; they were well practiced, having had done this for many years. A large fire was soon burning in a pit lined with stones polished by water.

Casius saw to his horse's needs and hobbled the animal in an area where the grass was thick and lush. He left the beast as it grazed contentedly on the verdant shoots. He wandered along the shore, and walked a short distance up the gorge. A wide trail followed the streambed, winding around large boulders that had fallen from the rim some thirty or more feet above.

The sound of rushing water grew louder the further he went until he came to a waterfall that plummeted from the heights above. Thick ferns lined the edges of the pool from which the stream flowed. The air was moist with blowing mist and smelled of rich earth.

The gorge beyond the falls was dark; its bottom lay in the shadow cast by the mountains. Casius remembered the Bard's warning and suddenly the area felt threatening.

He retraced his path quickly, cursing himself for foolishly wandering off on his own. When he entered camp the feeling of unseen eyes upon his back faded.

He joined the men at the fire eating a thick stew of beans and salted meat. Urbas said nothing of his foray but the look he gave him showed his displeasure at his venture.

All of the men bore arms now; their weapons clinking in the growing darkness as they moved about.

Casius lingered by the fire for a few hours listening to the songs of crickets, and the eerie croaks of frogs from the water's edge. His eyes grew heavy as sleep called him.

He moved carefully through the camp stepping around sleeping forms upon the ground. He found his bedroll and wrapped himself in the warm wool, and watched the dazzling stars above for a few minutes before slipping into a deep slumber.

In the early hours before dawn he awoke with a start, the camp about him was in chaos. Men were yelling and pack mules braying in terror. Above the din a deep primal roar pierced the darkness.

Casius untangled himself from his blanket, grabbing his short sword he raced through the camp to where a line of torch bearing men had gathered. He freed his sword from its scabbard as he ran.

What he saw at the edge of the camp filled his heart with terror. The men waved the brands and shouted, keeping a bear of nightmarish size at bay. The roaring mountain of dark fur and gleaming claws stood upon its hind legs, unsure as to whom to attack.

Infuriated by the fire it roared incessantly, blood and foam spraying from its cavernous maw twenty feet above the ground. Two men lay on the ground beneath it, mangled by the beast's ferocious attacks.

Arrows struck its breast, sinking deep into the heavy muscle beneath the blood-smeared fur. The bear roared in response, and lunged forward with incredible speed. Its twelve-inch nails narrowly missing a man's face as he frantically retreated.

The beast ignored the flames, and plowed through the line of men. Brushing them aside as if they were nothing more than a swarm of pesky flies.

More arrows struck the creature. The small game bows the men were using were incapable of piercing the muscle deep enough to do serious damage. The bear spun snapping at the painful barbs embedded in its side.

Two of the men stood their ground, firing arrows as fast as they could fit them to string. The bear fell upon them in its fury. Too late the bowmen realized their peril. They could offer little resistance to the bear as it attacked. One man's head was crushed within its gaping maw; his body was limp as a rag when beast shook its head. The second bowmen fared no better as the razor like claws tore open his belly, spilling his guts onto the ground.

Casius stared in horror, gagging as the stench of blood and bile reached him. Despite the gore he could not tear his eyes away from the scene, as the man struggled to force the hanging loops of tattered intestines back into his abdomen.

The shock on the man's face would be forever in his memory; the bear struck him a mighty blow to the back of his head snapping his neck. The crack of splintering bone echoed in the night.

The men renewed their attacks, tossing burning brands onto the bear. The creature's fur smoked several places, one man charged with a spear seeking to skewer the beast. The bear swatted the weapon aside and tore the man's arm from its socket with a vicious bite.

A loud clack was heard over the din, the bear fell dead pinning the dying man beneath its bulk. A single shaft protruded from its left eye. A cruelly barbed iron tip dripped gore from the back of its head.

Silence filled the camp, beneath the bear's corpse the feeble moans of the trapped man stopped as his life ended.

"How many men have we lost?" Urbas's voiced bellowed in anger, he stalked into view carrying the heavy crossbow he had fired with such deadly accuracy.

"Torel, Gawlen, Ednar, Vellon, and Kal." Kehvlor, the camp's cook spoke sadly. He was kneeling next to Kal, covered by the man's blood. He had attempted to staunch the flow of blood from the man's shoulder.

"Damn!" Urbas cursed, "and the animals?" He asked once he had regained control of his temper.

Several of the men spoke out at once. The bear had passed by the horses and mules. Choosing to attack the sentries, driving through them to fall upon the unfortunate men as they slept.

Urbas spat on the ground. "A man killer," He said in disgust. "He's probably followed our spore for days before attacking." Urbas looked to Casius, "This is a Fel'Tuin, they usually live in the higher reaches of the mountains. This bear is old and was driven from his range, probably by a younger male. They are rarely seen but once one has tasted a man's flesh they become man killers, forsaking all other prey. There are tales of entire villages terrorized by such beasts."

Casius shuddered, had he decided to sleep on the opposite side of the fire he too would be numbered among the dead.

"Double the watch." Urbas ordered tossing the crossbow to one of the drivers. "Break out your heavy weapons and keep them close at hand. Suddenly I have a very bad feeling about the remainder of our journey."

Casius felt out of place, he stood aside watching as the men followed Urbas's instructions. In short order the group no longer resembled a merchants caravan. It had been transformed into an armed encampment.

Casius felt more at ease by the sight of battle-axes and a large number of heavy crossbows. One of the men handed him an iron tipped spear longer than he was tall. Casius looked at the weapon and attempted to hand it back.

"I do not know how to use this," he said apologetically.

The man shrugged. "Just stick your foe with the pointy end," he said walking away.

Five graves were dug within the clearing; the men gently lowering the blanket wrapped bodies of their companions into the earth.

The graves were filled in silence; and in the morning the sun rose, falling upon five mounds of fresh turned earth.

Urbas built a small fire at the foot of each mound; into each he threw a handful of the bear's course fur. The acrid smoke coiled up into the still air. "Let the smoke of your fallen foe guide you to the houses of your ancestors." He intoned at each grave.

Although curious Casius knew this was not the time for questions. He was new to this group of trail-hardened men. Even though they had accepted him into their number he did not share their depth of grief. To these men, the fallen were brothers that they had known for many years, through both hardship and joy.

He glanced about him at the stern faces; only the moistness of their eyes betrayed their feelings. Of thirty-one men who had set out together only twenty-six remained. Now that number felt pitifully small when facing a very large and dangerous world.

One by one the men walked away and began to clear the camp. The animals were loaded. With a solemn wave of his hand Urbas led them from the clearing into the narrow pass.

Casius looked once more at the graves from the back of his horse. A parting glance to the men he had only just begun to know.

He felt sorrow; too much death had swirled about his life. Seeing the honored graves that these men rested in opened old wounds. He felt anew the loss of his father. If he ever did return to his home, he knew he would find no graves. Only crow pecked bones and fire scarred ruins would mark where his people had once lived. His eyes clouded with both rage and grief. He swallowed his emotions, and followed the last rider into the narrow gorge.

The man looked over his shoulder. "This is a hard life Casius," he said consolingly. "Each man here knows what is at stake, and yet we willingly accept the risk.

"We are not meant to be farmers or shop keepers; this is the life for such as we. Freedom and adventure are their own rewards." The man paused considering his words, "We have all seen friends die, and last night was a hard lesson for you to learn. Heed it well, this world cares little if you live or die. All we can do is be prepared and fight hard when the time comes."

Casius rode in silence for several moments before replying. "I am no stranger to death," He said somewhat more harshly than he intended. "She has touched my life before."

The man nodded, "Keep your eyes open, this pass is notorious for ambushes. If we are attacked stay close and do exactly what I say."

Casius nodded, his eyes now darting along the gorge's walls. He expected a hail of arrows from above at any moment.

Hours passed and the day grew warm, the air within the gorge lay still and heavy. The trail was narrow and treacherous affording no place for them to safely rest. As night fell torches were passed out. In their fitful light they continued on foot leading the weary animals. The faint bubbling of the stream's passage in the darkness below became a constant companion.

Dawn brightened the sky above. The faint light failed to reach into the depths of the grotto. The men and animals trudged onward, enfolded in the cold dark of the mountain's shadow.

Long weary hours passed, with the fears of ambush still foremost on their minds. Although they were weary to the point of near collapse, their eyes were sharp and alert. Searching the darkest shadows for enemies.

The early afternoon sun crept down the ragged stone. The path ahead brightened, and the shadows retreated. They came upon a roaring cataract that poured out of a cavern's darkened maw. It was the source of the stream they had been following. Flooding out from the mountain's roots the water sparkling in the sunlight. The grotto narrowed beyond the fall rising only slightly before sloping steeply downward.

The narrow path they followed led down into what once had been the stream's path long ago. Stones polished by the flow of water lined the channel walls, loose pebbles slid beneath their feet as they descended.

They traveled only a short distance when the walls of the looming cliffs ended. The Caravan stood at the grotto's opening. At the top of a long slope that led down into a land of gently rolling hills, dotted with thick groves of birch and oak.

A deep channel led down the slope ending in a broad shallow bowl like depression, that at one time had been a lake. The grass grew thick upon the hills, scattered with the tangled vines of wild berries heavily laden with fruit.

Urbas led them down into the bowl; here they made an early camp. The men were grateful for the respite. The watch was set and those not on guard duty slept soundly on the soft ground.

Casius stood the first watch and paced the perimeter. In the gathering gloom of nightfall he was reassured by the presence of so many men sharing his duty. As the midnight hour passed Urbas himself relieved him. He fell asleep within moments, and did not awaken until the first light of dawn brightened the sky.

The following morning he limped on sore feet to a small fire the men had started. He stood close, allowing its heat to drive off the dawn chill. He nodded to Urbas as the man joined them. The caravan master set a metal urn at the fire's edge.

"For tea," he explained when he noticed Casius's gaze lingering on the ornate scrollwork etched into the urn's metal. "It does wonders for wiping away the cobwebs of a long sleep."

Casius smiled, "I was wondering why I was not awakened for the dawn watch."

"Don't take offense," Urbas nodded to the men about the fire. "The hours before sunrise are the most dangerous, these men only trust a seasoned veteran to ward them during that time."

Casius understood. His father would have done the same when venturing out to sea on a new vessel. "I take only those men who have earned their salt." He would often say.

He shrugged, "I did sleep better knowing they were about."

"I as well," Urbas replied offering him a steaming cup of tea. "I hire only those men whom I feel to be trustworthy. I have too many other concerns to be wasting time watching my back. Believe me there are plenty of thieves and rouges trying to sign on with what they feel to be an easy mark." Urbas sipped his tea and smiled in pleasure. "These men have been with me for many years. I pay well and share the profits. This keeps them happy and loyal. A rare enough thing in this line of work."

Casius finished his tea, and listened to the complaining grunts of the men as they loaded the mules, in preparation of the day's journey. "I for one am looking forward to a warm bed and a bath." he said jokingly.

"Here now," Urbas laughed. "Just when I thought we had made a proper driver of you. You have to go and say something like that."

Casius wrinkled his nose in disgust. "Don't breathe too deeply Urbas. The pack mules smell better than us."

"Ah..." Urbas exclaimed making a show of inhaling deeply. "That's the smell of an honest day's labor. Besides my wife claims it keeps me faithful."

Casius laughed, "She's a wise woman."

"Aye, that she is." Urbas stood and raised his voice for all to hear. "Lets get these mangy curs on the road then. Five more days of easy travel lay before us."

It did not take long to get the train organized. Within the hour the line of mules and men were moving out of the foothills, and into the low lying lands of the Varsus Valley.

Unlike the plains that formed the heartland of Lakarra, the valley through which they trod was rich and fertile. The dark loamy soil supported thick woods, and fields of deep emerald grass.

They followed a trail that became a heavily traveled road. The rolling landscape became a patchwork of cultivated fields bordered with low walls of stone. Individual farmsteads were few. Most of the people of this land chose to live in walled compounds for their protection.

They passed these by under the watchful eyes of men upon their walls. Those working the fields would stop long enough to see if the men posed a threat.

"They're a wary lot," Casius commented as they passed yet another walled village.

"Aye," Urbas nodded. "It was not always so, but the roads are no longer as safe as they once were. These people have grown cautious."

They spent the night camped within a line of trees that bordered the fast flowing waters of the Koran River. The next morning they followed the road as it ran alongside the river for a few miles.

Through the trees, a modest house came into view. It stood upon the bank of the river, its stonework covered with patches of thick moss.

Next to the building a narrow bridge spanned the water. Constructed from stout planks, and supported by thick pylons. The bridge was well kept and appeared sturdy.

The fattest man Casius had ever laid eyes on stood outside the door watching them approach with interest. He was sweating profusely even though the day was cool, with a soft breeze blowing in from the west.

"C'arl Finnerson," Urbas muttered to Casius. "He collects tolls for the use of the bridge. A toad of a man who would slit his own throat if he could profit from the act."

"My good friend Urbas!" Finnerson exclaimed as they neared. Though his voice and smile were pleasant, his eyes held nothing but disdain and loathing.

It took Casius only a moment, but he knew there was nothing in this grotesque man that could be considered virtuous.

Urbas tossed a silver penny to Finnerson. "C'arl," he said in greeting with a slight dip of his head.

The man was huge but not slow; he snatched the coin out of the air and tucked it into a stained pouch at his hip. He leered at Casius as he rode by.

Casius felt the man's eyes burning into his back. He knew the man was foul in more ways than his appearance. "Why do you pay him?"

"He is the eyes of the Senatum and carries their protection. Men of his ilk are never alone; six of his kin lay hidden within the trees. A silver penny is not worth the loss of a single man to a coward's arrow." Urbas looked back over his shoulder as they clomped across the wooden planks. "Take care when you come back this way Casius, I do not like the way he looks at you."

Casius nodded, "Nor I."

"There are rumors that his brother serves the raider king as a captain of one of his black ships." Urbas said with a shrug. "From the look on your face I can see that you have had some experience with those sea devils."

"They murdered my father," He answered with a catch of emotion in his voice. No matter how many years have passed Casius's grief remained strong.

"Damn," Urbas muttered. He could sense the young man's pain. "I'm sorry," was all that he could say in consolation.

Casius nodded, "It was years ago Urbas."

"Aye, but that kind of pain lingers longest."

Casius said nothing; his thoughts had wandered back to his days upon the Isle of Kale. His gaze remained fixed on the scenery ahead but he noticed little of the land's beauty.

The road beyond the bridge cut through the wood, the leafy boughs overhead formed a shaded tunnel lined with rich ferns of deepest green. It was a large wood and took them the better part of the day to pass through its borders.

Over the next two days the road wound through rich fields and over low wooded hills. Several smaller paths joined with theirs and at almost every junction a small village stood. These were without walls, or defenses of any kind.

Other travelers began to appear on the road. Very few ventured alone; often they traveled in small groups. Their hands never straying far from the weapons they carried.

During the fourth day after crossing C'arl's bridge, they crested a small rise in the land. Spread out before them lay a low coastal plain. The silver ribbon of the Darkwater River sliced through the verdant fields below. In the distance they could see the city of Elkrun along the river's bank. The afternoon sun shining from its walls of polished stone.

The city stood a long ways off, yet but Urbas pushed the men. As the sunset, the caravan came to stand beneath the walls surrounding Elkrun.

Casius could see the maze of dark alleyways and litter-strewn streets just beyond the open gate. The buildings were low squatting affairs. Constructed from dark stone, they added to the oppressive atmosphere that hung over the place.

Elkrun was not built to be attractive; rather it was designed to withstand sieges, from the high wall, to the narrow winding streets. An army would be cut to ribbons trying to force its way into the city's heart.

After a moment's consideration, Casius decided to spend one more night with the caravan. He did not like the looks of the city. Or the appraising stares he had gotten from several shady characters, that lingered just beyond the guards' checkpoint.

Urbas had guided his animals into a fenced enclosure. He was delighted to have Casius's help, as they prepared the goods he would offer up in the market come dawn. It was several hours later when he collapsed exhausted into his bedroll.

The sounds of the men stirring awakened him; he sat up rubbing his eyes, when a bell began to ring from beyond the walls.

"The gate's are opening," Urbas commented once he saw the puzzled look on Casius's face. "Here," he said tossing a small pouch to him.

Casius caught the pouch, "What's this?"

"Two talents of gold as promised, payment for your work on my ledger."

"We agreed on one," Casius replied tucking the pouch into his belt.

"Think of the other as a bonus," Urbas said with a smile. "You've done a fine job."

"Where are you off to next?" Casius asked while saddling his horse.

Urbas shrugged, "Perhaps Lowfalls, it has been a long while since I have been there. What of you Casius?"

"I'll deliver my charge and find an Inn where I will sleep for two days straight."

Urbas laughed, "Maybe you should find a north bound caravan before you fall prey to the wiles of a soft bed and clean sheets."

Casius grinned at the man's advice, "That I'll do." He said his face growing serious. "Besides there is an air about this place that I do not care for."

"Aye there is that," Urbas said in agreement. "Stay to the main roads and keep out of the alleys. You'll be safe enough."

Casius gripped the merchant's hand firmly. "Good luck in your travels Urbas," he said in fluent Caleph. "May fortunes daughter smile upon whatever trail you choose to follow."

Urbas lowered his head slightly accepting the blessing from his homeland. "And with you as well young Casius." He stepped back as Casius swung up into his saddle.

"Look me up when next you come to Graystone Urbas," Casius said as he rode to the gate. "I'll gladly repair your books for you."

"I'll do that!" Urbas shouted waving farewell to the young man.

CHAPTER EIGHT

Casius passed through the checkpoint, one man among a throng of hundreds awaiting entry. The guards only gave him a brief glance before waving him through. As he passed down the crowded streets, he was stunned by the sheer size of the metropolis. The city of Graystone, which he had thought large, was not even half as big as this sprawling city.

The reek of cloistered humanity was powerful within the narrow streets. Open ditches lined the roads, filled with the stagnant pools of both animal and human waste. Casius stayed to the center of the street. He had seen several chamber pots simply dumped out of an open window, without a care should any passerby be underneath.

The merchant's office was located near the waterfront, close to the large market square. He had very little trouble finding it, and was shown into the private office by a servant.

The merchant was a rather fat and pompous man dressed in robes of lavender silk. He looked on Casius with disgust. He made a great show of holding a perfumed cloth over his nose as he read over the deed's details.

He may not have approved of Casius's appearance. But he was pleased with the document Casius had traveled so far to deliver. With a wave of dismissal, Casius was shown out of his office and back onto the busy street.

The hawker's calls from the market drew him; he left his horse at a nearby livery and walked into the large square. People by the hundreds crowded the narrow aisles running between the stalls.

They wore clothing from all across Lakarra. Elkrun was a thriving port located within the shadow of the Copper Hills. On the shores of the Dark Water River, a deep waterway that opened into the sea.

Through the maze of stalls he wandered, careful not to make eye contact with the merchants. He was not interested in buying and did not wish to draw their attention. The variety of goods amazed him, each stall offering wares more exotic than the previous.

He wandered the market for hours; he grew tired and began retracing his steps back to where he had left his horse.

As he neared the market's entry he noticed several men moving towards him at a brisk pace. They were hard looking men with skin darkened from many years spent at sea.

Casius's heart nearly stopped, there among them stood G'relg.

G'relg's eyes narrowed and then he recognized the somewhat familiar young man. "It's him!" he shouted.

The three men rushed forward, knocking aside any who stood in their way.

Casius bolted; he knew he could not make it to the stalls where Urbas and his men were busy setting up shop. He ran back into the heart of the market as fast as his legs would carry him.

Darting around stalls, and leaping over tables, he sought to lose the raiders in the confusion. Merchants' cursed him as he knocked their goods onto the ground in his careless flight. Hands tore at his cloak, but he was too fast for the men to capture.

Behind him he could hear renewed curses, as G'relg and his men in their pursuit added to the damage he had already caused.

He left the market and darted down a narrow alleyway. His hand wrapped around the hilt of his Ka'rich. The small blade was the only weapon he carried, all but useless when compared to the arms his pursuers carried. He cursed himself for his stupidity, he should have known better than to leave his sword strapped to his saddle at the livery.

Leaping piles of refuse and a sleeping drunk. He made for the opposite end of the narrow alley, and the street beyond. The raiders shouted for him to stop, as they spotted him in the alley. Boots pounded on the pavement, splashing through the fetid puddles in the shadows.

Casius did not look back; he knew the men were close. He only hoped that he was fast enough to elude them. He burst out of the alley's darkness and into the street. He spared a quick glance over his shoulder and slammed into what felt like a wall. He fell onto his back, momentarily winded from the impact. His small knife lay on the ground just beyond his reach.

A stern faced man stood over him, the barest hint of a smile on his thin lips. "Always look where you are going," he said with a chuckle. "You will find it less painful." The man's eyes were the color of steel and they narrowed menacingly as G'relg and his men rushed out of the alley.

"Friends of yours?" he asked without looking down. He flicked his wrist, opening his cloak of faded green. Revealing a long-sword hanging from a belt of bronze studded leather. Resting his hand on the sword's pommel he stepped between Casius and the men.

"Stay behind me," he said softly, his eyes never leaving the raiders. "What quarrel do you have with this man?" He asked them boldly.

"It is our own affair and does not concern you." G'relg said harshly.

"That is where you are mistaken," The man answered undoing the pin that held his cloak across his shoulders. "I have made it my business." he shrugged allowing the cloth to fall to the ground behind him. He wore a white linen shirt with voluminous sleeves, breeches of faded brown leather and sturdy riding boots.

G'relg smiled at the implied threat. "Who are you?"

"Who am I?" The man repeated brushing aside a strand of his long dark hair. "That is a question best suited for philosophers and men more learned than I. I am the sum of what you see standing before you. A pauper by most standards, owning little more than what I now wear." He patted the blade at his hip. "Save this well honed blade, my treasures are few."

"You are long on wind and short on sense." G'relg spat in disgust.

The man inclined his head slightly as if accepting a compliment. "Never the less," he said calmly. "What has this man done that calls for three raiders to run him to ground."

" He is my property and I will reclaim him!" G'relg's eyes burned with hatred as he spoke.

"I see no slaver's mark upon his head," the man spared Casius a quick look. "What say you?" he asked Casius.

Casius regained his feet, "I belong to no man." He was surprised at how calm he sounded.

The man winked, and faced G'relg. "There must be some mistake," he offered. "Perhaps you believe him to be someone else?"

"Stand aside!" G'relg commanded. "Too long have I walked these lands seeking him, to be denied now."

The man's sword flew from his sheath, a lightning fast blur of silver in the air. Before any could react, its point rested firmly on the raider's throat. "Now ask yourself this," He spoke softly, emphasizing each word with a slight amount of pressure to the blade. "How many men am I willing to lose to take him."

G'relg stepped slowly back away from the sword. He was stunned, never in all his days had he seen a blade wielded with such speed and accuracy. This man was more than a simple townsman.

"There are three of us," he said confidently, reassured by the men at his back. From the corner of his eye he could see in their faces, that they too had surmised the mastery that this man had of his blade.

"No matter," he laughed. "Come then Raider, death cares not, whether it is you or I that she drags into her twilight realm."

"Just who the hell are you?" G'relg demanded.

"Very well," he said with a shrug. "I am Connell Malkor."

G'relg's face paled and his men stepped back in fear.

"But what matters a name?" Connell asked stepping forward his sword now held casually at his side. "You can boast to your brethren in hell, who it was that sent you there."

The raiders gave ground keeping their hands away from their weapons.

Casius could not believe what he was seeing. Here stood one man backing down three murderous rogues.

A small crowd was beginning to gather. People were anticipating swordplay to begin at any moment.

G'relg saw the crowd, and knew if he backed down any further the raider's would lose much of the power that came with fear. "Be still!" He snapped at his men. "How do we know if this man is the Eagle of Kesh?"

Connell nodded, "Come then, slay me and remove my shirt if it is proof you want."

G'relg drew his blade and attacked. He was furious and swung wildly.

Connell's sword flashed in the sunlight, skillfully knocking G'relg's weapon from his hand. As fast as a striking serpent the blade flashed across G'relg's face. The Raider fell to his knees clutching at a deep gash across his cheek.

Connell stepped forward and grabbed the Raider's chin forcing him to look up. He compared the fresh cut with the old scar and nodded approvingly. "Once it heals, your face will have a touch of symmetry." He released G'relg's chin and shoved him onto his back.

G'relg scurried away, and with the help of his men he came to his feet and glared at Connell.

"Say nothing!" Connell threatened holding his sword up. "I will not entertain your petty threats. If you place any value on your hides you will leave. Simply walk away and bother me no more."

G'relg's face reddened but he held his tongue, with a final venomous glare at Casius. He forced his way through the crowd and back down the alley.

Connell slid his sword into its scabbard. Scooping to pick up his cloak, he turned to Casius. "You've made some dangerous enemies."

"Four years ago he led a raid on my village. He was going to kill me during the voyage to Cythera but I escaped."

"Escaped?" Connell asked raising an eyebrow in surprise. "How does one escape on a ship at sea?"

"I jumped overboard during a fierce storm."

"You say it as if it was as easy as crossing this street." Connell said laughing.

"I had few choices in the matter. He did have a knife at my throat."

"It was bravely done, none the less." Connell looked at the crowd, the people were beginning to depart, now that the excitement was over. "We must be going. They will not lick their wounds long. The raiders will return and in greater numbers."

"Damn!" Casius cursed. "G'relg has only to ask around and he will learn where it is I have been staying all these years."

"Then you cannot return, why would he go to such lengths to capture you?"

Casius shook his head, "I do not know."

Connell chewed his lip in thought for a moment. "Do you have a horse?"

"I left it at the livery, along with my sword."

"You are fortunate to have left it behind. More than your dignity would have been lying in that street. I won that fight by luck. Playing on the cowardice that darkens the hearts of men of that ilk. Raiders seek victims that are weak. They attack at night and rarely engage in open combat." Connell led him up the street towards the stables. "I will be leaving with the dawn. Heading north to the city of Tor, come with me and I will help you escape the raiders' clutches."

Casius did not know how to respond, he had only just met this man, but there was something about his face that made him trust Connell. He was confident and unimposing appearing anything but well versed in the art of swordplay. This man had traveled far, if he was truly from Kesh. "Have you ever been to Ril'Gambor?" he asked.

"Fond of knights, are we?" Connell grinned. "I've been there several times. It is a beautiful land, both wild and wondrous."

"Why did you help me?"

Connell stopped and looked him in the eye. "What is your name?"

"Casius Rhaine."

"Because Casius," Connell continued. "It was the right thing to do. My honor would not allow me to act in any other manner. Don't look so surprised, it is a rare enough thing in Lakarra but most men will do what's right if given the chance."

Casius doubted that, too many people had been willing to simply standby and watch the raiders. Only one man had put himself at risk for a complete stranger. "I am grateful that it was you that I ran into."

"Thank whatever god you believe in, for it was he that led you to me."

Casius snorted, "I no longer believe in the Gods or the workings of fate."

"Then call it chance, the outcome is still the same."

"Why did they fear your name?" Casius asked. He had seen the fear in G'relg's eyes.

"I have a rather dubious reputation among the fouler folk of this land. Mostly built on exaggerated tales and half-truths that have a way of spreading from inn to inn. I counted on it to aid me in the confrontation."

"You're a bold man Connell."

Connell grinned, "It did my heart some good to put that cut on his face."

Casius smiled back, "I too felt a small measure of joy in that. I fear that I have not seen the last of him. Especially now that he has been humiliated in public."

"I should have killed him," Connell mused.

"I want no deaths on my account," Casius replied quickly.

"Very well," Connell said. "But be forewarned, if he meets up with you again there may not be any choice in the matter."

"That I do not doubt," Casius said with regret. "I can always hope never to run across him again."

"While you draw breath there is always hope, never forget Casius. Many a Good man has gone into the ground in despair having never learned that lesson."

They reached the livery and Casius retrieved his horse and equipment.

Connell looked the horse over, apparently satisfied with the animal's condition. "Come," he said handing Casius the reins. "It is but a short distance from here."

Connell was true to his word. They followed a winding path through several alleyways, and came to a small Inn. The building had seen better days; it was a wooden structure sagging with age.

The sign above the door was carved in the shape of a running boar, and painted a gleaming yellow. From the open doorway the smell of freshly baked bread flowed out into the street.

Casius tied his horse to the porch rail and followed Connell into the inn's common room.

The room was small and empty; Connell seated himself at one of the less battered tables. Casius took the chair across from Connell, and nearly fell out of it as Connell slammed his open palm onto the wood loudly.

A large bellied man wearing a soiled apron rushed out of the back room. Wiping his hands on his apron he nervously came forward. "I...I..." he stammered. "I did not expect you to return so soon master Connell."

"Nor did I," Connell replied. "Have your stable boy attend to my companion's mount."

The man nodded, his heavy jowls quivering. "Will he be staying then?"

"For the night only." Connell tossed him two silver coins. "Put him in the room adjacent to mine."

The man frowned, "That room is taken."

Connell merely stared at the man.

The inn keep grunted clearing his throat. "I'll move the merchant then," he offered. Tucking the coins into his pocket he asked. "Will there be anything else?"

Connell looked at Casius, "My friend here needs a bath."

"I'll draw the water myself," the inn keep offered.

"Thank you Turlott," Connell said dismissing him. "A couple of ales before you go." He added as an after thought.

Turlott returned with two overflowing tankards, he set these down quickly and disappeared into the back room.

"Nervous fellow," Casius observed. "Does he always act this way?"

"No," Connell said picking up his tankard. "It would seem that word of our adventure has reached the inn before us. He is probably waiting for the Senatum to come rushing through the door at any moment."

Casius hadn't considered that possibility, he drank his ale keeping one eye on the open doorway.

Connell laughed, "Now don't you start playing the worried fool. The Senatum will do nothing in haste, and I doubt your friends have the weight in gold to necessary to pique their interest."

"We should stay alert," Casius said voicing his fear. "G'relg will go far for his honor alone."

"But will his pride allow him to seek aid in capturing one man?" Connell turned his attention to the open window. Through which, he could see back down the busy street.

"Connell," Casius said drawing his attention away from the window. "Why did they call you the Eagle of Kesh?"

Connell opened his shirt revealing a large raised scar on his chest. It was in the shape of a flying eagle with its claws outstretched as if attacking.

Casius grimaced at the thought of the pain he must have endured to receive a scar such as that.

"When I was a young, my cousin and I decided to test our budding manhood. By branding ourselves, with the very iron used by the king's smiths to mark the royal horses."

Connell closed his shirt hiding the mark. "The herd master followed the sound of my cursing, he arrived too late, as the brand had already seared my flesh. He chased us from the livery, the buckle from his belt biting our backsides." Connell smiled at the memory. "Needless to say my cousin never did prove his worth beneath the glowing iron."

Casius shook his head in amazement. What a strange man this was who sat across from him. Why on earth would anyone allow a piece of glowing hot metal, a full hand's span across to be pressed into his flesh was beyond him. This Connell was either a fool, or one of the bravest men he had ever met.

Connell finished his ale and stood adjusting his sword belt. "I have an errand to run, See to your bath and then get to your room. Open the door for no one until I return."

Casius nodded and emptied his tankard in one long pull.

With a slight tilt of his head Connell turned and left the inn. He moved silently with an almost catlike grace, quickly disappearing into the lesser-traveled alleys that riddled the city.

Turlott stepped into the room and at once seemed to be more at ease when he realized Connell had left. "The bath is ready," he said holding the door open for Casius. "It's none of my business," he said leading Casius down the short hall. "You seem like a decent enough fellow, too decent to be hanging around with the likes of Connell. Stay clear of him, he has a reputation and not all that I have heard is pleasant."

"Rumors have a way of growing Turlott, until little truth remains." Casius replied entering the small room where a copper tub stood steaming. "Connell stepped in where others would have let the raiders take me. For that I am grateful, his actions are proof enough of his character."

Turlott shook his head, "Keep your own council then. But ask yourself this, did he help you out of charity or for some other reason known only to himself."

"I guess time will tell," Casius answered closing the door and ending any further attempts at conversation from the inn keep. From beyond the door he heard Turlott mumble something about a damn fool as he walked off.

Casius stripped off his clothing and slipped into the steeping hot water. He scrubbed the weeks of travel away, the water growing murky with grime. Feeling human once more he wrapped himself in a heavy robe, and laundered his clothing in the tub.

He left the bath and carrying his dripping clothing. He called for Turlott, and had the sour faced man show him to his room. The inn keep was stoic and said little, he had said his piece and was slightly insulted at having had a door closed in his face.

The room was small but adequate; it was located on the second floor at the end of the hall. With a single window set within a wall of cracked plaster that overlooked the stables behind the inn.

Casius closed the door and hung his dripping clothing over the sill. Looking out onto the stable he counted twelve stalls beneath a sloping roof of moss-covered slate.

There were three horses present, one of them towering over the others. It was a powerful mount with a glossy coat of midnight black. Casius had never seen such an animal before; it had to be a warhorse. The kind found in the northern realms of Trondhiem and Kesh.

It must belong to Connell, he thought, such a horse would suit him well.

He found his saddlebags lying on the bed. Pushing them aside he collapsed atop the stained quilt and fell asleep in moments.

Night fell, and the city grew silent as the shopkeepers closed their doors and returned home. The temperature dropped and the evening grew chill. As a thin fog rolled through the streets, emerging from the waterfront where it was thickest.

Casius awoke in near total darkness, only the faintest light from a few stars shone through the window. He lay silently in the darkness for a moment, not sure if he had actually heard something.

Straining his ears he slid from his bed, his hand searching the floor for his gear. He found his short sword and slowly slid the sharpened steel free of its scabbard.

Casius jumped backwards as the door to his room suddenly opened. Blinking against the candlelight from the hall he was relieved to see Connell.

"You're up," he said looking at the sword Casius held. "Gather your gear and get dressed quickly, we're leaving."

"Now?" Casius asked blinking the sleep from his eyes. "It can't be much passed midnight."

"Closer to three actually," Connell whispered. "Now get dressed," he added with more urgency. "It would seem your friends are more influential than I would had thought possible. They have somehow enlisted the aid of the entire Senatum garrison. As we speak, they are searching every inn and boarding house within the city."

Casius pulled on his boots, "How will we get past the gates? They are sure to be closed and guarded at this hour."

"There are ways in and out of this city other than the gates." Connell answered with a grin. "This will not be the first time I have traveled those paths."

Casius finished dressing, and shouldered his saddlebags. His clothing was still slightly damp and only added to his discomfort. "It would have been better, if you had only looked the other way."

Connell shrugged, "The past is done, and nothing we do now can change it." He led the way to the rickety stairs. "Besides this is more fun."

For a brief instant Casius doubted his benefactor's sanity. Then he realized Connell was making light of the situation in an attempt to put him at ease.

At the foot of the stairs they were met by an irate Turlott wielding a meat cleaver. "What the hell are you two up too?" he said softly trying not to wake his other guests. "I thought you were thieves skulking about in the dark."

"We are leaving," Connell replied shouldering past the man. "It would be best if you forget that we have been here."

Turlott followed them out the back door. "What nonsense is this?" he demanded, stopping in the small yard near the stables. "There is a curfew in this town and the guards will..."

"The Senatum is searching in every hostel for us at this very moment." Connell hissed interrupting the man.

"The Senatum," Turlott stammered the blood leaving his face. "Be gone you fools!" He rushed past them fumbling with the latches securing the stall doors in his haste. "Damn you Connell for bringing this ill fortune down upon my household."

He quickly moved aside as Connell's horse stepped forward. "I must ready your rooms so that none may suspect that any have slept there." He fled back into the inn, his arms waving in agitation.

They saddled their horses quietly. Connell cut a saddle blanket into eight squares. He tied these about the horses' hooves to muffle the sounds of their passage on the cobblestone streets.

Connell's mount took this in stride, having been subjected to such treatment before. Casius's horse however cared nothing for this treatment and it took them several minutes to sooth the irritated beast.

"Stay close, and remain silent." Connell said slowly swinging open the wooden gate that led out into the street. He stood in the opening for several moments, ensuring the way ahead was clear. Without a word he led the massive horse out into the thin fog.

Casius followed, closing the gate behind him. Several blocks up the street he could see dozens of torches burning brightly in the dark. Their bearers stood outside one of the many inns along this avenue.

Casius only spared a moment to watch the heavily armored men forcing their way into the building. Angry shouts and the sounds of breaking glass reached his ears from the distance.

Connell led them into a narrow alley, one of many that formed a virtual labyrinth throughout the city. The alleys were dark and treacherous, littered with refuse. The buildings leaned over them blocking out all but a thin ribbon of starlight. They were forced to walk with care. Trying hard not to breathe too deeply, for the stench within the confined spaces burned their throats and made their eyes water.

Casius believed Connell to be witch sighted. The man guided them through the maze in near complete darkness. How he knew where and when to turn was a mystery to Casius. By now he was totally lost, and doubted he could ever find his way out again, even in daylight.

On occasion they were forced to cross one of the more heavily traveled streets. Here they would crouch in the deepest shadows, waiting, as a patrol of searchers would pass by. Even the Senatum knew enough not to venture into the alleys at night.

An hour passed in this fashion. Casius was growing sick to his stomach. The smells of urine and other waste assaulted his senses. He seriously doubted that he would ever get his boots cleaned of the filth. From the way his horse tossed its head he knew it was only a matter of time until it bolted, seeking to be free of the reeking confines.

The alley they followed was narrower than most, and led them to the very edge of the river. They emerged into the open, well away from the quays, and the flotilla of moored boats. The docks were bustling with activity even at this hour, with a curfew in place the merchants often raced to unload their wares. The city guard however seldom bothered them if a few coins changed hands.

"Can you swim?" Connell asked stepping close in the darkness.

Casius shuddered looking at the slow moving oily water. "If I could not I would have drowned when I jumped from G'relg's boat."

Connell chuckled, "Behind the warehouses the city wall ends in a high tower. There is a small strand of beach at its base when the tide is out. It is there that we will make our escape. If we are spotted before reaching the strand, we take to the water and make for the distant shore."

Casius looked off into the darkness. He knew the river was close to a mile wide at this point. He doubted they would get very far with all their gear. "Is the tower guarded?" he asked not wanting to consider the prospect of such a swim.

"There are guards enough, but I doubt they would be looking inward for danger. By the time they spot us we will be on horseback and riding away, well ahead of any pursuit they could mount."

"Let us hope our luck holds then." Casius held his horse's reins firmly while Connell cut the bindings that kept the cloth tied about its hooves.

They moved cautiously along the shore, keeping close to the sides of the warehouses. Litter lined the muddy bank, mostly discarded crates and rotting timbers.

The Tower rose fifty feet above the bank. The light from torches burning behind the merlons illuminated the fog rolling in off of the river. Through the haze the guards were visible as they slowly walked their rounds. As Connell had predicted they paid little, if any attention to the city. The soft sounds of the men laughing reached them from the Tower's top.

Connell patted his horse's flank, "They're tossing dice." He smiled, "It appears that our luck is holding. Move quietly should anyone look in our direction stand still. The light of the torches works against them."

Casius nodded his understanding, and together they moved out into the open. The Tower loomed over them; the ground about its base was soft and wet. They sank deeply into the mud with each step, at times coming almost to their knees.

Connell stopped directly beneath the Tower, the laughter above them continued unabated. Casius's heart hammered in his chest so loudly he was sure the men above could hear it.

Beyond the Tower, a mere stone's throw away. The night swathed landscape of low rolling grassland faded quickly away into darkness.

"Our goal lies a mile to the northwest," Connell whispered. "There stands a thick grove of trees lining a hilltop." Connell stopped speaking as a thin stream of liquid rained down from the Tower top nearby. It splattered loudly on the ground and ended as abruptly as it had started. "Let's go before he decides to relieve himself further."

Connell led them out from beneath the Tower at a full run. They had gone several hundred feet when shouts broke out from the guard.

Casius hunched low in the saddle, he had never felt so exposed in all his life. He expected to feel the stinging bite of an arrow at any moment.

The horses tore into the night grateful to be free of the city and its constricting buildings. Connell's mount was surprisingly fast for a horse of such size. He led them due north. Once they were well beyond the sight of the guards, he veered northwest. Slowing to a stop when they came to the edge of the wood.

Connell sat in silence listening, "They are not pursuing," he said with a grin. "But that will not last long, word will spread, and the Senatum will know we have escaped. We can not linger here long, they will search far and wide."

Connell swung the mount eastward, and they raced along the wood's edge. Casius gripped the reins tightly as they moved along. A low stonewall appeared out of the gloom. The horses leapt it easily, and now ran through a field of green wheat. The stalk's thrashed at their legs as they passed scouring most of the offensive mud from their clothing.

On their right, a small grouping of huts flashed past. A dog barked in the distance. Followed by the angry yells of a man who was not happy at having been awakened at such an hour.

Connell kept the pace brisk until the sun was beginning to break the horizon. They came to fallen oak, its bark long gone and the wood bleached white by exposure to the elements.

Connell dismounted, and reaching into the shadows beneath the trunk he pulled out a heavy satchel. Reaching in once more he withdrew a bow of black horn and a quiver of arrows.

"You sneak about often?" Casius asked dismounting and stretching his back.

"More than I would care to admit," Connell answered pulling on the shirt of mail that was in the satchel. "It suits my lifestyle." He donned his cloak and picked up the bow slinging the quiver over his shoulder. "We walk from here," He said using the bow to point out a game trail cutting into the wood. "The boughs' hang low and the horses need the rest."

They spent the morning walking through the quiet wood. The only sounds were the rattle of their equipment, and the soft sighing of the wind as it rustled the leaves above.

They left the wood before noon, and passed down into a land filled with the patchwork of farmer's fields. From the distant houses they could see men moving about busy with their labors.

Crossing several fields, they came to a rutted road running northwest between low walls of dry set stone. Connell allowed time for them to rest the horses, and eat a quick meal of dried fruit and a loaf of bread he had taken from the inn.

Casius ate in silence; he was too weary for conversation. He knew this was going to be a long day. They had to put many miles between themselves and any pursuit coming out of Elkrun.

After what seemed only a few minutes, Connell got them moving again. They pushed their mounts hard, and by nightfall they had covered many miles. As the sun disappeared below the horizon they came to an isolated farm. With a few copper coins Connell convinced the farmer to allow them to hold up in his barn for the evening.

That night it rained until Casius thought that the barn would surely float away. He was grateful for the shelter that the thatch roof offered. Once the horses had been tended, Connell took the first watch while Casius slept.

After two day's of hard travel the land had risen gently. Until they reached the western most ridge of the Carec Mountains. Unlike their brethren further east, these were far less imposing. Little more than a line of steep faced hills cloaked with a mantel of thick woods.

The road they followed climbed one of the gentler slopes. Switching back and forth until it disappeared within the trees. They spent the night within a ring of broken stones. The shattered foundation of what had once been a small fortress. Built by a forgotten nation long ago upon the hill's summit.

The following morning they descended down out of the hills, and Casius was once more out on the vast sweeping grasslands of the Greensward. Mile after mile of waving grass stretched to the distant horizon, appearing at times to touch the very sky. Through this emerald sea ran the road, arrow straight into the distance.

The sky remained clear and the weather fair as they journeyed. On their fifth day a messenger riding hard from the south overtook them. As he passed them by, he stared at Casius for a long time

Connell reined in. Looking on in disgust at the foam-lathered beast, whose flanks had been switched bloody by its rider.

"He's going to kill that animal," Casius exclaimed in disapproval.

Connell stared at the man's retreating back. " He bears urgent news indeed to ruin such a horse." Standing in his stirrups he looked back the way they had come. "We've lingered on this road too long. From the way he looked at you I fear he may be spreading word to other garrisons. There will be an ambush awaiting us in South Fork."

Casius cursed, "How are we to cross the Brae River then?" He asked. "The only crossing is at South Fork."

"There is a place that will suffice for our needs." Connell said turning eastward out onto the trackless grasslands. "I know of a ferry man who will bear us across, he asks few questions, and remembers even less."

Casius frowned, he knew of no other crossings within a hundred miles. "Lead on then Connell, I know little of this land."

Connell laughed, "You will learn much before our trek is done."

They rode far out into the trackless land, with neither road nor markers for guidance. Casius was beginning to wonder if Connell was lost.

With an hour of sunlight left Connell stopped and dismounted. They set up a cold camp, "Firelight travels far on the plain." Connell had warned him.

"Once we reach Haven," Connell said while dolling out the last of their food, "We will purchase supplies enough for our journey."

"Haven?" Casius asked. "I do not know of any town by that name."

"As you have said Casius, your knowledge of these parts is somewhat lacking." Connell reminded him. "Tomorrow will be a long hungry day but by nightfall we will be dining at an old friend's hearth."

"Why are there no roads leading into this Haven?"

"Not all men who live in Lakarra care to draw attention to themselves. Haven is exactly that, a refuge."

"A town of rogues and outlaws, you're leading us into a den of vipers!" Casius said hotly.

"Not so," Connell said placating. "A rogue in Lakarra is someone who defies the king and the Senatum. They live in secret to prolong their lives."

"Then how do you know of this place?" Casius asked still somewhat skeptical.

Connell smiled, "For I am counted among their number. I have been marked for death by the crown for fifteen years now. The price on my head would make a man wealthy." Connell stood and slid his sword from its scabbard. "Come draw your blade."

"What?" Casius asked surprised by Connell's actions.

"I did not take you all the way out here to kill you." Connell said with a grin. "I would know where your skill's lie ere we enter battle for real."

"My skill is poor," Casius said coming to his feet. "In fact non existent to be exact."

"Never the less draw your blade." Connell smiled at Casius's hesitation. "Humor me in this, I vow not to draw any blood."

"What is the word of a rogue worth?" Casius asked drawing his short sword.

Connell shrugged, "Not much these days."

Casius drew his blade, the metal shining brightly as it reflected the red light of the setting sun. "I was afraid you would say that."

Connell stood at ease the point of his long sword resting on the toe of his boot. "Attack me." He said.

"I cannot, you are not ready." Casius replied.

"In real life men are seldom granted the luxury of being ready. Attacks come swiftly, more often than not when unlooked for.

"Often with surprise, a man can kill where his skills alone would not suffice." Connell nodded in encouragement. "Attack Casius, I would not be much of a swordsman if I let you injure me."

Casius took a half hearted overhand swing aimed for Connell's head.

There was a flash of silver and Casius's sword flew through the air.

Casius jumped back holding his hand. Connell had struck his knuckles a sound blow with the flat of his blade. He massaged the injury glaring at Connell hotly.

"I said attack," Connell said ignoring the anger in Casius's eyes. "You came at me as if you were swatting a fly."

Casius retrieved his sword, "You are at an distinct advantage Connell. Your blade is twice the length of mine."

"A short sword is a good weapon for close in work Casius. In properly trained hand's it is as lethal as the weapon I hold in mine. Out here, in the wilds however, you will find most of your opponents prefer longer blades. It is against these, you must learn to defend yourself."

"Then I should get myself one," Casius said looking at the weapon in his hand.

"Even with a longer sword your opponent may have some sort of an advantage. He could be taller, faster, stronger, or more skilled. Sometimes, it may come down to simple luck.

"Instinctive fighters rarely better one who uses his head, as well as his arm. If you think fast enough you will see an opening and be able to use it to your advantage. Outwitting your foe is as important as your swordplay."

"Mastery of the blade takes years, Connell."

"A lifetime, Casius. I will teach you if you wish. You will find me long on criticism and short on praise. It will not be easy, and you will rue the day that you ask this of me. But I will enable you to defend yourself, even against the likes of G'relg." Connell sheathed his sword in a single fluid motion.

Casius lowered his blade letting it hang at his side. "I have never aspired to being a swordsman Connell. I have no desire to take a life or to prove myself on the field of battle."

"No man of honor wishes to Casius, but there are times in one's life when he must."

"Aye Connell," Casius agreed. "If I am ever to live without fear, I must abandon the path I have chosen. To follow the way that you have offered."

"You are a good man Casius, were it otherwise I would not teach you. With skill lie options, many of which do not lead to death's door. Remember good intentions will not turn the blade."

"When do we start?" Casius asked.

"We have already begun, in Haven we will find you a better sword. For now let us focus on balance, the key element to the art of the blade."

While the light lasted Connell had Casius leaping about on one foot then the other. He taught him several practice patterns, and had him repeating them over and over. Casius felt like a fool. He feared that someone would walk into their camp and laugh at his antics.

Connell as if sensing his discomfort drew his sword and repeated the patterns, emphasizing each movement with feints and attacks. He moved with amazing speed, his sword becoming a web of flickering steel.

Casius was awed by his skill, no wonder the raiders feared him. The sheer speed and agility of Connell was surpassed by the total control he maintained over the weapon. When he had finished, Casius noticed he was not even breathing hard.

"Where did you learn to do that?"

Connell sheathed his sword. "In Kesh, the art of the sword is taught at an early age. I was fortunate to have had one of the finest swordsman of the realm as my teacher."

"Who was that?" Casius asked sitting down on the lush grass.

"My father, Connell replied. "It was both good and bad. Imagine trying to live up to his expectations. I grew up in a household of strict discipline, living a life devoted to duty and honor above all else." Connell stretched out his saddle blanket and lay down. "Still it was a better life than most, from what I have seen in my travels. There are many men who consider themselves fortunate if they go to bed with a full stomach."

"We can never go back can we Connell?" Casius said feeling the loss of his family weighing down on him.

"I'm afraid not Casius," Connell answered. "Such is life, always changing. You have little choice if you are to succeed." Connell paused rising to his feet. "Don't rush tomorrow Casius, it will come on its own accord soon enough."

"You speak as if you were a wise man, Connell."

"Nay Casius," Connell laughed softly. "I am as big a fool as ever did walk this green earth. I remember bits and pieces of the wisdom spoken to me in my youth. Seldom have I ever heeded the advice given me by others.

"Get some sleep Casius, I'll take the first watch." He walked off into the deepening darkness, checking on the horses.

Casius lay back and watched the stars slowly emerge from darkening sky. Despite all that was on his mind he drifted off to sleep quickly, the weariness of his body taking control.

Connell awakened Casius shortly after midnight by placing his hand across his mouth to keep him silent.

Casius knew something was dreadfully wrong, the excitement casting aside the cobwebs of too little sleep. In the darkness he could see the stars reflecting from Connell's sword, small flickers of light upon the gleaming steel.

Casius drew his short sword and followed Connell crouching low in the grass.

They crawled slowly forward; the night was still and silent. Only the soft whistle of the wind through the grass kept them company.

Connell stopped, and they sat in the dark their ears straining. Faint snorting sounds came from the darkness ahead. Something was sniffing around moving in short rapid burst as it approached.

Casius had heard pigs making such noises before; he was about to laugh at Connell's mistake when a new sound reached his ears. Faint mumblings, whatever it was, it was speaking in hushed tones. Half formed words drifted out of the blackness, Casius strained to hear, but he could not make out what was being said.

Intrigued by the sound, he lifted his head slowly above the waving grass. He was greeted by a most peculiar sight. Not more than twenty feet away, the dark form of a very thin man was crawling about on all fours. His head held close to the ground. In the gloom he could only discern the man's shape. He gasped in surprise as the silhouette raised its head, and two eyes of gleaming amber pierced the darkness.

At the sound of his gasp the man sniffed loudly. The amber lights narrowed. Then with a terrifying scream the figure leapt forward, its long thin arms held out at its side.

Casius struggled to pull his sword up but the long grass had become entangled in the weapons guard.

The figure was almost upon him when Connell launched up out of his concealment. Striking the attacker in the chest with his shoulder. They staggered backwards, the force of the blow knocking them both off their feet. The air whistled as the figure lashed out with one of its hands.

Connell rolled out of the way, the figure's hand thudding into the ground with incredible force. He got to his feet and struck the figure across the chest as it stood.

Ignoring the wound the figure attempted to work its way around Connell, seemingly intent upon Casius.

Connell's sword formed a barrier, the flashing steel forcing the figure back. Several times Connell evaded the figure's attacks. Stepping out of the way, and countering with attacks of his own. He had struck solid blows. Each of them capable of killing a man, but the only effect they had on this figure was to enrage it further.

The creature howled, and ignoring the blows that Connell delivered. It charged and struck the man across the chest.

Connell was lifted several feet into the air. He landed on his back, the breath knocked from him.

Casius abandoned his sword, and pulled the Ka'rich from his belt as the figure drew closer.

The gangly form moved with incredible speed, running on all fours.

Casius threw the blade with all his might.

The two amber lights suddenly became one, the being howled in anguish and fell to ground. Thrashing wildly in the grass. Its piercing cries did not last long, with a final gurgling moan it ceased to move.

"By the Gods!" Connell exclaimed drawing close to it. He held his sword ready not trusting it to be completely dead. "What the hell is that thing?"

Casius was shaking; it took him a moment to find his voice. "I don't know," he croaked, his throat suddenly as dry as a desert. "I thought it to be a crazed man."

"As did I," Connell sheathed his sword and squatted beside the body. "Until I saw the light burning in its eyes."

"My sword struck true more than once, but it felt as if I was hewing timber instead of flesh. How did you manage to kill it? No strike of mine so grievously injured it."

"I threw my Ka'rich into its eye," Casius answered moving closer to get a good look at it. "Remind me to thank the caravan master, should I ever see him again."

"A Calephean throwing knife?" Connell laughed. "And you were worried about the reach of your blade?"

Casius could not help but smile, seeing the irony of it.

"A good throw Casius," Connell complimented him.

"Pure luck and desperation."

"Nonsense you hit your mark."

The figure was not a man. It was man shaped, but its skin was covered with thick knobs of bone and scale. Completely naked, without clothing or hair on its hide. The head was small with a broad toothless mouth.

The eyes were spaced wide and lidless. The light in the undamaged one was gone; all that remained was an orb of pallid flesh devoid of any sign of a pupil.

The long arms ended in a single wicked claw, where a hand would be on a man. From its tip a thin bead of yellowish fluid seeped out onto the ground.

"Poison," Connell commented tapping the claw with his knife. Connell stood sheathing his blade. "I have no idea what this is, but let us pray it was alone." He looked up at the sky, "There are a few hours of darkness yet. We'll come back once the sunrises and see if the light reveals more."

They returned to their camp, neither man felt like sleeping after their harrowing encounter. They sat watching the sky brighten in the east as the sun slowly crept skyward.

Finally they could wait no longer, retracing their steps they came upon a macabre scene.

The body was little more than a pile of bones lying within a pool of bubbling slime. As they watched the roiling slime evaporated into a thin cloud that reeked of corruption. Within minutes, even the bones themselves had turned to dust and were carried away by the plain's ever-present wind.

No sign of the creature remained, only the flattened grass were it had lain, and the glittering blade of the knife that had killed it.

"This is foul work," Connell said picking up the small blade and passing it to Casius. "In all the year's I have traveled this land I have never heard of such a thing. Why would it decay so quickly?"

Casius shrugged, "Perhaps it is the sunlight." He guessed. "After all it had lain unchanged through half the night."

"I fear you may be right, and that only makes this all the more disturbing."

They returned to their camp in silence and started packing their meager supplies.

"Urbas, the caravan master told me once, that there are things out on the Greensward that men have never seen. Old things that have outlasted their time." Casius said to break the silence.

"Yesterday I would have scoffed at such a statement."

"What of today?" Casius prompted.

"Today," Connell paused lifting his saddle onto the black's back. "I would say heed Urbas's words, he may know things of worth." Connell finished tightening the straps, and swung up into the saddle. "Let us be away from here, I will sleep better once we reach Haven."

They started off at a brisk trot both men looking back on the scene with unease.

CHAPTER NINE

The door to Gaelan's chamber burst open flooding the darkened room with light. A giant of a man with a dark beard streaked with gray, and a wild mane of hair to match stood in the doorway. In his thick-fingered hand he clutched a wildly swinging lantern. The light it cast sent shadows racing across the walls.

"My Lord," he hissed loudly. "Wake up!" He kicked the bed firmly.

Gaelan covered his eyes, shielding them from the offending light. "Burcott," he groaned. "It is not yet dawn."

Burcott closed the door, "I know what the hour is." He pulled at the linen bed sheets, uncovering Gaelan. "Now get dressed. There's something afoot in the king's tower. If I was a gambling man I'd lay good money to say that cur, Goliad is involved in this."

Gaelan sat up rubbing the sleep from his eyes. "You do gamble Burcott, have you been drinking?"

Burcott grabbed Gaelan's clothing from the floor and tossed them onto the bed. "Of course I have. Why else would I be up at this hour?" Burcott tossed Gaelan's boots onto the bed as well. "But that doesn't mean I don't have my wits about me.

I just passed Lord Vernal and a dozen of his men running full out across Galloglass hall. The weasel even had his sword drawn!"

Gaelan jumped out of bed, pulling his clothes on frantically. He had never trusted Lord Vernal, he was known as a troublemaker. As one of the most powerful lords of the lesser houses he carried much influence, and often used it for his own financial gain. If he was about and openly involved in something, no good could possibly come from it.

Buckling his sword belt about his waist he shoved Burcott out of the room.

They raced through Thorunder Hall, the lantern's light dancing in the darkness. They slowed as they came into Galloglass Hall. It was dark and gloomy with only a few oil lamps burning. Servants had packed the hall, many of them still wearing their bedclothes.

Burcott's massive frame and harsh glares quickly cleared a path for them to the stair that led up into the king's tower.

Climbing the broad stair to the levels above, Gaelan began to feel a sense of impending doom. The royal guards were missing on the landing. In their place stood a heavily armed group of warriors. Gaelan recognized them as Lord Vernal's men by the yellow crosses on their hauberks. The men did not block the doorway to the king's chambers but the expressions they bore were just short of murderous.

The king's parlor was filled with people. Lord Vernal, along with other members of the lesser houses stood at the entry to the bedchamber. There were at least twenty armed guards loyal to Vernal in the room.

"What goes on here?" Gaelan demanded annoyed to see so many armed men in his father's chambers.

Lord Vernal looked into the prince's eyes. A faint smile pulled at the corners of his mouth as he spoke. "The King is dead, your Highness."

Gaelan drew his sword and the crowd pushed back away from him. "You would bear such ill tidings to me with a smile upon your Jackal's face?" Gaelan shouted in his rage. He shrugged off Burcott's restraining hand and stepped forward. "I should run you through for such callousness."

"Has there not been enough killing tonight?" A thin voice spoke from beyond the darkened doorway. "Or does your blade yet require more blood to quench its thirst."

Blood pounded in Gaelan's temples, he knew that viper's voice. It belonged to Goliad, the spreader of lies. A worm of a man who hung within the shadows, fearing the touch of daylight. Why his sister had allowed such a villainous man to wed her he would never understand.

"Goliad!" he shouted pushing past Vernal. Gaelan stopped in the doorway, there lying on the floor was his father. His white robe stained scarlet from a dozen stab wounds. Gaelan staggered backwards, grief and rage seeking to over power him.

Goliad stood over the body his boots planted within the dark pool of spilt blood. Goliad smiled sadly, his black goatee hardly moving as his lips curled. "Could you not wait for the fullness of your father's time to pass, Gaelan?" He spoke softly his voice low and soothing, though his eyes burned with hatred.

Gaelan tore his gaze from his father's body and looked into Goliad's face. "What are you hinting at?" he asked in disbelief.

Goliad arched an eyebrow in surprise. "You would deny having a hand in this? When you come in here bearing the very blade that took your father's life."

"I had no part in this treachery!" Gaelan snapped.

"Does not your blade yet bear the dried gore from your father's wounds?" Goliad indicated the weapon Gaelan held with a casual wave of his hand.

Gaelan looked at the blade and cursed. Along its three-foot length dried blood marred the polished steel. "This is impossible." He muttered in disbelief.

"Then perhaps, someone else used your weapon while you slept." Goliad said mockingly. "I have heard it said that you sleep with your sword at hand. A pity your father did not as well. Then perhaps it would be your corpse we are standing over and not his."

"Where are his guards?" Burcott demanded. "They will know the truth of this matter."

"Dead," Goliad responded. "Apparently poisoned, one of them survived long enough to tell Lord Vernal that it was Gaelan, who entered his father's chamber while the king slept. Lord Vernal came upon this grisly scene too late to save his liege."

Gaelan had heard enough. He spun to face Vernal. The sound of a dozen swords being drawn stopped him.

"Do not be foolish," Goliad admonished. "Drop your blade or you will be cut down, adding your blood to your father's."

Burcott glowered his hand on his sword's hilt. He looked to his prince awaiting the command. He was not afraid of death, and would take out more than a few of these traitors before he fell.

Gaelan looked his friend in the eye and shook his head. The sound of his sword ringing upon the stone floor echoed loudly. Turning to speak he opened his mouth, and a heavy sword hilt slammed into the back of his head. The room spun and he fell to the floor. His last sight before darkness overtook him was that of Burcott charging forward, his sword cutting a bloody path through the guards.

Gaelan awakened a few minutes later, his head ached terribly. He tried to move and found that his hands had been tightly bound across his back. In the darkened room he could hear Goliad and Vernal whispering behind him.

"What nonsense is this?" Lord Vernal exclaimed. "This is not what we agreed to!"

Goliad laughed, an empty sound devoid of emotion. "Gaelan is marked as a king slayer. When he swings from the gallows, it will be his sister who takes the throne. Through my wife, I alone will rule Trondhiem."

"But it was I who was to be named regent!"

"Lord Vernal," Goliad said softly. "The Deal has changed, is it not enough that the lords of the Landsmarch will lie in chains. Your house will rise up, and their lands shall be yours." Goliad raised his hand silencing Vernal's protest. "Hold your tongue, there are more than one set of chains in the dungeons."

Vernal clenched his jaw, "Very well Goliad, just ensure nothing else changes this day."

Goliad nodded, "Smile Vernal, after today you will be the second most powerful man in all of Trondhiem."

Vernal grunted and waved his guards over, "Take this traitor and his companion to the dungeon. Let them spend some time together before we hang them in the morning."

Gaelan was yanked to his feet roughly and shoved towards the door. "You will pay for this treachery!" He shouted.

"Gag him!" Vernal commanded. "Lest he wakens the entire keep."

He was thrown to the ground and a cloth was shoved into his mouth and tied behind his head. Once it was secure he was wrenched upright and ushered roughly from his father's chambers.

More guards joined them. Under armed escort he was taken from the tower, and down into the labyrinth of tunnels that riddled the earth beneath the Keep.

He was tossed into a narrow cell. As soon as he had hit the rough floor a great weight fell across his legs. The guard slammed the door and locked it from without.

Gaelan blinked in the darkness, the weight pinning him shifted and groaned. He rubbed his cheek against the stone, working the gag free of his mouth. He spat out the cloth and moistened his lips. "Burcott are you hurt?" He whispered.

Fullvie grunted rolling over onto his back, and off of Gaelan's legs. "Save for a knot the size of a goose egg on my head, I'm fine."

Gaelan winced, "I bear one that would rival yours in size." Shifting around he leaned against the wall. He inhaled deeply and instantly regretted the action. The air of the chamber was damp and reeked of sewage. "These cells have stood vacant for more than fifty years, you would think the smell would have faded over time."

Burcott laughed softly. "Thorunder's garderobes empty into these levels. Just try not to sit anywhere that's damp. The smell is sure to improve once the Keep's populace awakens."

Gaelan shook his head in wonder at his companion's twisted sense of humor. "With what Goliad has planned for us come daybreak I think that will be the least of our worries."

"Goliad and Vernal will have much to answer for once we are released." Burcott said threateningly.

"We will never be set free," Gaelan said dejectedly. "Goliad has seized the crown and will never willingly relinquish it."

"What has Vernal gained for his treachery?"

"Vernal thought he would gain the throne, Goliad however betrayed him as well. He will instead become lord over the Landsmarch."

"Your father's life was brought for a high price," Burcott mumbled. "The people will not follow Goliad."

"No," Gaelan agreed. "But they will follow my sister, and through her he will rule. He controls her as easily as a bard manipulates a puppet."

They sat in silence for a few moments listening for any sounds in the darkness. The steady drip of water and the scratching of foraging rats kept them company.

Gaelan could take it no more, "We need to escape Burcott, any ideas."

"We wait," Burcott answered. "My men will be here soon enough, once they learn of our fate."

"How many men?" Gaelan asked his hope returning.

"Thirty two, not enough to take the hall. But they should suffice in getting us free of this place. Between Vernal and Goliad they have over one hundred men. With the lesser houses support they may have as many as five hundred."

Gaelan rested his head on his knees. He could not count on the palace guard. If they believed him to be the killer, they would only support Goliad. There was no way they could retake the Keep. Goliad was too well entrenched. "Where do we go if we win free?" He asked, unable to come up with any plan for the moment.

"We go east, to Carich," Burcott answered. "My men hold that Fortress."

Gaelan closed his eyes. "We might as well get some rest, it will be well after sunup before your men notice you are missing."

As Gaelan finished speaking the sounds of fighting reached his ears. A door was ripped from its hinges nearby.

"I forgot to tell you," Burcott spoke over the noise. "It was with my men that I was drinking." He laughed, "I would take any drunk from my household over a sober guardsman any day."

The sounds of fighting stopped and a dim light shone through the opening in the door.

"Lord Burcott?" A voice called out from the hall.

"Over here!" Burcott shouted in response pressing his face against the iron grill set in the door.

A crowd of men had gathered beyond the door, the lock clicked as they tried the keys one by one.

As soon as the lock opened Burcott was through the door. His eyes blinking against the light of the torches they carried. One of his men cut the cords' that bound them.

"Garm!" Burcott shouted, slapping the man on the shoulder. "Well done!"

The man smiled enduring the blow. "We must go milord, our men hold the corridor above, but the alarm is being sounded."

Burcott nodded his face growing sober. "Lead on then, we will need horses if we are to live out this day."

"That's already done," Garm shouted as they ran down the passage. "Lord Hurin and his men hold the courtyard and the memorial gate."

Gaelan smiled, they may actually succeed. "How many men are with him?"

"Close to thirty, most are his retainers, but a few of the palace guard are with him as well, milord," Garm answered suddenly aware that it was Prince Gaelan at his side.

"That gives us more than sixty men," Gaelan mused. "Could we capture Goliad with so few?"

"Perhaps," Burcott replied. "But..."

"Nay," Garm interrupted them. "There are at least twice our number in Morne about the keep."

"Morne!" Gaelan shouted. "Are you certain?"

Garm stopped at the stairwell leading upward. "Black robes," He said panting. "I got a close look, they are not men. Goliad greeted them at the gate himself. When I saw this I went in search of Lord Burcott. It is for this reason that many of the palace guard are with us."

Burcott spat, "Does his treachery know any bounds? I'll gut him like a fish for this."

"That will have to wait," Gaelan said cooling Burcott's temper. "We have to escape and rally our people. We cannot allow the Morne to get a foothold in Trondhiem. If they do all of the east is doomed."

They took the stairs two at a time quickly arriving at the landing above. Where a number of Burcott's men stood guard, several of Vernal's men lay dead on the ground. Having failed to fight past them.

Burcott searched the dead for weapons. He passed a sword to Gaelan. "Stay behind me if we run afoul of any of Vernal's men."

"I will do nothing of the sort," Gaelan answered angered by the suggestion.

"It is my duty to protect you," Burcott argued. "I have failed one King this night I'll not fail another."

"Then watch my back," Gaelan said with a grin. "As to my father's death you cannot take on that burden."

Burcott frowned, a deep furrow creasing his brow. "I am a member of the Landsmarch, it is our duty to protect the crown."

"We will argue this point later, for now get us the hell out of here."

Burcott nodded to Garm who took the lead. "I always wanted to be an outlaw." He said falling in step beside Gaelan.

Taking a side passage, Garm led them through the kitchens and into the dining hall beyond.

At the opposite end of the room several of Vernal's guards were entering through the large double doors that opened onto Galloglass Hall. They shouted and charged.

The fight was furious but short lived; at the end, six of Vernal's men lay dead as well as two of Burcott's own.

From the Hall beyond came the sounds of running men.

"This way!" Garm hissed, leading them through a servant's entrance away from the large doorway.

They ran down the narrow passage, and turned into a short corridor that led to the king's courtyard.

Chaos greeted them as they rushed out of the building. A fierce battle was taking place, members of the palace guard stood alongside Hurin's men. They were fighting Goliad's forces pressing them back into the Keep.

Lord Hurin had gathered fifty horses, and some of his men held the reins of the frightened mounts near the gate.

Gaelan wasted no time; he vaulted onto a horse's back. He led the mounted charge that smashed into the usurper's men. The mounted warriors became a wedge between the forces. Giving the men on foot a chance to mount up. They did not have horses enough and a few had to ride double.

The men within the Keep rallied and pushed forward. Lord Hurin led the way as they retreated out the gate and into the twisting paths of the royal downs. Around ancient burial mounds the horses charged. Until they reached the low wall that surrounded the graveyard, with a final leap for freedom they entered the city of Rodderdam.

Rodderdam stood atop a steep sided hill known as Cal'Arev. Its streets were narrow and paved with rough sided cobbles. The iron-shod hooves rang loudly on the damp stones as they hurtled through the night.

Coming to the edge of the hilltop they hardly slowed. The horses plunged over the brink. It was steep and treacherous; four horses fell, their legs flailing wildly as they rolled. Three men were crushed beneath them, the fourth was lost in the darkness.

At the base of the slope they called out for the missing, but no reply was heard. They were either dead or rendered unconscious. No matter their condition, the men could ill afford any further delay. From the city above the alarm bells rang and lights were kindled in many of the darkened windows.

"We can linger no longer," Burcott charged eastward trusting that the others would follow.

The land about Cal'Arev was a low smooth plain of rich soil that supported many farms. Driving their horses hard they crossed many miles of open farmland. One of Hurin's men died on the ride. He had taken a sword thrust to the belly; there was little anyone could have done to save him.

Burcott took the man's sword and plunged it into the earth. The rising sun reflected from the polished steel, a beacon upon the field marking the resting place of a fallen warrior.

"We have no time for a proper burial," He said apologetically. "The farmers will see the deed done for us."

After a few moment's rest they set out once more their number now fifty-three. They rode northwest at a slower pace, their fears of pursuit somewhat lessened. The plains about Rodderdam were vast, and Goliad could not allow his forces to search them out until his hold on the palace was secure.

On the morning of their third day since escaping Rodderdam, they reached the banks of the Rildrun River. The waters were deep and swift. From Lake Valdecar the river cut across the land, until it merged with the salt marsh on the shores of the Southern Sea.

There was no way to cross the raging current. Lake Valdecar was swollen with snowmelt from the Raobahn Mountains. With the lake flooding and the river swollen it would be weeks until the torrent lessened.

To the west lay the only crossing, and towards it they rode. It took most of the day, in the late afternoon the bridge of Galtor stood before them.

The bridge spanned the river, in a single graceful arch of cut stone. On the opposite shore stood the village after which the bridge was named.

They crossed the span surprising the guards who warded it. They snapped to attention saluting the two Lords and the Prince who rode with them.

The townspeople turned out to see the bedraggled royalty as they rested their mounts at the livery. The hour was late and the men spent the night in the small inn that served as a barracks for the bridge guard.

With rested horses and supplies they set off shortly after daybreak. They made good time, and left the plains. Climbing into the rising hills within the shadow of the Raobahn Mountains.

They followed a well-worn trail leading into the dense pines that shrouded the lower slopes of the mountains. The air was brisk and the wood bursting with the songs of birds. The trail followed the lay of the land in its climb up into the pass.

The pass itself was a deep groove cut into the high cliffs of the mountain. It opened at the upper limit of the forest, barren of trees with only a few skeletal bushes to mark its entrance.

Nestled within the shelter of the mountains, stood the citadel of Carich Tower. Rising a full one hundred feet above the trail its upper level pierced by narrow lancets spaced evenly about its diameter. Armored men could be seen behind the battlement that encircled its top.

The Tower's base was hidden behind a stout wall of dressed stone. Rising thirty feet it contained only one gate, framed by two bastions. Within the gate a heavy iron portcullis had been raised, only it's lower edge was visible to the riders as they approached.

Above the tower a large banner snapped in the wind, a golden stag rearing upon a field of sapphire. It was the standard of the house of Fullvie, and Gaelan felt safer seeing it.

Two men rode out of the gate as the riders entered the pass. They trotted slowly down the steep slope. When they recognized that it was the prince accompanying their lord one of the men returned to the Keep driving his horse at a dead run.

"Prince Gaelan," The remaining rider said bowing his head slightly. "This is most unexpected, we have received no word of your coming. I am afraid we have no welcome prepared for you."

"There will be little time for ceremonies and feasts guardsman," Gaelan replied with a casual wave of his hand. "The reason for our visit is not something to be celebrated." The prince spurred his horse past the bewildered guard and up the berm towards the open gate.

Gaelan rode into the bailey. Hastily assembled, the thousand men of the guard stood in orderly ranks awaiting his inspection. He looked at the men's faces. Many of them were too young to have seen combat. They looked eagerly to their prince, expecting some word from him.

Gaelan reined his horse to a stop directly in front of them. He took a moment to gather his thoughts before speaking.

"Men of the house Fullvie!" He said loudly, his voice echoing from the surrounding stone.

"I bear news most dire, seven days ago my father, your King was murdered in his very chambers. Slain by a traitor's blade in the dead of night." The men began shouting questions, hundreds of voices crying out at once. Gaelan sat in his saddle waiting for them to grow still.

"Silence!" A voice bellowed from the gate, it was lord Fullvie, his face reddened with anger. "Are you men? Or old women who cannot hold their tongues to save their very lives!"

The men snapped to attention, an eerie silence filled the courtyard. Only the sound of the sighing wind mixed with the snapping pennant broached the stillness.

"This foul deed was perpetrated by the lesser houses, united by Vernal and Goliad." Gaelan continued. "They have seized the throne and have either killed or imprisoned the Lords of the Landsmarch. To make their deed all the more grievous, they have allied themselves with the Morne. As we sit here the enemies of our forefathers walk within the very house of your King."

All sense of order vanished. The bailey rang with the angry shouts of these men. Swords were drawn and a thousand blades flashed like lightning in the bright sunlight.

Gaelan's horse spun about unnerved by the commotion. As he fought for control of the unruly beast Burcott stood in his stirrups' his drawn sword held high above his head.

"Death to the traitor's!" Lord Fullvie shouted. "Long live Gaelan, King of Trondhiem!"

The men took up the call, shouting it until the very stone of the mountain seemed to shake from their anger.

Gaelan held his hand out, and after several moments the men quieted. "The road ahead is perilous, we will be branded as traitors. Our names will be slandered in our own homes. I will have no man among us who does not wish to be. There is no shame or dishonor, the gate stands open. If any should wish it, he may leave now in safety with his head held high."

The men looked about, but no one moved. They were warriors of Fullvie, sworn to the service of their King.

Gaelan nodded in approval to Burcott. The old lord was smiling proudly.

"For Trondhiem!" Gaelan shouted, the men roared in approval taking up the new call. "Seal the gates!" He ordered dismounting and passing his reins to a nearby guard.

"Return to your duties!" Burcott bellowed above the din. "Sharpen your blades and remain vigilant. Our enemy will come to us soon enough."

Burcott dismounted and strode confidently through the organized chaos of men rushing off to ready the small keep for war.

Gaelan gripped Burcott's shoulder. "These are fine men."

"You'll find none better, my King." Burcott replied with pride.

Gaelan frowned, "I will not be called King until all of Trondhiem is free of Goliad, and Vernal's filth."

Burcott nodded in acceptance. "As you wish, Gaelan."

"Prince Gaelan," Lord Hurin interrupted. "I must return to my house in Eramat. My people must be forewarned of the coming danger."

"By all means," Gaelan answered shaking the lord's hand firmly. "I owe you a debt of gratitude Lord Hurin."

Lord Hurin bowed, "I only did my duty as all who are loyal to the crown should sire. My house and men are at your service prince Gaelan. I shall return with the men at my disposal." Hurin looked to Burcott and shook hands with the large man. "Hold fast until I return old friend."

Burcott laughed, "Don't worry we wont go off and win the war without you." Burcott pulled his signet ring from his finger. "Would you be so kind as to swing south and tell my brothers what has transpired." He tossed the ring to Hurin. "Give them this and they will know what is to be done."

Hurin tucked the ring into the pocket of his leather-riding cloak. "I will do as you ask."

He mounted up and with a short wave farewell. He led his men out through the gate.

Burcott led the way into the Tower. A great Hall comprised the entire lower floor. Thick columns of worked stone supported the upper floors. Oil lamps hung from the ceiling, their light flooding the room, reflecting from the hundreds of polished shields that lined the outer wall.

The officers of the guard rose from their chairs, many of their faces filled with doubt.

Burcott laughed and slammed the palm of his hand down upon the table. "Why the long faces?" He exclaimed. "This is War!"

"Januel," Burcott pointed to one of the youngest. "Have ale brought and see that scouts are posted on the trail. I want warning should any of Vernal's men have followed us."

The young warrior bowed quickly and left the hall in a rush.

Prince Gaelan crossed the room to where a detailed map of Trondhiem hung upon the wall. "Where to start?" He mused looking over the familiar lands of his father's kingdom.

"Send messengers to the other houses of the Landsmarch," Burcott suggested, "Not all of the Lords were at Thorunder, a few may yet be free and will come to your aid."

Gaelan nodded in agreement. "We must marshal every man who can swing a blade or bend a bow to our cause. Have them gather here, Carich will be our foothold."

"Aye," Burcott agreed. "Carich will not easily fall."

"How do we keep the north lands open should Goliad and Vernal lay siege to Carich? If he bottles us up here we can never gather enough men to rid us of these usurpers."

Burcott touched the map resting his forefinger on the name Galtor. "We hold the Bridge, the span is the only crossing an army can use. The Rildrun's waters run fast and deep this time of year. Any force brought against us either crosses the span, or circles around Lake Valdecar. Those are Lord Hurin's lands that lay against the Raobahn Mountains. If Goliad's army attempts that passage they will pay dearly for each foot of ground they traverse."

Gaelan could see the wisdom of Burcott's plan. He was fortunate indeed to have such a seasoned warrior as his advisor. "How many men would holding the bridge require?"

"One hundred could do it," Burcott replied. "Send two, and it will be as secure as we could make it. Should they come that way the men can hold long enough for us to arrive."

"Very well, gather what men and supplies you need and see to it."

Burcott pointed to one of the waiting captains. The man straightened and bowed, turning to leave.

"Good luck," Gaelan offered.

The guard smiled and touched his fist to his heart in salute. "We will hold the span Sire." He turned on his heel and left the Tower's Hall.

"From now on this pass is closed," Gaelan continued after the officer had left. "Trondhiem will remain cut off from the Eastern Kingdoms."

"Can we not call on your uncle in Kesh for aid?" One of assembled men blurted out. He flinched as Burcott shot him a hot look.

Gaelan shook his head; "If he receives word of my father's death and believes the lies of Vernal, we may have the entire Keshian army on our back's."

"Then it is imperative that we reach him first." Burcott passed him a mug of ale. "If we're lucky, we may receive aid in regaining the throne."

"Luck," Gaelan snorted. "Why would it suddenly change?"

The first war council lasted throughout the night. Plans were made and scrapped, as new ideas flitted about the room. Even the most outlandish were considered.

With the rising sun one hundred and twenty men rode out the gate, each to ride to different parts of the kingdom, spreading the call to arms. Two of the men were tasked with overtaking Lord Hurin and charging him with the defense of the northern lands.

Gaelan watched the men leave his room on the fourth floor afforded a view of the bailey below, from a narrow lancet set within the wall. He stood looking out the small opening watching the long shadow of the mountain shrink as the sun climbed high into the sky.

The grief he felt was a small pang buried deep within him. His sense of duty overwhelming any desire for revenge. "I pray father that I am up to the task set before me." He said to the empty room as he turned from the narrow opening.

He fell onto the simple bed and closed his eyes, he lay for a long while but sleep would not come easily to his troubled mind.

CHAPTER TEN

Lord Vernal stood within the king's private audience chamber. The room was dark and cold, far colder than he had ever felt any room in the Keep being.

Goliad paced the chamber in a rage, his passage disturbing the flame of the single candle upon the table. Its feeble fire offering the only source of light in the chamber.

The collar of the formal tunic he wore irritated his neck, but he made no move to adjust the offending fabric. In the darkest shadows stood the Morne guards, their golden eyes never leaving him. He shuddered beneath their inhuman gazes, wondering if he would live out the next few moments.

The brutality the reptilian warriors had shown in the last few hours was beyond comprehension. The passages of the keep were red with the blood of their victims. The same blood stained the broad snouts that poked out from beneath their ebon hoods.

Goliad slammed his fist down upon the table, startling Vernal. "How many have we captured?" His pale face was uncolored by his rage. His eyes however burned with both hatred and loathing.

"Three of the Landsmarch are in the cells below us." Vernal spoke softly hoping to quell Goliad's wrath. "Lords Colven, Lewitt, and Grindorias. Lord Ol'kie was slain when we attempted to apprehend him."

"The others?" Goliad prompted him, his breath hissing through clenched teeth.

"Of Lord Deneb there has been no sign, Hurin and Burcott escaped with the Prince as you already know. Lord Neros has gone south with a large force of the King's guard."

Goliad grunted at the news, "Because of your incompetence four of the most powerful Lords are running free."

Vernal's back stiffened at the rebuke. "You have twenty two of the lesser houses," he said defensively.

"What of the other eight?" Goliad countered. "You promised all of them?"

"It was not I who brought the Morne here." Vernal spoke his mind, instantly regretting it.

"Kill the fathers and grant title and lands to the sons. Only if they swear fealty to me."

Vernal paled his mouth going dry with fear. "That's a bit drastic," he stammered. "You will only create more enemies if such a plan is put into motion."

Goliad smiled, "Fear is a tool Vernal. I do not seek their love, only their obedience."

"Wait," Vernal urged. "We need to gather our forces, and strengthen our position here first."

"And in that time will not Gaelan do the same?" Goliad replied.

"He has fled north, seeking out his uncle's aid I would guess." Vernal said growing more confident as Goliad's rage lessened.

Goliad laughed, "I have taken steps to see that Kesh remains within its borders. Their King should be in the nether world with his brother by now."

The lengths Goliad would go to too gain the throne shocked Vernal. "There are treaties between our lands, you simply cannot assassinate their King with out plunging us into war."

Goliad sat down, his dark eyes bored into Vernal, harsh and unforgiving as if they searched the man for weakness. "You would quote the law to me Vernal? Where were your laws the night we slew your King? Or do we just obey those that suit our fancy?"

Vernal had no reply. The fiend before him was correct. He would live out his life knowing he had betrayed every oath he had ever taken.

"I'll take your silence as a sign of agreement with me on this matter. Now, you will take your men and round up those fugitives. Leave Gaelan to me." Goliad motioned to the door with his hand. "Go now before I consider having you replaced."

Vernal's eyes burned with anger but he bowed and stomped from the chamber into the dim corridor beyond. "Go ahead play at being King Goliad." Vernal muttered beneath his breath. "I will have the throne yet," he vowed silently.

CHAPTER ELEVEN

The town of Haven was located on the shores of the Brae River. Its buildings lay hidden from the waterway by a thick screen of trees. A wooden palisade erected upon low earthwork surrounded the village. They rode up to it and Connell dismounted, motioning for Casius to do the same.

They stood there for several long minutes before the gates opened. A small group of riders advanced, crossing the hundred yards of intervening space cautiously.

They were hard faced men, and bore their weapons in hands well accustomed to their use. The lead rider smiled and exchanged a firm handshake with Connell.

"Bal'Zar," Connell said with a smile. "It has been a long time."

"Two years," the man said with a nod towards Casius. "Can he be trusted?"

"With my life," Connell said vouching for Casius. "We wont stay long. We need supplies and a warm meal."

"You never stay long in any case." Bal'Zar said with a smile. "Your both welcome to stay in Haven. Any man Connell would speak so highly of is a man I can trust."

They remounted and followed the men to the palisade.

"Bal'Zar we were assaulted last night by something strange. Some creature that I have never encountered, or seen the likes of before."

"Strange things have a way of showing up in the plains now and then." The gray haired man said with a shrug. "You look none the worse for it, did you slay it?"

"Casius did," Connell answered. "We thought to see it in the daylight but the light of the sun destroyed it, turning it to dust and smoke before our eyes."

Bal'Zar looked at him strangely.

"Tell your people to take care, Bal'Zar." Connell warned. "This thing was tough as iron, it resembled a thin man with glowing eyes that burned in the darkness. Creeping about on all fours, it moved like lightning when it needed."

"I'll spread the word, Connell." Bal'Zar replied disturbed by the description. "I pray that you have destroyed the only one of its kind in our area."

"I do as well," Casius said. "I hope never to come across another again."

They crossed through the gate and dismounted on the barren ground within the shadow of the wall.

"You have told him of our ways?" Bal'Zar asked Connell.

"I saw no need," Connell replied. "It is not within him to violate the laws of Haven."

"Whether it is within him or not he must know." Bal'Zar answered. He looked into Casius's eyes as he spoke. "Within these walls a man's past is forgotten. You will not draw your weapon unless attacked. Nor will you steal or otherwise cause harm to befall another.

"This place will not be spoken of nor will you lead another to Haven. Secrecy is held dear by all of us, and should we ever doubt your ability to keep quite. You will never leave this town alive. Connell has vouched for you, do not betray his trust."

"I wont," Casius replied.

Bal'Zar nodded, "Should Haven fall under attack you will come to her defense, and stand upon the wall alongside all others who reside here."

They led their horses into a large livery, two eager boys rushed out to take the reins.

"Grab your gear," Bal'Zar prompted. "You can stay beneath my roof this night."

"I was looking forward to sharing your fire old friend," Connell said with a grin.

"Bah!" Bal'Zar exclaimed. "Your more likely looking forward to my wife's cooking."

"Always," Connell laughed throwing his saddlebags over his shoulder.

Bal'Zar's house was warm and comfortable. His wife greeted them warmly, and was genuinely pleased to have the company.

Casius and I would pay a visit to your smith before he closes shop. We will be gone but a short while.

Bal'Zar saw them out. "Don't miss diner." He reminded them.

It was a short walk to the smith's forge. A small building that radiated heat from its open doors. A large man with a bent back stood in the yard wiping his hands with a stained cloth.

He was broad shouldered, with a baldhead that gleamed with sweat. His arms bore many scars, each brand earned in the pursuit of his life's work. His deeply lined face brightened as he recognized Connell.

"It's good to see you lad!" He exclaimed.

"It's good to see you as well Gall," Connell shoved Casius forward, "This is Casius."

Gall nodded in greeting, "I see you still carry the sword I made for you."

Connell patted the blade hanging from his hip. "I have never seen better, you are a master of your craft."

Gall laughed, "With a silver tongue like that you must need something."

"A sword," Connell said. "My friend here needs a blade more suited to our lifestyle."

Gall looked Casius over; "I may have something for you." He stepped into the building and returned in a few moments with a long sword in hand.

"I don't have much money," Casius said apologetically as Gall handed him the blade.

"No one ever does," Gall said with a sigh prompting Connell to laugh.

Casius looked the blade over, its mirror like sheen flashed in the afternoon sun. It was a simple sword void of decoration but it was well made and razor sharp.

"How does it feel?" Gall asked after Casius had taken a few swings with it.

"A bit heavy but the balance is perfect."

"You'll need to toughen him up a bit before he gets hurt Connell."

"We've already begun, Gall." Connell replied taking the blade from Casius. "As fine a blade as a man can ask for," he said complimenting the smith's work.

"I only have two Talens with which to pay you." Casius offered up the two coins to the man.

Gall reached out and took one of them. "And that pig sticker you're wearing as well."

"Done," Casius quickly removed his sword belt and handed the blade over.

Casius fastened the belt Gall handed him around his waist and slid the new weapon into the scabbard of dark leather. "It fits well but feels somewhat odd."

"You'll get used to it," Connell said. "Just try not to trip over it when you walk." Connell shook Gall's hand. "You're getting soft old man, and you let him get the best of you."

"Nonsense," Gall grunted. "I figure if he's traveling with you he's going to need protection. Besides my days of venturing are over, and I have little need of money." He led them across the yard away from the forge's oppressive heat.

"Now tell me, what have you done? You never come here unless someone is on your tail."

"For some reason a Raider has taken a personal interest in Casius here. The man even bribed the Senatum into capturing him." Connell explained, "I only helped him to escape."

Gall spat, "Damn raiders!" He handed Casius his gold coin back. "Keep the blade, I can not stand the likes of those men and would aid any man who has run afoul of them."

Casius pocketed the coin, "I don't know what to say Gall. I will cherish the blade."

"Don't cherish anything of its kind Casius." Gall said, "It is a thing made to kill and maim. Respect it and learn its use, and it will defend you."

"I will ensure that he does Gall." Connell said. "Once again you have proven yourself to be an honorable man with a good heart."

Gall waved them away, "Go on I've got work to do for paying customers," he said with a grin.

They returned to Bal'Zar's house, despite the awkward feeling of the swinging blade upon his hip Casius actually felt taller.

"You are fortunate," Connell said as they walked. "Gall has a collection of lesser blades. He could have passed one of them on to you."

"Why would a smith of such skill live here in seclusion?"

"Many years ago Gall had a fair daughter named Morwen. Her beauty was unmatched; she was a kind and gentle soul without blemish. Gall worked for the King, forging the blades used by the Senatum.

"A Senatum Captain took a fancy to Morwen, he pursued her night and day. Morwen rejected his approaches and the man grew angry, one night in a drunken rage he brutally attacked her. She was beaten so severely that she did not survive the night.

"Gall gave in to his rage and slew the Captain, and the entire garrison that attempted to protect him. Thirteen men lay dead within the guardhouse when he was finished. He fled the capital of Cyndra after setting fire to the guardhouse. For two years he wandered the wild. After his rage had abated, he found his way here." Connell paused at Bal'Zar's door. "It is only one of the many tragic tales that can be found within this settlement."

Casius shook his head. Gall's tale awakened the grief that he kept buried in his own soul. "So much evil in the world." It was all he could say.

"There is much good left as well Casius," Connell reminded him. "Its just harder to find these days."

Their mood brightened when Connell pulled open the door and the heady aroma of fresh bread and roasted duck greeted them.

After their meal they sat before the crackling fire until late in the evening. Bal'Zar entertained them with many tales. Casius learned much about Connell that night.

He learned of the failed uprising that Connell had led in the north. The small army that he had gathered was not enough to overcome the Senatum. On the field of Dal'Entor the full weight of the King's army crushed the rebellion. They offered no quarter slaying any who opposed them.

Connell and a few men escaped into the Nallen wood. They watched helplessly as the Senatum razed the city of Tor. In that battle Connell had stood alone upon a narrow footbridge. He faced ten of the Senatum's best swordsmen, defeating them one by one. His actions had given many men the time needed to flee the field.

"You slew ten men?" Casius asked looking at Connell.

"More," Connell replied. "It was a dark day Casius, one which I try not to remember."

"A heroic feat all the same Connell," Bal'Zar said. "It made you a legend."

"And a wanted man as well, Bal'Zar."

"Aye, as are we all who were with you that day." Bal'Zar stood and stretched. "Dawn fast approaches friends," He said through a yawn. "I'm off to bed ere the sun catches me dawdling about the fire."

They retired to the rooms that Bal'Zar had provided them. Casius was exhausted and fell to sleep within minutes, his new sword propped against the wall at his bedside.

Two hours later Connell stepped out of the shadows of Bal'Zar's house. He moved silently a shade within the predawn mists that blanketed the streets.

He came to the palisade. The gates were locked and guarded by two men. Above them on the wall stood seven more, their eyes turned outward searching the grasslands.

Connell climbed the ladder to the narrow allure upon which the watch stood. Looking to where they were staring intently. He could see nothing but mist swirling in the darkness a few feet beyond the wall.

"What is it?" he whispered to the man closest to him.

"I'm not sure," the man whispered back. "An animal perhaps."

"I know of no animal with eyes the likes of those, they burned as if afire." another man added.

The hairs on Connell's neck stood on end. "Where is it now?"

"The beast drew close and froze watching us for awhile before retreating back into the mist." The guard pointed to the left. "I think it may be kin of the one your companion slew last night."

I should hope not," Connell said staring off into the dark. "Do you have any heavy crossbows?"

"Aye down in the guard shack below."

"Fetch them, and iron tipped bolts as well." Connell suggested.

"Iron tips on an animal?" the man nearest him asked.

"When we encountered the beast my sword bounced from its hide hardly damaging it. An iron tipped bolt may fare better."

The guard nodded and descended the ladder.

The captain of the watch placed a small brass horn to his lips and blew three sharp notes into the darkness. After several moments a whistle sounded from the gloom. "Two of our best trackers went out in search of the beast. I've just recalled them," he said for Connell's benefit.

A short while later two men emerged from the darkness. They ran quietly with short bows in hand.

Once through the gate, they joined the men on the allure.

"Did you see it Cheval?" the captain asked.

"I do not know what it is," Cheval answered. "It moves as if it were an animal, and at times as if it were a man. Sneaky thing. Here one moment, gone the next. I never got very close to it. It's akin to chasing a whiff of smoke, damn peculiar."

"Do you think it's dangerous?" one of the men asked visibly shaken by what he had seen.

Cheval rubbed his neck. "It could have attacked me easily at any time. It is searching for something, or someone and fortunately I was not it. To answer your question I would say yes, it is probably the most dangerous creature I have ever encountered in my life. That thing out there is a hunter, and damned good at it."

The captain looked at Connell. "Perhaps this thing tracks you and your companion. After all, you first encountered one on the plain."

"I am of the same mind," Connell agreed.

"You are safe enough here the wall is well watched and nothing can enter Haven without the guard seeing it. But I fear for you should you leave Haven."

"When we leave we will have the river between us, that alone may prevent it from following. Once on horse we will move quickly, a difficult catch for something that slinks about in the dark."

Connell remained on the wall throughout the night but the creature did not show itself again.

The sunrise was a splendid display of red and deep yellows. As light returned the trackers went out once more, but they returned a short while later. Having found no sign of the visitor. This was what Connell expected, and he did not bother to take part in the search. He left the wall and returned to Bal'Zar's home.

As he approached he could see Casius practicing the sword patterns he had shown him. Connell stopped beneath an ancient Willow; from within its shadows he watched the young man practice.

He stood there for the better part of an hour watching. Casius impressed him with the ease that he had mastered the patterns. He had been gifted with a natural sense of balance and coordination that most swordsmen would spend a lifetime trying to achieve. Casius finally tired, and sheathed the blade. Taking a long drink from a bucket near the well, he poured the remaining water over his head.

Connell left the sheltering shadows of the tree, and entered the yard. "I am surprised to see you up so soon." He said in greeting.

"I would say the same, had you slept last night."

"I was at the gate, it appears our attacker was not alone. Its companion spent the evening trying to find a way past the guard."

Casius felt a chill run up his spine. "Why?"

Connell shrugged, "It may be tracking us, or it is just a coincidence. We must assume it is us it pursues. I don't want to be caught unawares on the trail." Connell looked up at the clear sky overhead. "It is a good day for travel, we will cover as much ground as possible today."

Casius pointed to the packs on the house's porch. "Bal'Zar had those prepared for us."

"Go ready the horses, I will take my leave of Bal'Zar."

Casius walked to the livery shouldering the heavy packs. He saddled his mount with no problems, but Connell's black was less than enthusiastic on leaving the comfortable stall.

Casius managed to get the saddle on the mount but he was unnerved when he looked into the brute's hard eyes. "Lets hope he doesn't take too long," he said to the stallion.

The horse snorted loudly in response, stomping its thick hoof in the dust.

Connell joined him within a few minutes. Together they led the horses out the gate and down to the riverbank.

It took some doing but they eventually got the horses onto the large raft that served as a ferry. The crossing was quick and uneventful. The Ferryman and his sons were familiar with the ways of the river, and guided their craft expertly to the opposite shore. The horses were eager to be free of the craft and once it had entered the shallows they leapt onto the bank.

They rode hard and fast throughout the day. Moving north through the trackless fields of waving grass. They walked the horses often after nightfall, preserving their strength. Something drove them onward a feeling of being pursued, although no signs of it were evident.

Two days they traveled in this fashion. Sleeping little, even when they had stopped for the night. Connell kept a wary eye on the horizon behind them, expecting to see riders in the distance.

The grasslands gave way to gently rolling hills, which grew larger, the father north they traveled. Scattered copses of trees and rills of clear water dotted the landscape.

On the third day they entered a thick wood, and traveled within the shade of the trees. Deer were plentiful as well as other creatures. Small furtive animals, that darted for cover as the men approached. Their feelings of pursuit faded and for the time being they actually felt safe.

On the fourth day, the wood ended on the crown of a rock-strewn hill. Stretched out before them lay a large body of water, its placid surface reflecting the colors of the sky above. The water's stretched out as far as the eye could see.

"The ocean?" Casius asked even though he had never seen the great body of water lying so calm.

"Lake Nall," Connell replied leading his horse down the slope. "The largest lakes in Lakarra, its waters cover hundreds of miles. We will follow the shore north, the town of Bent Oak lies but a few hours away. It is there that we will rejoin the road."

Casius was relieved; the long days of crossing open country were wearing thin on him. "Won't that be dangerous? The Senatum may discover us."

"They may not watch the roads this far north. We're outlaws and I have often found the best hiding place is out in the open. Besides we are entering dangerous country, there are worse things than the Senatum out here. These lands are thick with outlaws and two men provide an easy mark."

"Outlaws and Senatum," Casius said in disgust. "Will there ever be a time when people can safely travel the countryside?"

"When justice returns to these lands once again." Connell answered sadly.

It was dark when they came to the road. The thin sliver of the moon above shed little light. It lay hidden away behind a thin blanket of clouds.

Ahead of them through the gloom burned the lamps of the town of Bent Oak. It was large, sprawling along the shore of the lake. The stone buildings crowded close together behind a stout wall of stone.

"Are we stopping for the night?" Casius asked hopefully.

"Remember the Messenger?" Connell reminded him. "There is a large garrison here, I'd rather not draw their attention."

"A bit out of the way for a Garrison isn't it?"

"The people of this land have a long history. They are proud and resent being under the King's rule. Only his firm hand keeps them quiet."

The darkness covered them, and they stayed within the deepest shadows of the trees that bordered the road. Moving slowly on foot they passed by the walled town and disappeared into the hills beyond.

Leaving the town far behind they rode until well past midnight. The road wound its way higher into wooded hills shrouded in mist. Fires burned in the distance, a merchant train had made its camp near the hilltop. The wagons and animals blocking the narrow path ahead.

Connell dismounted, and with Casius following they walked into the light cast by the nearest of the fires.

Five men sat about the fire. They were supposedly keeping watch but the chill of the fog had brought them to the fire. They jumped, startled to find two trail weary strangers emerging from the dark to stand among them.

"We seek only to share your fire." Connell said calmly keeping his hands away from his sword to put them at ease.

One of the men eyed them warily; the size of Connell's horse clearly bothered him. Only warriors rode beasts of such breeding. "A bit late to be out riding," he said skeptically. "There are more than twenty men in this caravan, it would be unwise to do anything foolish."

"Brigands and raiders don't often announce themselves before attacking." Connell secured his horse's reins to a low hanging bough.

"And honest men don't go about slinking in the dark."

"Lets just say we do not want to draw the Senatum's attention to ourselves." Connell said with a grin.

"No sane man would," the gruff driver replied nodding to the fire.

They seated themselves close to the fire, its warmth driving off the chill that seemed to have settled in their bones.

Connell could tell these men had come down from the north by the way the heavily laden wagons were pointed. "What news from the road ahead?"

The driver shrugged, "The road is the road." He replied dismissing the many rumors he had heard in his travels. "Though the nights are growing colder which is unusual for this time of year."

"It is much the same to the south, there are strange things moving on the plains these days. It would be wise to keep a sharp watch."

"If your business is with the Senatum I would turn away from the north. The road is watched and travelers are being searched. If you carry contraband, I would lose it before reaching Deepwell."

"My thanks friend," Connell said. "We travel north seeking work nothing more."

The man smiled, he could see through Connell's tale. "I've heard there's more to be had in the south."

"We travel north nonetheless."

The driver laughed, he knew he would get no more information from the man. "Suit yourself," he said with a shrug. "You have an honest look about you. Stay 'til morning if you'd like. We leave with the rising of the sun."

"We are most grateful," Connell stretched out making himself as comfortable as one could on the rocky ground.

Casius did likewise and fell fast asleep in moments.

Connell smiled at his trusting companion, although he lay down he remained awake his hand resting lightly on his sword's hilt.

The camp stirred to life as the sun broke the horizon. Casius opened his eyes briefly. Shutting them he lay listening to the familiar sounds of the men breaking camp. A few of the drivers were cursing while attempting to harness the uncooperative mules and oxen.

He was about to drift off back to sleep when his feet were kicked softly. Casius opened his eyes and looked up at Connell's face. The sky was the color of fire, the clouds blazing above the treetops.

"Get up." Connell said drawing his sword. "We will practice a bit before moving on."

Casius got to his feet groaning; his back was sore and stiff.

Connell laughed at his discomfort. "Life on the road can make you old before your time."

Casius stretched and drew his sword.

"This will loosen you up a bit." Connell said swinging his blade towards Casius's head.

Reacting quickly Casius brought his blade up. The sound of metal striking metal echoed loudly as he deflected the blade up and away.

Under the curious eyes of the workingmen they sparred for close to an hour. Connell always attacking while Casius strove to parry the blows. After Casius had received several bruises from the flat of Connell's blade he sheathed his sword.

"That's it," Casius gasped his arm burning from exertion. "I'm not worth a damn at this!" He said rubbing at the newest welt upon his shoulder.

"You're a worthy student Casius," Connell said while sliding his blade into his own scabbard. "It has been only twenty days. I have spent a lifetime learning my skills. I've held a blade since I could first walk."

"Who would give a weapon to a babe?" Casius scoffed.

"A wooden one," Connell corrected. "Fastened about my waist, I learned to walk with a scabbard at my side.

"You do not have the time to learn as I did however. Slow and steady with many teachers. Instead I am trying to make it so you can survive, and you are learning far faster than I would have thought possible.

"Just practice what I have taught you, when you no longer have to think about where your sword is then you will have nothing more to learn from me. Until then nurse your pride and learn from your mistakes."

"What if we encounter the Senatum near Deepwell?"

"Run," Connell said jokingly. "That news is two weeks old at best. No messenger from Elk Run could have made it there so quickly. I doubt it has anything to do with us. By the time we reach Deepwell the Senatum should be long gone."

"Then we have nothing to fear." Casius stated in relief.

"On the contrary," Connell replied. "We have much to concern ourselves about."

They mounted their horses, and bid the drivers farewell. The hills ahead were losing the thin shroud of fog that hid them from view.

Connell set a fast pace letting the mounts stretch their legs on the trail.

CHAPTER TWELVE

They followed the road up into the rugged highlands, which bordered the towering heights of the Weyre Mountains. The snow-clad shoulders of the mountains filled the northern sky. Their peaks were invisible, hidden within the heavy gray clouds that darkened the day.

For two days the road had narrowed. Becoming a well-marked trail that bordered a racing river as it plunged from the lands above. The water rumbled as it descended in steep falls and narrow rapids. The water was frigid, carrying with it the cold from the snow pack above, from which it sprang.

As the ascended the trees grew shorter, becoming gnarled, wind twisted mockeries of their taller brethren in the lower altitudes.

A town of dreary gray stone buildings greeted them as they left the tree line. The structures clung to the face of a steep ridge. Rising several hundred feet above them in a series of four broad terraces.

The buildings were low, with thick walls and small lancets for windows. Many of them were roofed with copper that had turned green with age. On the lowest terrace a broad curtain wall protected the settlement. In places thick mats of moss had all but obscured its large stones. Towers rose along its length, seemingly placed at random.

The settlement was far from elegant; in fact it was depressing to look upon. There were no bright colors to be seen. It was built for strength. Able to withstand the worst weather the mountains could throw against it, a bastion against the harsh winters and cold summer nights.

As they neared the curtain wall the river veered eastward. Ending at the bottom of a low waterfall that pierced the rocks above. It was from this landmark that the town of Lowfalls had gotten its name.

Casius looked to the open gate in the curtain wall a half-mile away. "A long way to haul water," he commented.

"You can't build any closer," Connell answered. "In spring there are flash floods as ice dams in the mountains break free. The resulting walls of water are fierce and powerful. Anyone foolish enough to build in its path is swept away. Long ago a hidden aqua duct was cut into the rock, it provides all the water the town could possibly need."

The road to the gate climbed to the lower terrace. In several steep switchbacks that were so narrow that the two men could not ride abreast.

Casius clung tightly to his reins; he had looked down and regretted it. The trail skirted the edge of a deep ravine that plunged hundreds of feet into a darkness, which the dim sunlight could not penetrate.

"Why would anyone wish to live in such a place?" Casius wondered aloud.

"Two hundred years ago this was the border of a kingdom named Haego. A small keep stood here, it became a refuge for the people fleeing the Senatum.

"For twenty years it was besieged and eventually it fell to the Lakarrans, as disease and starvation forced the survivors to surrender. These are proud people and many of them remained building the town you now see."

A deep rumbling echoed across the mountains. To the west the sky was darkening and the smell of rain rode the stiff breeze.

"A storm is approaching, we will wait it out in one of the town's inns."

"Will that be wise, Connell?" Casius asked, the last thing he wanted was to run into the Senatum.

"Safer than facing a storm on these trails," Connell answered. "Besides the Senatum are not welcomed here. The last time I passed this way there was no garrison within the walls.

We will keep a low profile nonetheless," Connell added. "You can be assured that spies are about. The Senatum would not let this town stand unwatched. Rebellions can spring up quickly in places such as this."

Casius looked up at the threatening sky, "We should pick up the pace then," he said, as the first drops of rain began to fall. "I hate riding in wet clothes."

Connell laughed, "Such is the life of a vagabond Casius."

The sky released its pent up fury as they entered the common room of the first inn they came too. Lightning and hail pounded the mountainside. Many of the inn's patrons flinched with each deafening blast of thunder. At times the stone building shook as the wind roared through the narrow streets.

The proprietor calmly closed the shutters to the narrow windows. He had seen many such storms in his long life, and this one was no different than the others.

Casius ignored the raging weather. He was busy wolfing down the first decent meal he had eaten in many days.

Connell sat with his back to the wall, enjoying a tankard of ale while watching the inn's patrons.

Casius finished his meal and leaned his back against the wall, a cup of warm spiced wine in his hands. He flinched slightly as thunder roared outside, shaking the building's very foundations.

He glanced over to Connell somewhat embarrassed by his reaction. He was not sure, but he thought his companion was somewhat displeased. "What's bothering you?"

Connell shrugged, "I hadn't planned on staying here long. But this storm is powerful and may last several days."

This did not seem to be a bad thing to Casius. He knew they both could use a few days of decent food and rest. "It will end eventually," he said consolingly. "When it does we will move on."

Connell raised an eyebrow at Casius's remark. "Have you forgotten the creature you slew? If its mate pursues us I do not think this weather will slow such a beast."

"We do not know if it has followed us. It may have been nothing more than sheer coincidence that led it to," Casius paused, he had almost blurted out Haven's name. "Bal'Zar's house," he said quickly. "Besides I doubt our spoor could be tracked through such a storm."

"That thing was no animal Casius. I feel it is something entirely different." Connell grunted over his tankard, taking a swift drink he continued. "Perhaps you're right, but I haven't lived this long by being careless. We will remain vigilant just in case my fears should be justified."

During the second day of the storm's assault upon the mountain community, an old man entered the inn accompanied by his two daughters. They wore heavy cloaks of leather that kept out the worst of the rain. He must have been a local man of some notoriety, for the inn erupted into applause as he lowered his hood. He waved his wide brimmed hat to the crowd in acknowledgement. As one of the patron's drug a stool over to the hearth.

His daughters sat on the floor at his feet; one carried a small flute of silver. The other bore a drum of brass and dark wood.

Lighting a long stemmed clay pipe, the man tossed his hat onto the floor with a flourish. It landed top down and had barely stopped moving, when several coins landed within it.

He smiled at the generosity, "What story would you hear?" He asked the crowd.

Many people shouted their requests lost in the rumbling peal of thunder. The old man raised his hands for silence, "There is but one tale that should be told on a night such as this." He took a long pull on his pipe and exhaled a cloud of pungent smoke. "Tanuth the axe?" He suggested, smiling as more coins fell into his hat.

The drummer tapped out a steady cadence that seemed to compliment the rumbling thunder outside. The flute joined in, the notes soft and plaintive.

"More than two hundred years ago," the man said in a low voice that captivated everyone. "Our forefathers faced their darkest hour. King An Ahkman ruled Haego. He was a sickly man. His veins filled with the blood of a coward."

The audience hissed and booed, many curses came from the mouths of the drunkest men.

The bard waited until the noise subsided. "His leadership of Haego's army was ill inspired, and doomed to fail. The Lakarrans overran our borders, and spread destruction across the land. They moved as locusts, an unstoppable force that consumed all that lay in its path.

"Our men fought bravely, but all they could do was slow the enemies approach. The Lakarrans paid dearly for each mile they advanced. Blackened fields and burnt ruins marked their progress.

"Women, children, and the old fled before them. Those that faltered were run down and slaughtered. Their life's blood turning the fertile fields to mud."

The music changed growing softer and full of grief.

"Those that fled to these mountains fared far better than the kin who took to the upland plain. Tanuth came here onto this very mountain. In those days all that stood upon this crag was the lone tower of Le'ach Tol, and the curtain wall that surrounded it. The guards within would suffer no one to enter, for the small keep was filled with refugees and there was no room for others.

"Tanuth pounded upon the gates, shaking them in his fury. Go out! He cried to the men upon the wall. Strike down these invaders and keep your oaths."

The bard paused, inhaling from his pipe deeply. "The men within the walls refused. After all, their families were within the walls, and they would not abandon them. For five days Tanuth assailed them with curses and challenges. On the fifth day he threw up his hands in disgust.

"He left the mountains, and entered the Nallen forest. He journeyed far into that dire wood. By secret trails and hidden paths it is said that he found his way to the forest's heart. He stood within the shadow of Asua Tuell, the mother of all trees. There he struck a bargain with the spirits of the forest. What the terms of that bargain were is not known.

"Tanuth left that dark wood bearing a great axe, the very haft was fashioned from one of Asua Tuell's limbs. Its black iron head glowed with power, and struck fear into those who looked upon it.

"He combed the countryside for several months, gathering freemen who would follow him. Using little known passes and trails they moved through the mountains. Often attacking the Lakarrans in the dead of night.

His reputation grew and word of his exploits spread throughout the land. Men came from far and wide to fight beneath his banner, a green tree upon a field of black.

"Night Blade, the Lakarrans named him, they believed he was a spirit, a being that neither sword nor arrow could touch. Some claimed that he stood ten feet tall and wielded an axe wreathed in flame. His very footfalls were said to shake the earth for miles.

"The King of Lakarra upon hearing of this man placed a great bounty on his head. Many a fool sought to collect it, and their blood was spilt adding to the legend.

"The war had gone badly for our people and the last dregs of our army was trapped within Com's Girdle. With the mountains on three sides, and the largest host Lakarra had ever fielded to the south. The weary men prepared to make their last stand in the deep valley.

"Day after bloody day the Lakarrans charged. The ground was treacherous, and our men held the heights above the Valley's opening. Men died on both sides by the thousands, the remaining warriors of Haego could not hold onto the pass much longer.

"On the fourth day it looked as if the Lakarrans would finally break through. A great horn sounded from hills, Glorien it was named. Its echoing call pierced the morning air. The Lakarrans' advance faltered, for they knew the sound of the trump of Night Blade.

"Pouring forth from the highlands, two thousand strong came the host of Tanuth. They smashed into the startled Lakarrans flank. The ordered ranks disintegrated, many of the Lakarrans fled before them. At the charge's head came Tanuth, his great axe dropping men by the dozens."

Casius leaned forward in his chair his ale all but forgotten. This man was a master at his craft and for the moment no one remembered the raging storm outside.

"His chain hauberk was stained with the blood of the Lakarrans," the bard continued. "A dark helm hid his face but through the visor his eyes burned with rage. The Night Blade had come, and the Lakarrans died before him.

"Two score fell dead at his feet, and many more lay wounded. The Lakarrans flank collapsed, and our army rallied charging into the fray.

The drumming ceased and the flute faded. "The tide of battle was turning. The Lakarrans were about to break when the unthinkable happened." The bard held his pipe up as if it were a dagger. "It was then that Tanuth felt the sting of cold steel sliding through his ribs." The narrator lowered the pipe slowly.

"The fire within the axe faded as it fell from his hand. The dark bladed head sank deep into the fertile earth at his feet. Falling to the ground, he could see the bloody dagger in his best friend's hand."

The crowd hissed. Allowing the man to take a quick drink from a sweating tankard that had been set at his feet.

"Yourid, the traitor knew Tanuth's weakness. The axe protected him from those he saw as enemies, but not his friends and companions. Yourid had sold his loyalty for a steep price, not to the King of Lakarra, as one would believe.

No this treachery was rooted in a far darker place. For it was Tanuth's own King who had ordered his death. An Ahkman feared the warrior. In his paranoia he believed Tanuth would soon seize the throne. In the darkest hours of night he had come to see Tanuth as a threat more dire than the Lakarrans.

"With Tanuth's fall our forces fled the field. The Lakarrans pursued them until every man that could be found lay dead. Hacked to pieces by the invaders. A few days after the battle the Lakarrans found an ancient oak of dark wood had sprung from the earth, growing tall and stately its branches shadowing the very spot where Tanuth had fallen.

"The Lakarrans searched the field for many days but no sign of the great axe or Tanuth's body was ever found. Some say that the oak had sprung from the haft of the enchanted weapon. It grew anew, watered by the blood of our fallen heroes. Somewhere within the sheltering wood of its bole it cradles the body of our peoples last hope."

"King An Ahkman surrendered a few weeks later and was executed by the Lakarran General Telque. His body was tied behind the General's war chariot, and drug through the streets of every sizeable town in our realm.

"A few men survived the battle of Com's Girdle, and word of Yourid's treachery spread. Until one day a mob swarmed his estates, and drug him down into the valley where he had committed his foul deed. He was hung that day from the very oak that marked Tanuth's grave.

The audience cheered, the bard waited for the room to grow quite once more. "The tree still stands upon the hillside. Surrounded by its offspring, a new forest has slowly taken shape, a wood where no man's axe would ever fall.

If you ever venture to the valley, do so in the early summer for on the day of Tanuth's death every leaf of the wood is said to turn blood red at sunset. As if the trees remember the treachery of that day."

The music stopped and the old man bowed accepting the applause that came from his audience. The hat quickly filled with coins, his tale had earned him a goodly sum. He emptied it into a small pouch, and with a flourish he set it upon his hoary head.

"I thank you all for your generosity!" he proclaimed over the applause.

"Another!" Came a call from the audience, it was taken up by others.

The old bard bowed once more. "I am touched my good friends, but there are other inns where the storm holds people at bay. It is my calling to spread good cheer and I cannot forsake my duties."

He wrapped his sodden cloak about his shoulders, and held the door for his two daughters. "Look for me on the morrow, whether this storm still blows or not." With a final bow he stepped out into the darkness.

Casius returned to his seat and took up his half emptied tankard. "That was a tale worth hearing," he said to Connell.

"Aye," Connell replied. "He told it well."

They sat in silence enjoying the warm room, and listening to some of the men as they sang bawdy drinking songs. As the hours passed and more ale was downed the songs became lewder. It had gotten to the point where the serving girls were blushing with each chorus.

The inn keep held up his hands, and began to tell a tale. It was the ballad of Raegash the bald and the hounds of Corrin. A vulgar tale better suited for the dockside taverns frequented by pirates.

The men loved it, and to the inn keep's delight they cheered him on.

The door opened, and a gust of frigid air ripped through the room causing the lanterns to flicker madly. Standing in the entry, a shapely woman in her early thirties was shaking out the water from her dark cloak. She wore her golden hair long, tied into a single braid that hung down her back.

Beneath her cloak she wore a linen tunic of deep green over breeches of dark leather. A simple belt of faded leather girded her waist. Tucked into the belt were two of the longest knives Casius had ever seen. Across her back hung a quiver of arrows; the shafts were long and fletched in scarlet.

Resting her unstrung longbow against the wall she turned and surveyed the room. The firm set of her jaw and the steely fire in her blue eyes convinced most men to avert their appraising looks.

Casius however did not look away, her bold demeanor fascinated him. Their eyes met and Casius could see no pleasantries in her gaze. She seemed to judge him in an instant and moved her eyes to Connell.

Frowning slightly she crossed the room gracefully her deer hide boots silent on the rush strewn floor. She wove through the rowdy crowd and settled on the bench across the table from Connell.

"Hello D'Yana, it's been a few years," Connell said in greeting.

"You're a hard man to find Connell," she said softly, barely above a whisper.

"What good is being an outlaw when everyone knows your whereabouts?" Connell answered with a slight smile.

"Half the Senatum is out searching for you. I've looked from Glycea to Garm to find you."

"The bounty must be high indeed for you to cover such a distance."

D'Yana smiled, a brilliant flash of white in the gloomy rooms interior. "To go against you is suicide, and every man hunter in Lakarra knows it."

"That doesn't stop them."

D'Yana spared a glance at Casius. "So this is the slave you have stolen, I hope he's worth it. The price on your head has tripled."

"I am no slave!" Casius snapped.

D'Yana laughed, "I'd say not," she said. "With a tongue like that I doubt you have ever worn chains."

"D'Yana, this is Casius." Connell said introducing them.

"If you did not come for the bounty. Then why have you searched for me?" Connell asked returning to the point at hand.

"Not for old times sake," D'Yana replied coldly. "I have been commissioned to find you. My employer seeks your skill at arms, and wishes to speak with you. Our camp site is not far."

Connell shook his head, "I have pressing business of my own, and little time to spare. As you have said half the Senatum is out for my head."

D'Yana smiled, "He pays well." She said softly, "Very well indeed." Opening her hand she allowed ten Imperial Crowns to fall onto the table. The heavy gold coins were twice the size of a Talen, and worth five times as much.

Casius gasped he had never seen such wealth in his life. What lay on the table between them was more than most men would earn in their entire lifetime.

Connell covered the coins with his sleeve. A quick glance around assured him that no one had seen the gold. "That was foolish D'Yana," he whispered sternly. "It would serve you right if a thief makes off with your fee."

"The gold is for you," she said sliding the coins into a small pouch. "All you have to do is meet with my employer."

"This smells of a trap," Casius warned.

Connell nodded, "Had it been anyone else who brought this before me I would be inclined to agree. I have always trusted D'Yana and I know she would not steer me wrong." Connell took the pouch from her, "Who is this employer of yours?"

"He calls himself Marcos," she answered. "He travels with a companion, the oddest man I have ever seen. With strangely shaped eyes, named Suni. They hail from distant lands and seem to be fair and honest men."

Connell leaned back and tucked the pouch into his belt.

"Be wary of Suni, Connell." D'Yana added as an after thought. "He has the demeanor of a warrior, a damned dangerous one if I judge him rightly."

"Then what need has this Marcos of me?" Connell asked.

"Marcos has need of a Swordsman. From what I gather, Suni uses no bladed weapons," D'Yana shrugged. "Some sort of code he follows."

"We will accompany you." Connell said accepting her offer. His curiosity was fueled by her description of this Suni.

"We?"

"Where I go," Connell nodded to Casius. "He goes as well."

D'Yana shrugged, "He asked for you alone, but I can see no harm in Casius coming along."

"Thank you," Casius said sarcastically, not sure if he had been insulted by her statement.

"Where is your Camp?" Connell asked heading off a sharp reply from D'Yana.

"Just beyond the Westerling trail, a short distance within the forest."

"Your employer is an idiot, with a fool for a guide!" Connell exclaimed. "No sane man would place himself at such risk."

D'Yana's face reddened in anger. "It was he who insisted on it. Over my most vehement objections." She snapped back defensively. After a moments hesitation she let go of her anger with a deep breath. "Does this change anything?"

Connell paused, feeling the weight of the coins tucked in his belt. He had no desire to walk beneath the boughs of that haunted wood, but he had need of coin. This money would make their trek easier. "Nothing," he answered.

Casius watched the change in his friend with interest. Connell held a fortune in gold, and had actually considered setting it aside at the mention of the forest. "What could be in this forest that poses so grave a risk?" he asked. "A few bears and wolves perhaps?"

"There's more than bears in that accursed wood Casius," Connell replied coldly. "You can be sure of that."

"Bah," D'Yana scoffed. "Mostly shadows, and stories from what I've heard."

Connell smiled knowingly. "A few days in it's depths and you would think differently. I've traveled those forgotten roads, and prayed I would never have to do so again. Nallen Forest is not for the faint of heart."

"The wood where Tanuth was given the axe?" Casius asked.

"The same," Connell answered. "There are many legends wrapped about the wood. At one time its trees were even worshiped by the people of these hills."

"When do we leave?" Casius was looking forward to moving on. The forest did not frighten him after all he had survived his own trial in a gloomy wood back on Kale.

"We leave as soon as possible, the storm will cover our departure." Connell looked about the room. He had noticed several shady looking characters taking more than a casual interest in them. "The trail will be treacherous in this weather," he warned.

"It is not as bad as you would think," D'Yana said. "The cliffs shelter it from the worst of the wind and rain. It is slow going but passable." Just as she had finished speaking, the entire building shook from the powerful thunder of a nearby lightning strike.

"It is not the wind or rain that concerns me," Connell said once the echoing rumble had died down. He turned to Casius. "Get your things together we leave within the hour."

CHAPTER THIRTEEN

Casius flinched as another bolt of lightning lit up the darkness. He held tightly to his horse's reins as the mount tossed its head in fear. He stood within the meager shelter offered by the stable's overhanging roof. It kept the worst of the slashing rain at bay, but he was already soaked to the core. He doubted if anything in his saddlebags was dry.

Connell was nearby, tightening the straps on his saddle. The black warhorse rolled its eyes angrily with each peal of thunder.

Casius took another step away from the brute; he had already been bitten once by it. For some reason it blamed him for the raging tempest. The dull ache in his shoulder was a painful reminder of the horse's strength.

D'Yana appeared at the gate leading a gray mare. She waved for them to follow. Between the echoing rumbles of thunder and the howling of the wind, any spoken words would soon be lost in the tumult.

Connell led his mount out of the shelter, and into the storm. Casius followed, making sure he stayed far enough back so that Connell's mount could not reach him. A kick from those powerful hooves could easily kill a man.

Through the rain swept streets the trio traveled, and to the guard's amazement they passed out the open gates. The walls of the town vanished quickly, swallowed by the whirling sheets of water.

D'Yana led them down a narrow trail that veered westward. The wind blew at their backs, plastering rain soaked cloaks to their bodies.

Ankle deep mud pulled at their boots, slowing their progress. Every step became more difficult as the muck clung stubbornly to their feet.

Casius pulled his cloak tighter. It was a futile gesture, doing little to ward off the chill from frigid water that assailed them. Stinging droplets tore at his face, forcing him to shield his eyes with his left hand. A few times he lost sight of Connell and after a tense moment, the wind would lessen and the hulking dark form of the warhorse would appear out of the gloom.

The path they followed led over the edge of a cliff. Carved from the stone it descended, switching back and forth along the rock face. In some places water poured from above, cutting across the trail in powerful torrents that at times were knee deep and dangerous to cross.

Casius kept close to the wall, praying that the wind would not blow him off the edge. Several times he had slipped on the damp stone, only his firm grip upon the reins had kept him on his feet. The world beyond the trail had disappeared, becoming a dark chasm etched with fiery fingers of distant lightning.

D'Yana had spoken truly for the wind had grown weaker. It was disorganized and blustery no longer the fierce blow that battered the town far above them.

After what seemed to be an eternity to Casius, dark shapes appeared in the void below them. Becoming the wind tortured canopies of immense trees. Leaves torn from the swaying branches swirled around them, sticking to their wet clothing and faces.

Branches cracked and trunks groaned in the wind. Down into the treetops the trail passed growing broader and less steep.

The wind died down dramatically, its force unable to penetrate the verdant ceiling overhead. The gloom about them lessened. It seemed that the entire forest was aglow with a faint silvery light that shone from the massive boles of the trees.

Casius stared in awe. The tree trunks spread far off in the distance, resembling the towering rows of columns in a temple constructed by a madman. They grew arrow straight out of a thick carpet of ferns, bare of limb for well over two hundred feet. Their tops lost to sight, vanishing in the canopy far above.

The rain still fell, absorbed by the trees until it became little more than a gentle drizzle. The air was cool, filled with the rich smells of wet earth and decaying leaves.

The rumble of thunder faded until it only faintly reached their ears. D'Yana smiled, her voice cutting through the silence.

"Stay with me," she advised. "It is easy to become lost in this wood." She mounted her horse and led them through the towering trunks, following a trail that only she could see.

Connell rode with his back rigidly straight. His senses straining, his hand wrapped about his sword's hilt.

At first Casius could not understand his friend's anxiety. Then the feeling of suppressed hatred and malice overcame the wonder of what he was seeing. The trees became threatening. To his eyes, they appeared the same. Unchanged since he first saw them, but in his heart he could feel their anger.

The forest floor sloped downward, away from the mountains. They followed the lay of the land, walking their mounts along the bank of a swift flowing rill swollen from the heavy rainfall.

The trees grew taller the further west they ventured. Becoming towering monoliths of wood whose canopies hung shrouded in mist.

Dead branches reached down from above, festooned with long pennants of damp hanging moss that brushed their shoulders as they rode past.

"I see no signs of felled trees?" He asked Connell compelled to speak softly by the brooding malice in the air. "With such a vast forest nearby you would think that the people of Two Falls would have need of lumber."

"They never cut these trees, and few of them would venture as far as we have. To enter this land with axe or fire is to court disaster," Connell replied knowingly. "There is more to this place than meets the eye."

"You've traveled through here and remained unscathed."

"I was more foolhardy back then and in a dire circumstance which offered few if any choices." Connell spared him a look. "As to being unscathed," he said with a small shrug. "I don't think so, this wood has left its mark upon my soul."

"And yet here we are?"

Connell grinned, "I am still foolhardy I suppose. Besides we have need of coin and this is well away from the Senatum's reach."

Ahead of them, out of the gloom loomed a tangled wall of twisted roots. The roots of many of the giants were knotted together forming a barrier twenty feet high in places. Some of the larger roots measured seven feet in diameter. Wrapping about its neighbors in a tight embrace that could never be broken.

Suddenly Casius understood Connell's trepidation. This barrier was too uniform to have been a mere coincidence. This was the work of a thinking mind; placed here to keep even the most determined explorers away. The knotted wall filled him with dread, and he had no desire to see what lay on the other side.

"Well that tears it," Casius muttered. "How will we get the horses over that?"

D'Yana shook her head, confused by what she saw before them. "We have followed the markers I left but the opening through which I passed is no longer here."

"Such is the way of this Forest," Connell said. "It is forever changing, with paths appearing and disappearing on their own accord. It is almost as if the trees themselves move about."

Casius laughed at the suggestion. The giants resembled oaks but their leaves were tinged with silver and the bark upon their mighty trunks was pale and smooth. He did not know what they were called, but they were trees, with deep roots, immobile sentinels of the forest.

Connell ignored Casius's snort. "We could go north a short ways, perhaps we will find an entry there."

D'Yana looked to the south and frowned. The trees seemed huddled, standing closer together than where they now stood.

"South holds no promise, we will go north and see if it is any better." From her saddlebag she produced a handful of small white stones. They gleamed in the dim light as if they had been polished. She placed two on one of the roots forming the wall. "Only a short way mind you," she warned Connell. "I have no desire of becoming lost in this place."

They headed north, and had gone only a small distance. When the sounds of groaning wood and rustling leaves stopped them. They spun about in time to see a narrow pathway opening in the tangled wall.

The large twisted roots slowly unwound, drawing back into the earth with a low sucking sound.

"As I said the trees move," Connell reminded them. "Do we dare the passage?"

D'Yana chewed her lower lip considering their next move. "I don't believe we have any choice." She looked to Connell for conformation. "If we turn back, will another such wall stand in our way?"

Connell shrugged, "I do not know," he answered.

"Then let us go forward," D'Yana guided her horse to the opening. "Our business lies ahead."

"Have you both lost your minds?" Casius asked, exasperated by the bravado of his companions. "Did you not see the same thing as I? Why should we go deeper into the embrace of this evil place?"

"Because," Connell answered him with a nod back to the east, "We have no choice."

Casius turned in his saddle and his heart sank, behind them a writhing wall of roots was erupting up from the damp loam. There would be no turning back; the Westerling Trail was lost to them now.

"Damn," Casius muttered looking to Connell he could see his own concerns mirrored in the warrior's eyes.

D'Yana led them through the narrow passage, their legs brushing against the quivering tips of the roots as they passed.

Casius flinched at their touch, he imagined that at any moment they would leap forth like a striking snake and crush him in their cold embrace.

Beyond the dense barrier the forest opened up. The massive trees spread their boughs over a thick carpet of lush ferns.

Scattered among the undergrowth lay the trunks of fallen trees, giants that had succumbed to old age and disease. Their bone white boles draped with thick carpets of moss, festooned with vibrant yellow flowers.

Thin vines climbed the standing trees; from these long bouquets of white and gold flowers shed loose petals into the air.

The heaviness of the air lightened, and the sense of malice faded. A small touch of it remained however, making them feel as if their intrusion was being tolerated.

The rain had finally ceased and a gentle breeze carried the falling petals and their vivid perfume towards them.

"Reminds me of a garden." Casius said opening his drenched cloak, relieved that the rain had finally ended. "From your description I expected a far more gloomier place."

"Looks can be deceiving Casius," Connell answered.

D'Yana pointed to several brightly shining stones placed upon a mossy trunk nearby. "We're back on my trail." she said with some relief.

"As long as no one has moved your markers." Connell said jokingly.

"You have become quite the pessimist over the years, haven't you?"

"Having a price on your head tends to make a man a prudent."

"Or is it the guilt that you carry from Dal'Entor?" D'Yana asked. "You cannot continue to blame yourself. Haven't you paid a high enough price?"

"What happened at Dal'Entor was no ones fault." Connell answered coldly. D'Yana had opened an old wound and he was loath to discuss it.

"Who would have thought that the King would have thrown his full strength against such a small rebellion? He risked losing his entire kingdom. Had any of the other lands decided to rise up and join us." Connell paused the battle coming fresh to mind. The faces of friends lost in the bloody conflict passed before his mind's eye.

"Yet you continue to live your life fighting the Senatum?" She asked.

"I do what I can," Connell agreed. "Not from a sense of guilt. My fallen comrades wanted more for this land, and I have tried to better it in their memory."

D'Yana smiled, "Perhaps you have not changed much." She turned her horse and set off west once more with the others following close behind.

"You know what's odd? I hear no bird calls, nor do I see any living thing other than us," Casius said bringing his horse along side Connell's. The gelding shied slightly, nervous to be so close to the powerful Warhorse.

"They're here Casius, our presence keeps their voices still. In a few hours time under the cover of darkness they will let themselves be known."

Casius looked at the eerie silver lit gloom. "Then the light from these trees will fade?" he asked not looking forward to spending a night in the wood.

"Yes," Connell answered him. "This light will end with the setting of the sun."

Casius could see the haunted look in his friend's eyes. "Just what happened to you in here?"

"We were routed by the King's forces. Those who escaped the slaughter reached the Forest edge. Not daring to enter too far into its shadowy depths they clung to its border using the gloom of the wood to escape to the west.

"The Lakarrans were cowed by the wood's reputation. Out of fear they did not pursue us, and many of my comrades lived to see another day.

"A small number of us, five altogether, became lost. Separated from the others. We followed narrow trails that appeared before us. Those pathways were often an illusion, always shifting and changing. Herded by the trees, we had become hopelessly lost deep within the wood by nightfall.

"You have felt the malice of the trees when we first entered," Connell reminded him. "That was a mere taste of the anger and hatred that assaulted us. During that first night two of our number disappeared. We could hear their distant calls, and no matter how hard we tried. We could never reach them. Sound does strange things in here. One minute they are to the north, the next to the south. After many hours their calls simply faded away and we heard them no more.

"The nights were the worst, long dark hours filled with such sounds as to freeze your very blood. Feral things prowled in the shadows. Silent stalkers, with burning eyes that watched our every move."

"You did manage to find your way out though."

"It was the wood itself that allowed us to do so. I think it tired of the game it was playing, and drove us from its depths."

"But you survived," Casius reminded him. "Were you the only one?"

"Three of us came out," Connell replied. "I alone remained whole of mind. The others went mad from fear during the journey." Connell said no more, sadden by the memories the tale had brought to mind.

Casius looked on the wood with new respect. What could dwell in this place that could ruin a man's mind? He wondered.

Connell could tell that his tale had unnerved Casius. "If we keep our heads, and use caution we will be safe enough. We are far from this Forest's heart, and that is where the true dangers lie." He said reassuringly. "D'Yana does not often play guide, whomever this employer of hers is, he has attracted my interest."

D'Yana led them deeper into the tranquil corridors of the forest. Where they forded a slow flowing rill of cold spring water.

On the opposite bank she reined her horse in suddenly as a man stepped out of the shadows before them.

He was of small stature, barely five feet in height. His hair was dark as midnight. He wore it long, and kept it in a neat single braid that hung down his back.

His clothing was strange as well, a sleeveless tunic of dark gray that barely reached his knees in length. With a sash of dark green cloth tied about his narrow waist. Tucked through its folds on his left side were two rods of dull black iron, their ends wrapped in worn leather bindings.

He moved silently, almost ghost like. His sandaled feet scarcely disturbing the leafy litter of the forest floor. His almond shaped eyes narrowed somewhat as he scrutinized Connell and Casius. With a short nod he greeted D'Yana.

"Connell, and Casius," she said introducing them. "This is Suni of the Anghor Shok, my employer's protector."

Suni nodded to each in turn his narrow face devoid of any emotion. "You are expected," he said in a soft voice. Before any of them could respond he turned his back to them and disappeared once more into the shadows.

"Talkative isn't he?" Connell quipped.

D'Yana nodded her head in agreement. "That is the most I have heard him say at one time." She motioned for them to dismount, and led them through a narrow gap between the soaring trees.

Casius searched his memory, somewhere he had heard of the Anghor Shok. Then it came to him, "Of course!" he said aloud recalling the old poem he had read long ago.

"Of course?" Connell prodded him.

"Anghor lies far to the west beyond the great waste, a land of warrior priest. They are said to dwell in palaces of crystal and gold, their realm hidden within mountains of jade."

Connell looked skeptical, "For a man from such a wealthy land he hides his riches well."

Casius laughed, "I did not write the poem Connell, I merely read it."

"Don't believe everything you read Casius," Connell said with a smile. "Bards have a well earned reputation for often embellishing the truth."

D'Yana laughed, "Heed his advice Casius, if anyone among us understands reputations. It would be your roguish companion, the Eagle of Kesh indeed."

"Some of its true," Connell said defensively. "In part anyways."

Casius smiled at their banter.

They entered a small clearing, created when one of the giants had fallen. Through the ragged opening in the canopy high above them, they could see dark clouds scudding across a steel gray sky.

Two hobbled horses nosed through the undergrowth for tender shoots within the shelter of the fallen giant's trunk.

Suni stood talking to a tall dark haired man, beneath the branches of a young sapling scarcely ten feet in height. He faced them as they entered the clearing, his eyes shined brightly in the gloom.

"Welcome," he said in a soothing voice. "I take it you have at last found our elusive quarry D'Yana?"

D'Yana inclined her head slightly in greeting, "Marcos this is Connell," She said motioning to him with her right hand. "He insisted that his companion Casius come along."

Marcos shrugged as if it was of no importance. "I'll be with you in a moment," He said turning his attention back to the young tree. He sang a soft wordless song for a few moments, while watching the foliage of the sapling sway in the breeze.

"It is such a sad time," he said to his audience. "The trees are silent now, the old no longer teach the young how to speak. Once long ago their songs filled this wood with wisdom" Marcos laid his hand softly on the sapling's bole. "A strange darkness has fallen over this wood. A wound to its very heart has taken away much of its strength."

Casius shook his head, had this man lost his mind? Trees singing indeed!

"This forest has always been dark," Connell countered.

Marcos lowered his hand and looked upon Connell. A strange sadness seemed to fill his gaze. "It has not always been so," he said. "This is an old wood, it has stood proudly for ages beyond reckoning. Back in its youth it was many times its present size, sheltering much of this land beneath its verdant boughs.

"Men once lived here, wise and powerful. They dwelt in harmony with the wood. Then an ancient evil grew in power and corrupted their hearts. No longer were they content to live in fellowship. They grew ambitious and sought dominion over the forest.

"With axe and fire they strove to conquer, until the forest could no longer see any good left in the heart's of man. In those dark days its spirit awakened and in its wrath destroyed them. Casting down the lofty towers and homes of those prideful people. The few remaining survivors fled to the mountains. Their golden age destroyed by their arrogance and greed.

"You are tolerated now for my sake, do nothing to give the forest cause to destroy you," Marcos warned. "I can barely make myself heard through its pain, and if truly angered I fear I could do nothing to protect you."

Connell looked at him as if he were mad, "You speak with trees?"

"It is a gift that at one time was shared by men," Marcos answered ignoring the look Connell gave him. "Before the breaking, the blood of man was strong in the ways of this world." He paused in thought, "Perhaps there are a few yet who know the secret. The blood of old is yet prevailing in the men of Ril'Gambor." Marcos stopped speaking for a moment his eyes grew distant. "You've been here before Connell," he announced. "This wood knows you."

Casius gasped in amazement. "He can speak with the trees."

"Easy Casius," Connell said, shaking his head at his friend's gullibility. "Many men know of my passage."

Marcos smiled, "Your caution and skepticism is worthy of a man twice your years."

"Gray hair and a crooked back does not a wise man make." Connell said quoting a favorite saying of his father. "Many a fool has been led to disaster following the words of a mad man."

Marcos laughed and the color of his eyes began to shift from violet to deep blue. "Am I a senile dotard then?" he asked.

Connell took a step back; the man's eyes surprised him. He had only heard of their like once. Told to him by his grandsire long ago.

"The colors of the sky danced across their wizened orbs, and the fires of knowledge burned upon their brows." His grandfather had read from an inscription found on a slab of stone near his home in Kesh. It was part of the ruins of an ancient monument dedicated to the fabled Tal'shear.

"You think I'm quite mad don't you?" Marcos asked Connell.

"Eccentric perhaps," Connell answered looking away from his disturbing eyes. "I promised D'Yana that I would hear you out," Connell said with a slight shrug. "I make no promises beyond that."

Marcos slowly nodded his head, understanding this man's reluctance. "Very well, I have need of your sword arm, Connell. For four frustrating long years we have searched for you, time which I did not have too spare."

Connell looked to D'Yana, "Four years?"

"I have been in Marcos's employ for two of them." D'Yana answered somewhat defensively. " As I have said, you are not an easy man to find."

"Your prowess with the blade is said to be unsurpassed."

"There are plenty of men who are known for their skill." Connell countered. "More than a few of them are willing to sell their arm and are easier to find."

"They are men of questionable character, Connell. I need a man of integrity as well."

"What is it you wish me to do?" Connell asked. "I am no assassin, and I will not fight a duel in your stead to protect your honor."

Marcos laughed, "Nothing so mundane. I seek a talisman, an object lost in antiquity. I need your services to help me in its recovery."

"D'Yana is a fair enough guide, she could lead you as well as I."

"D'Yana has never ventured beyond Lakarra." Marcos pointed at Connell. "You have traveled far, and know the lands of the north.

"It must be you Connell. For what I seek only a skilled swordsman of honorable character can lay claim to it."

"Are you so certain of my character?"

"You have a reputation for standing against tyranny and defending those who cannot defend themselves," Marcos replied looking at Casius. "Did you not lead the ill fated rebellion?"

"Aye," Connell nodded. "I swore an oath that never again would I allow my name to become a call to arms. Too many good men," Connell paused. "Men far better than myself died that day."

"Many more good men are about to die Connell. Should I fail to recover what was lost so long ago," Marcos said ominously. "A darkness is gathering in the west, an ancient evil that stands poised to strike into the very heart of the eastern lands. For three millennia it has worked its foul craft in the shadows. Growing stronger, waiting until it has become powerful enough to leave the darkness that has sheltered it for so long.

"No longer is it content to lurk in the shadows, gnawing on its own ambitions. It has grown powerful. With its might it will throw down all that remains of the old world, and spread its malignant shadow over all the lands." Marcos looked into Connell's eyes, his color shifting gaze holding the warrior's without flinching. "You have felt its touch, even here in Lakarra it has gained much influence. Through its dark agents it prepares the way for its final conquest."

Connell could not look away, the man's eyes bored through him seeking to touch his very soul. He could not argue the point. He too had noticed the changes that were taking place. Men had become fouler, quick to anger and even quicker to kill. It seemed that good honest folk were becoming harder to find.

"You seek sanctuary in the north," Marcos continued looking briefly at Casius, thus releasing his hold on Connell. "You will find only death. The price put upon your heads is far greater than you can imagine. Brothers would turn against one another for a chance at such wealth."

Connell's brow furrowed in consternation, he knew Marcos spoke truly. If the bounty on them was high enough, there would be no safe haven for them.

"It appears that we may have little choice Casius," Connell said after a moments thought. "We may have to leave Lakarra altogether."

Casius nodded, he had grown weary of the life that Connell led, and did not relish the thought of being on the run for the rest of his days.

"I tire of playing the outlaw." As Connell spoke he noticed the look of satisfaction cross Marcos's face. "This does not mean that I will blindly follow you on your quest," he added.

Marcos held up his hand in a placating gesture. "Of course, will you at least join us on the first leg of our journey?"

Connell turned to Casius. "This choice I will not make for you. Do we go, or take our own road wherever it may lead us?"

"I would go with Marcos," Casius said without hesitation. "There is safety in numbers. Moreover the Senatum are searching for two, not five travelers."

"It looks as if we are to accompany you at least part of the way," Connell informed Marcos.

"That will have to do for now," Marcos said, looking somewhat disappointed. He had hoped for more of a commitment from them.

Suni drew his staves from his belt in a rapid motion that caught everyone's attention. "We are not alone," he said flatly his dark eyes fixed to the south. "They have been followed."

Connell drew his long sword and motioned for Casius to do the same. "If we have been trailed, then someone has gone through great hardship to do so."

Marcos raised his hand motioning everyone to be silent. From the shadows they could hear a faint rustling within the undergrowth.

A dark hunched form emerged from behind the roots of a nearby tree. It stopped, freezing in place knowing that it had been seen.

Casius's heart was hammering in his chest; he recognized the way the thing moved. The twin burning lights of its eyes confirmed his suspicions. It was the companion of the creature he had slain outside of Haven.

Before anyone could react the beast leapt out of the shadows with amazing speed. It ran upright its large sickle shaped claws held out at its sides. Charging straight for Casius it roared in anger and defiance. Smoke streamed from its shoulders as the dim light of the obscured sun struck its knobby hide.

Marcos waved his right hand, and the ring upon his finger burned with an intense argent light.

Small Vines thrust up from the moist earth wrapping about the loping creatures legs. It staggered and with a sweep of its claws it severed the impeding vines. Before it could resume its charge more vines wrapped about it. Lightning swift they burst from the soil, growing thicker as rose. They completely enshrouded the beast, and pulled it violently to the ground. The mound of knotted stems writhed as the creature trapped within them fought violently to be free.

Suni stepped forward his staves held protectively before him.

"Stop," Marcos ordered, his tone halting Suni's advance. "It is a Naz'Haruk, one of Sur'kar's most loathsome and dangerous creations."

Casius let his sword tip touch the ground. The weapon all but forgotten in his shock at having seen what Marcos had just done. "Are you a Warlock?" he asked carefully, if he was one he did not wish to draw his ire.

Marcos kept his eyes on the writhing bundle, "No Casius I am not," he answered.

Connell took a step away from Marcos, keeping his sword in hand. "An enchanter then?" Connell pressed.

Marcos shook his head, "I am not known by the titles of man."

The bundle thrashed violently, the trapped creature within released a howl that echoed in the wood.

"Kill it!" Connell demanded. He did not know if it traveled alone or with others. But with the noise it was making if it had companions they would be sure to find them.

"I will not become that which I strive against." He lowered his hand the argent gleam fading away as roots from the trees roiled up out of the ground. They ensnared the bundle and drug it down into the dark earth. "Let the forest have its due, the kin of this creature have done much damage here and the trees crave revenge."

"Then how did it come so far?" D'Yana asked once she had recovered from her shock.

"The forest is gravely wounded, its spirit is dying," Marcos answered. He swung up into the saddle of his mount. "I have awakened only a small part of the wood. It is beyond my power to revive the entire forest."

Suni cocked his head to one side, "I hear the calls of hunters," He said softly, his eyes closed as he strained to hear. "Three...no four brass horns."

Marcos nodded, "As I feared, the calls of the Naz'Haruk have drawn the attention of Sur'kar's minions." He motioned for the others to mount up. "We must make all haste away from this place."

"Why run?" Casius asked. "You can use your power to stop them."

"The Phay'ge is not to be used lightly. What I have already done has placed us in grave danger. There are stronger and deadlier enemies, drawn to such power as a moth is to a flame."

Casius looked to Connell, and then they too heard the thin high note of a horn in the distance. Needing no further urging they mounted their steeds, and followed Marcos as he led them racing off to the northwest.

They wove through the trees for several hours until the sounds of the hunters could no longer be heard. The sun had set, and the gloom of the forest darkened, until the world had become nothing more than a land of deep grays and black.

Taking shelter within a hollow between two of the towering giants. They set up a cold camp. It was uncomfortable and cramped but it was as safe a place as any to wait the dawn.

As the darkness became nearly complete Suni left their shelter and disappeared into the night.

Connell searched the darkness with his eyes but he could see no sign of him. He admired the man's skill; he was a master of stealth. He nodded to Marcos as the man came to stand next to him.

"My words are true." Marcos said. He knew this man had many questions, and perhaps now was the time for a few answers. "There is an ancient evil stirring Connell, the doom of man draws nigh. The object I seek is our only hope. A weapon forged long ago, with the strength to thwart Sur'kar's might.

"I seek Aethir, the sword forged by Ma'Rail, the greatest of the Tal'shear smiths to walk this earth. It was lost three thousand years ago when the world was reeling from the breaking.

"Before he died, Thoron'Gil carried it to a distant land and it rests there. In his tomb hidden from the eyes of the world."

"And you know where this tomb is?" Connell asked. This man really did believe in those old legends and myths. Connell was trying to decide if he posed a danger, he was either a Warlock or an Enchanter of some power.

Enchanters by their very nature are recluses and seldom interfere with the affairs of men. Warlocks on the other hand were ruthless men who care for nothing, but their own ambitions. The expansion of their power and knowledge is the sole driving force behind their evil.

Connell doubted that Marcos was a Warlock. Suni did not have the look of a bonded man, and he had shown no ill effects from Marcos's earlier use of power. Marcos may be an Enchanter but one who has lost some measure of his sanity, and that alone may make him very dangerous indeed.

"I was there when the blade was cast, Connell. A small part of me lies within it. I know roughly where it is hidden and as I draw closer, its whereabouts will become clearer to me."

"I am having a hard time taking you seriously," Connell said softly, looking directly into the man's disturbing eyes. "There are many things about you that defy explanation. But do you really expect me to believe that you are three thousand years old?"

Marcos's eyes flashed brightly in the darkness. Whether it was out of anger or amusement Connell could not tell.

"You are a straight to the point man," Marcos said with a smile. "Actually I am far older than that Connell. I was born upon the great ship Tel'Ganduil as she sailed the Darkling Sea that lies beyond this world. I am the last of the Tal'shear Warders. I chose to remain behind after my people had returned to the great void between the stars. To guard against the return of Sur'kar."

Connell shook his head in amazement at this man's audacity. "You speak of legends, created by primitive people to explain that which they could not understand."

Marcos let out a long sigh of exasperation. "Has the race of man fallen so far that he has forgotten the greatness of his forefathers?"

"Perhaps," Connell answered. "If you are who you claim to be, can you not simply destroy this Sur'kar?"

Marcos looked over his shoulder he could see that Casius and D'yana had both fallen asleep. "Even at the height of my power I was no match for him. He was beyond the combined strength of the eight Warders who opposed him.

"It was a desperate act born in despair by one of my brethren that defeated him. So'san's deed nearly destroyed this world, it took all the strength at our command to save what we could." Marcos stopped speaking for a few moments, as dreaded memories replayed themselves through his mind.

"I have grown weaker over the centuries Connell." He continued after gathering his thoughts. "My power fades as my spirit grows weary. Though my people are long lived, we do eventually tire of this life and pass beyond the veil into the next world."

"What of the blade?" Connell asked. "Was it not forged for his destruction?"

"It was, but I am Tal'shear and my kind cannot suffer the touch of iron." Marcos laid his hand upon the blade at his hip. "My own weapon is forged of brass. With enchantments placed upon it, so that it is sharper and stronger than any iron forged by man."

"Ma'Rail forged four great blades. Two of bronze for the Tal'shear, Lo'Wyren and Bel'Lendil they were named. Dawn singer and North wind, as men knew them. Carried into battle by Na'Boal and Ce'Loth, the greatest warriors ever born of my people."

"On that day he undertook his greatest work, the forging of Aethir and its twin Alagond from the iron of a fallen star. Great enchantments had been placed upon Black Thorn and Storm Biter. These were to be wielded by the Captains of the armies of men, Thoron'Gil and Caen.

"The forging of those two blades were the last creations of Ma'Rail, for working with the cursed metal cost him his life.

"Aethir was never used, So'san's devastating blow fell before Thoron'Gil could face Sur'kar. In the aftermath of the destruction all of the blades were lost. Thoron'Gil had wandered far into the west, and secluded in some dark place he passed from this earth. His strength was great, but the fires of destruction wreaked such havoc upon his body he could not hope to recover."

"Now you wish me to step in and recover this weapon? A blade that was never forged to face an ancient enemy that was never born." Connell asked.

Marcos frowned; he had failed to convince him. "Connell, there is little time left to us. For as we speak his armies gather, and the hammer will fall ere we are prepared for it. The salvation of this world rests upon another's shoulders. If I alone could do this task I would. But I need you Connell, you have to take up Aethir and fulfill its destiny."

Connell shook his head, "This is nothing more than a fool's errand."

Marcos eyes flashed in the dark. "Then forgive me," he said.

The world before Connell disappeared in a flash of brilliant light. A hot wind blew against his face making his eyes water profusely. He blinked away the tears, and found that he was standing in a circle of men. They surrounded a white-hot glowing blade upon an anvil of burnished bronze.

As his vision cleared he noticed that these were not men that he stood among. They were tall powerful beings with fair skin and pale eyes, which shone with great intellect. Each one held aloft his right hand, a glowing orb of brilliant white light enveloping their fists.

He could feel the power coursing through him, the very air crackled with energy. Through eyes that were not his own he watched in fascination, as tendrils of ethereal fire snaked through the air to merge with the blazing metal of the sword.

The room blurred and with a gut wrenching twist, he was standing on a low hill overlooking a vast plain. A Mountain of fire blackened stone rose high above the lowlands, several miles away. Crowned in roiling flames it belched black soot and ash high into the dark sky, while rivers of molten stone flowed down its craggy sides.

Writhing branches of lightning that strived to reach the ground broke from the gloom above. Each flaming filament was accompanied by a deafening peal of thunder that shook the very earth with its ferocity.

Connell wanted to gag. The air reeked of sulfur and the pungent aroma of burnt flesh. Through the rumbling could be heard the sounds of pitched battle, the clamor of swords, the screams of the dying, and the harsh brazen blasts of trumpets.

Spread out on the plain below him, two massive armies merged, locked in combat. Men in brightly gleaming armor faced a foe many times their number. Huge ice and Trolls wielding enormous cudgels led the charge. Behind the ponderous Trolls came the Morne. Rank upon rank of dark robed fiends. They licked their scaly maws, anticipating the taste of man flesh.

The two captains of the dark horde were plainly visible, dressed in heavy plate armor the color of midnight. They rode among the foremost ranks. Upon reptilian steeds with horned heads that spewed forth fire.

The power of these beings was evident, even the heroic men could not stand before them. Connell knew them; he had heard the legends of Sur'kar's servants. The Balhain, cursed to live in the darkness. They were strong beings, second only to the Dark One himself in power.

Connell's heart sank; he could see that the armies of men and Tal'shear could not hope to stand before this foe. They were losing men by the thousands. Soon the ranks would break and they would be routed.

The gloom brightened, and with a tremendous roar. A great flaming orb tore through the clouds. It struck the mountain and the sky brightened. Connell was forced to shut his eyes against the flash.

The shock of the impact blasted the men across the field. The very air burned and the earth bucked violently. The Tal'shear Warders worked their magic, and sought to redirect the power of the cataclysm. The ground heaved and a terrible rending sound echoed across the plain. It was as if the earth itself screamed in torment. Heavy ash and soot darkened the sky until it was darker than the darkest night.

The land about the flaming mountain was blasted up into the air. A ring of smoldering mountains thrust their heads up from the tortured soil ringing the deep depression. In its midst sat the ruined remnants of the volcano. Its great Calderas surrounded by a low wall of stone that once had been the grand peaks foundations.

Within the churning magma of the Calderas stood a low islet of black stone. Perched precariously upon it, the ruined walls of what once had been a massive keep glowed with heat.

Nausea nearly overwhelmed him as he was pulled from the hilltop. When his sense of balance had returned, he found that he was now standing on the shore of a large frozen lake.

The sky above was dark and brooding, only a faint glow showed that the sun was actually quite high in the sky. Connell could not tell if it was late morning or early evening.

Thick snow covered everything, not the blanket of virgin white that one finds in winter. It was gray, marred with the soot that darkened the heavens above.

Nothing moved on the surface of the snow. The only sound was that of the chill wind whispering, as it passed through the barren branches of lifeless trees that bordered the shore.

Connell knew he was looking at the results of the breaking. The decades long winter that had nearly destroyed the world. How people had managed to survive was beyond him. It was a time of hardship, a dark age that had stripped away the great nations. Man had forgotten much of his history and was forced to rebuild the world from the few scraps of knowledge that remained.

He knew he was seeing the past. These were memories shared by Marcos. He was Tal'shear and he had spoken truly. Tales that Connell had believed to be nothing more than epic yarns, spun by storytellers over the ages, was in fact rooted in truth.

His surroundings shifted once more, this time his sense of vertigo was diminished. He was becoming accustomed to the sensation.

It was night, and he was standing in grove of poplar trees. A light wind carried the rich smells of spring to him. It was a clear evening with a thin sliver of a moon hanging high overhead. Its light competed with the countless stars for brightness.

He watched in fascination as a huge ship of bronze and gold rose noiselessly into the air over the treetops. Iridescent sails unfurled and filled with light. The vessel shone as bright as the sun. The proud ship slowly accelerated and was joined by two more as it rose.

Higher and higher into the sky they climbed, gathering speed until they became mere specks of light disappearing into the vast field of stars lining the heavens above.

Connell nearly wept with the sense of loss he felt. He was struck with a terrible sense of loneliness as the ships faded from sight. Tears of grief blurred his vision. He had no regrets however, he was confident in the decision he had made.

The world spun violently once more. Connell blinked his eyes and as his vision cleared he could see that he was once more standing in the dark Nallen Forest.

He felt violated and his anger grew as he realized what Marcos had done. He clenched his jaw several times before speaking, swallowing his ire. "You entered my mind," he said accusingly.

Marcos shook his head, "No Connell, I would never do something so invasive without your leave. I merely projected some of my memories. Forgive me for my rashness. I needed to convince you, and my time grows short."

Connell rubbed his temples; a dull ache had begun to throb behind his eyes. "That was risky Marcos, another man may have attacked you for such a deed."

Marcos smiled, "I was never in any danger."

Connell was about to respond when Suni stepped out of the shadows. The warrior had been within arms reach the entire time. He nodded once in greeting and walked off into the darkness.

"A handy man to have around," Connell stated. He was both surprised, and somewhat dismayed that Suni had managed to stand so close to him without being detected.

"The Anghor Shok should never be dismissed as ordinary men," Marcos stated. "They are formidable opponents with abilities that are beyond most mortals."

"As I see," Connell grunted in agreement. He would have to be more wary of the odd man. He was evidently a highly skilled fighter.

"I have shown you but a small part of what I've seen," Marcos said changing the subject. "You now know I have spoken truly, will you aid us?"

"Before I decide, I would know why you have remained behind. I shared the pain and sorrow that tortured your soul when those vessels left." Connell held the Tal'shear's gaze. "Your decision stranded you here, forever alone. Exiled on an alien world."

"Alone?" He repeated shrugging, his shoulders slightly. "I do not believe so, others of my kind cherished this world as well. Perhaps they live in the wilder places, following their own callings. Shunning humanity in the pursuit of their destinies. Sometimes when the night is still, I can touch the echoes of their thoughts upon the ether."

"Yet you do not seek them out?"

"I am the last Warder, sworn to defend this green earth and its people," He said proudly, his eyes flashing with power. "You know the sense of duty I feel. You have already taken your first steps down the same road as I did long ago."

"Perhaps," Connell answered. "But I have never given it much thought."

"Live as long as I, and you will find the time to ponder many of life's enigmas."

Connell smiled at Marcos's remark. "The number of my days will never equal yours."

"True," Marcos responded. "But they are your days, given freely by the creator. Revel in them waste not a single hour. For all life is fleeting, a mere heartbeat in the pulse of eternity."

Connell turned and looked down at his sleeping companions. As he looked on D'Yana's peaceful face he felt the stirrings of emotion in his heart. The old flame of what they had once shared was rekindled. It was long ago but his heart had never forgotten.

"The Naz'Haruk that attacked us was not the first you had seen." Marcos stated. "I could tell by the way you and Casius reacted. Only D'Yana was surprised by its appearance."

Connell turned and faced Marcos once more. "We slew one two weeks ago on the plains."

"The Naz'Haruk do not die easily," Marcos said in surprise. "It seems your skills are not exaggerated."

"It was Casius who dropped the fell beast not I."

Marcos looked at the sleeping young man with a new measure of respect. "Perhaps I have been rash in my judgment of him."

"He is stronger than he appears," Connell added. "I will consider all you have shown me, and will give you my answer in the morning."

"Consider carefully Connell, if two of the Naz'Haruk have tracked you. Then Sur'kar has already deemed you to be a threat to him, and he will not stop until you lie dead." Marcos paused allowing his words to sink in. "If I fail all that you love will be destroyed."

"Then I have no choice," Connell said regretfully. "I will aid you," Connell answered. He was trapped by his sense of honor and could not stand by and do nothing.

Marcos lowered his head in acceptance. He was grateful for the man's pledge of aid, but he wondered what would make him so hesitant to do so. This Connell was puzzling, he had proven himself many times over to be a man of honor and compassion, capable of taking great risks if needed. "Sleep now Connell, Suni and I shall keep watch until dawn."

Connell settled down against the trees bole, his sword lay across his lap. "Wake me at the first sign of trouble."

"I will," Marcos said reassuringly.

After Connell had fallen asleep Suni stalked out of the gloom. "Rock Trolls," he whispered to Marcos. "They are several miles west and moving away from us. They follow a pack of Fell hounds."

"Our pursuers?" Marcos asked, even though he already knew the answer.

Suni nodded, "I followed their spoor, they came from the direction of our earlier camp."

"Rock Trolls and Fell hounds," Marcos said distantly his thoughts elsewhere. "Did you see nothing else among their number?"

Suni looked puzzled, "I would have seen if anything else moved among them."

"There is something dark and powerful moving out there. It goes cautiously always staying just at the edge of my awareness."

"I will seek it out then," Suni said, turning to leave.

Marcos stopped him with a hand to his shoulder. "I will know if it should draw nearer. You are Anghor Shok but I fear this will be beyond your skills to cope with."

Suni lifted an eyebrow in what was an uncharacteristic show of emotion for him.

Marcos regretted his words; he had unintentionally offended his friend. "I cannot allow you to take an unnecessary risk Suni." He pointed to the west. "It is a long way off and poses us no real danger at this time. I would prefer to pass it by unnoticed, in secrecy lies our best defense."

Suni nodded in acceptance, "I live and die to serve." He said repeating a small part of an ancient oath he had taken long ago.

Marcos leaned against one of the trees roots. Through its bark he could feel its tremors of pain. A seeping foulness was spreading through the wood. Slowly it traveled tainting everything it touched.

It was within his abilities to relieve the tree's torment for a short time, but he dared not. For such a display of power would shine as a beacon in the dark, and the nameless evil would fall upon them.

"The Forest's heart pulls at me Suni, I cannot leave this place without finding the cause of its distress."

Suni said nothing. He accepted his charge's decision. He was Anghor Shok and would follow Marcos into the very fires of the underworld if need be.

CHAPTER FOURTEEN

Marcos awakened them as the first light of the rising sun touched the sky. The glow of the forest brightened, rekindled by the golden light above the leafy bowers.

Connell's headache had disappeared, and he felt all the better after having a full night's sleep. He told Casius and D'Yana about his encounter with Marcos, and the shared visions. He spoke softly, desiring a private conversation away from Marcos. He described the shared memories down to the finest details he could recall.

"Then you believe him?" Casius asked when Connell had finished.

"I felt the pain and anguish he carries within him," Connell answered. "I believe he has spoken truly."

"I knew him to be different," D'Yana said sparing a quick look over her shoulder. She could see Marcos was busy saddling his pale mare. "But I would have never dreamed this."

Marcos smiled at her comment and led his horse over to where they sat. "I must inform you that the ears of my people are especially keen. There is no call for whispering."

Connell laughed softly in surprise, and D'Yana's cheeks reddened in response.

"There is a large party of Rock Trolls hunting us. They are using Fell hounds as trackers." Marcos said passing on Suni's warning.

"Where are these Rock Trolls?" Connell asked standing upright his hand falling to his sword's hilt.

"A few miles northwest, and moving away," Marcos said reassuringly. "They are no threat to us at this time. However it would be prudent for us to move cautiously, and leave no trail behind."

"A wise precaution," Connell said approvingly. "There may be more in the wood that we do not know of."

Marcos nodded, "It is what we don't know of that worries me."

"Where do we go from here?" Casius asked. He did not wish to remain in an area where Trolls wandered the countryside. Although he had never seen one, he had heard enough tales to know that he did not want to meet one of the dim-witted giants. Slow thinking and quick to anger the Rock Trolls and their larger cousins Ice Trolls were creatures to be feared. They killed out of pleasure and would gladly eat any man that had the misfortune of crossing their path.

Two to three times the size of a man they are incredibly strong, with thick hides tough enough to turn aside an arrow. Unless it was shot from extremely close range.

At one time Rock Trolls could be found throughout the eastern lands. They preferred to dwell in damp caves and usually hunted only at night. Trolls would often raid homesteads during the darkest hours, and slay every living thing. Carrying off the bodies of their victims to their hidden lairs.

When such a raid occurred, the local men would ban together and track the Troll. Using Mastiffs they would set the dogs on the beast, enraging it to the point where it would come out of its hole. Men on horseback with lances would then charge the brute cutting him down if all went well. There were many tales of such outings going horribly wrong, and few if any of the men surviving the attack.

Years of such attacks however had the desired effect, and there were now far fewer Trolls. Those that still existed stayed hidden in the most inaccessible places, far from the likes of man.

"I have to find out what has happened to this forest," Marcos answered. "We will go to the Wood's heart, for there will my questions be answered."

"Will it be safe?" Casius asked recalling Connell's tale.

"There are no safe places left, Casius." Marcos answered swinging up into his saddle. "In days such as these, only the dead have nothing left to fear."

Suni rode up, his gelding tossing its head, anxious to be moving. "Come, it is a long way and we are wasting daylight." He waited for them to mount, and led the way north into a broad path between the trees. It was as if the forest had cleared the way ahead to hasten their progress.

For nine days they rode, the trail ahead never shifting. It was an arrow straight corridor, slicing through the heart of the verdant giants.

The land changed subtly, large boulders lay along their path. Gray monoliths entrapped by entangling roots. The way before them rose gradually, becoming steeper as the days progressed.

The higher they climbed, the larger the trees became. Towering giants with trunks so broad that fifty men holding hands could not encircle them. Among these behemoths they ventured, crossing many fast flowing rills of icy cold water. The gurgling call of the passing water added the only sounds to the eerily silent forest.

On the ninth day they came to a steep boulder strewn hill. The massive trees crowded its face, their roots weaving about the boulders and each other. To Casius it resembled a fishermen's net. Cast by some wading giant, ensnaring a small part of the forest.

Brilliant rays of sunlight streamed through the trunks upon the hills crown. The golden light was alive with clouds of small swarming insects.

The clear light was a welcome sight to Casius. As they picked their way up the slope, he could see small patches of sapphire blue sky showing through a break in the canopy.

At the top of the rise they emerged from the line of trees, and stared in awe at the view before them.

They stood on the rim of a large shallow valley. A perfectly circular lake lay within the vale; its tranquil water's reflecting the clear sky above.

A light fitful breeze out of the north sent ripples across its mirror like surface. Riding upon its currents, colorful birds wheeled in the sky. Their boisterous calls echoing in the valley, adding life to the wood.

Their approach disturbed the smaller birds, which flitted among the branches chirping incessantly.

"Glin'eress," Marcos announced breaking the silence. "The heart of Nallen Forest." He pointed to the east where a craggy pinnacle of stone rose several hundred feet into the air. The narrow top crowned by a giant tree whose leaves shined golden in the sunlight.

The base of the Tor straddled the shore, the water's of the lake caressing its rough walls. A waterfall fell from the heights issuing out from within the gnarled roots of the lone giant squatting upon its peak. The cataract plunged into the lake. Shrouding the hill's base with clouds of mist that drifted with the breeze along the shore.

Marcos pointed to the tree atop the Tor. "There lies our goal, the great tree Asua Tuell. Heartwood of this land and mother of the forest." He lowered his arm slowly; "A great wrong has been done here, a betrayal of all that is good. She is dying. I can feel her agony, it is almost to much to endure, I only hope that we are not too late."

"We are too exposed here," Suni said with a shake of his head. "We should await the cover of night fall before making our approach."

"Our enemies eyes are sharpest at night," Marcos said looking up at the early afternoon sky. "The task before us is safer done while the sun yet shines."

Marcos took the lead, staying within the tree line they clung to the forest's shadows making their way along the valley wall.

"What do you make of that?" Connell asked drawing everyone's attention. He was pointing through the trees to a spot on the shore near the pinnacles base. A huddled form lay there swathed in rags.

"A man?" Casius guessed. He could just make out what looked like twisted limbs.

"Not from the distance," D'Yana added squinting her eyes. "If it is a man, then he is a giant."

"Troll," Suni said. "Or what remains of one."

"We must be vigilant," Marcos cautioned. "Trolls seldom travel alone."

"And they rarely welcome surprise guests," Connell added, loosening his sword in its sheath. "If we are attacked, stay close together. Facing a Troll alone is a sure path to the after life." He pulled his bow from behind his saddle and slung the quiver of arrows across his back.

D'Yana drew her bow as well and knocked an arrow. Seeing the giant's carcass on the shore had reminded her of the dangers they faced.

It did not take them long to reach the spire's base. The roots of the stone outcrop stretched away from the shore to merge with the ridge that bordered the valley.

Casius looked up the nearly vertical side of the rock. It would be an onerous climb. The narrow ledges and deep clefts were passable, but they would have to proceed with caution.

They left their horses in a small clearing that Suni had found nearby. With the mounts secured they returned to the Tor Carrying only their weapons.

They encircled the rock base looking for the easiest way to make the ascent. The body of the Troll lay nearby and could easily be found by the fetid stench coming from it.

There was not much left of the brute. A thick boned skeleton eight feet or more in height. Clothed in rags and tattered bits of dried flesh.

Its rib cage was shattered, a stout branch wedged firmly in the wound.

"The Tree attempted to defend itself," Connell remarked after looking down on the body.

"It's so large," Casius remarked. "How does one kill such a thing?"

"With luck and a large number of men." Connell answered. "It is only a Rock Troll, Ice Trolls are twice this size and twice as hard to kill."

Casius stepped away from the reeking body and looked up at the peak high above them.

"What's wrong Casius?" D'Yana asked. "Scared of heights?"

Casius smiled, "Only falls."

"Climb with caution then, the rocks above are slick with moss." Marcos advised them.

Suni took the lead, he moved across the rock face as if born to climbing. He was a skilled climber and led them up the easiest paths possible.

Marcos ascended after him with D'Yana and Connell close behind. Casius swallowed his fear and after a moment's hesitation he followed his companions upward.

The climb was arduous and on two occasions they were forced to retreat down a short way before attempting another route upwards.

Casius's arms ached, and his fingers were stiff from gripping the slick rock.

Near the summit Suni had found a narrow ledge and they rested. They were all breathing hard and sweating profusely in the cold air. All that is except for Suni, the climb seemed to have no effect on him at all.

Casius sat with his back against the stone, attempting to wipe the dark green stains from the moss off his hands. The color remained firmly embedded in his skin, only a small part transferred to his shirt.

The roar of the waterfall less than a hundred feet away discouraged any attempts at conversation. The sun hung low in the western sky and the forest's shadow stretched far out onto the lake.

Marcos was not pleased; it had taken them longer to climb than he had thought. With a nod he sent Suni up the remaining twenty feet. A few moments later, a length of rope dropped down onto the ledge.

Casius groaned as the others ascended the rock face with the aid of the rope. When it was his turn he wondered if he would have the strength to finish the climb let alone descend back to the valley floor.

Casius climbed over the edge and entered into a thick tangle of tree roots and brush. Suni stood there motioning him to be silent. Once Casius was past he coiled the rope, leaving it upon the ground.

The air atop the Tor was foul, reeking of sulfur and decay. It assaulted their senses, burning their throats and stinging their eyes.

Connell grimaced and Casius fought to hold down what was left in his stomach.

Although the top of the hill was little more than a hundred feet across, the thickness of the brush made it hard to see beyond twenty feet. The sky above them was hidden from view by the gnarled branches of the great tree that grew here.

The damage to Asua Tuell was evident; its leaves were stained yellow, their edges turning dark brown. The bark of the branches was festooned with patches of grayish mold that oozed a thick yellowish fluid.

The ground below their feet was a thickly knotted mat of tree roots, and jagged bits of stone. In a few places giant slabs of rock stood out of the tangle, leaning precariously over them.

"We will not move quickly in this," Connell whispered disapprovingly as he readied his bow. "Not without risking a broken ankle."

Casius couldn't agree more, he had already stumbled once when a thin loop of root had entangled his foot. From beneath his feet he could hear the flow of running water.

Marcos could see where his attention was drawn and stepped closer to him. "The rock below is riddled with fissures through which the water flows. It is only the roots that holds the stone together." He said softly. "Come, what we seek is near at hand." He motioned them onward with Suni once more taking the lead.

They crept carefully forward. The thick brush ended suddenly. A clearing stood before them. It bordered upon a small glittering pool of water, which lay between the outstretched roots of a giant tree.

Its bark was gnarled and dark nestled within its cracks and crevices, large ferns grew. The trunk was so thick it was hard to believe it was a living thing. The bole was easily two hundred or more feet in diameter. Rising overhead it spread its low hanging canopy over the entire peak.

The tree's lower branches were devoid of leaves. Little more than twisted skeletal remains of once verdant boughs.

The dark bark hung in tatters, stretching to the ground in places, leaving the bone white wood exposed.

Marcos hissed in anger "Asua Tuell is defiled!" He pointed to the source of his ire for the others to see.

Two huge iron spikes had been driven deep into the tree's heart. The black metal still smoked where it met the wood.

Runes etched into the iron glowed with a sickly green light along their length. Pulsing as the malicious enchantment bore down into the tree's defenses. The spikes were massive things, as thick as a man's leg and twice as long.

"Touch them not!" Marcos warned. "They are forgings of Sur'kar's, and nothing from the furnaces of V'rag should be taken lightly."

"What purpose does it serve to destroy this wood?" D'Yana asked. The site of the wounded tree offended her greatly.

"It is a remnant of the old world," Marcos answered. "In days long past it too stood against Sur'kar, and would have done so again. Man may have forgotten what has gone before, but not this place. The trees have deep roots, and deeper memories. The spirit of this place would never bend knee and serve the darkness, and therefore it must be destroyed to prepare the way for Sur'kar's coming."

"Ware the shadows!" Connell shouted as his bow thrummed, shooting his arrow beyond the tree.

A blood chilling bellow of anger sounded from the gloom. The ground shook and limbs snapped as a monstrous giant burst into the open.

Clutching at the arrow lodged in its neck, its single eye fixed upon them burned with pure hatred. Towering over them at ten feet in height, to look upon it was to know fear.

Powerful muscles rippled across its chest, beneath a dark craggy skin. Despite its size and awkward appearance it moved with surprising speed. It roared in challenge, exposing a mouth full of yellowed teeth behind two enormous tusks that jutted up out of its lower jaw.

The shaft snapped as the Troll ripped it free. Tossing it aside the Troll lifted a massive hammer and charged. The weapon smoked darkly, and pulsed with the same sinister green radiance as the smoking iron spikes lodged within the tree.

Connell wasted no time, and released another shaft at the beast as it splashed through the shallow pool.

The arrow buried itself deeply in the Troll's heaving chest. Another shaft appeared next to it as D'Yana recovered from her fear, and loosed one of her own.

The Troll staggered, and blood flecked foam stained its lips.

Casius stood immobile with fear, his sword raised in a futile gesture to ward off the Troll's attack. Something grabbed his collar and pulled him clear of the Troll's descending hammer.

The Ground he had stood upon erupted in a spray of shattered rock and earth. The force of the impact staggered him. Throwing him into Marcos who still pulling at his collar.

He was regaining his feet when Suni suddenly leapt over him. Staves in hand, the agile warrior dashed forward and struck the beast in the face. The force of his blow actually pushed the Troll back a few paces.

The Troll brought his hammer to bear, but Suni was moving to quickly for it. The hammer slammed into the earth once more with a deafening boom that shook the Tor to its roots.

Suni rolled behind the Troll, and kicked with both feet. He connected with the giant's knee, and the Troll screamed as it gave way with a resounding crack. The knee was ruined unable to bear the Trolls great weight; it fell onto its side with a heavy thud. More arrows appeared in its hide as Connell and D'Yana continued their attacks.

The Creature thrashed violently and attempted to roll over Suni. The Anghor Shok leapt high into the air and landed on the Troll's back. He drove both his staves into the creature's neck just below the skull.

The weapons did not pierce its hide but they did damage nonetheless. The neck of the brute snapped under the onslaught and with a violent shudder the Troll ceased to move. A long shuddering exhalation was the last act of the brute before death claimed him.

Casius sheathed his sword and took a deep breath to calm his hammering heart.

Suni tucked his staves into his sash and stepped down off of the Troll as nonchalantly as one would step down from a porch.

Connell and D'Yana looked on the man in wonder. Suni had just killed a Troll with nothing more than his bare hands and two simple iron staves.

Marcos stood near the hammer and shook his head in disgust. "More of Sur'kar's treachery."

Casius felt ashamed. While his friends had fought he had stood paralyzed by fear. Only by Marcos's quick action was he even yet alive. He walked over to the trunk of the great tree, too embarrassed to even look at Connell.

As he neared the great trunk he saw a dried out corpse of an old man. Dressed in gray robes, with simple leather sandals upon his shriveled feet. The hair upon his head was snow white and obscured the gaping vacant sockets of its eyes.

About the withered neck hung a thick collar of gleaming gold. Utterly seamless and without blemish it shone brightly in the gloom.

"Have a look at this," Casius called to the others.

"Warlock!" Marcos said in disgust. "This poor soul was bonded to one of the Dark men. He paid dearly for the casting that so wounded the great tree."

"Warlocks and Trolls," D'Yana muttered. "What next?"

"Aye," Marcos agreed. "What next indeed. Evil things are stirring and old alliances are being revived. As Sur'kar emerges from the dark, many old enemies of man are stirring. Coming forth from their hidden lairs."

"What of the Warlock?" Casius asked. "Should we not search him out?"

Marcos shook his head. "No, he is either dead or so weakened he poses no threat to us." Marcos covered the corpse with his cloak. "His bond was broken when this man died. The cost of power would have befallen upon him at that moment. Unless he was well prepared, he too lies dead."

"Then the Troll was left here to guard the tree." Connell guessed.

"It is more likely that the Warlock died, and the Troll merely stayed not knowing what else to do." Marcos surmised. "The Hammer it bore is too great a weapon to leave here. A thing so powerful would have taken centuries to fashion."

Marcos laid his hand upon the wounded trees trunk. "Stand back," he advised. "The spikes are protected and will kill any who attempt to draw them out. There is a slim chance that I can strengthen the tree and give her the power to force them out."

They stepped back a few paces not sure how far to go.

Marcos closed his eyes and the ring upon his finger flared to life. The brilliant radiance cast the gloom aside and burned clean and pure. The tree shuddered and thin veins of light gleamed within its bark.

For several long minutes nothing seemed to happen, then a low creaking sound emerged from the wood. It grew louder until it became a shrill screech as the Iron spikes were slowly forced back.

The Runes upon the spikes brightened and the emerald light fought to overwhelm the pure light that now shown brightly where the metal entered the bole. The iron began to glow a dull orange that brightened to red. The heat coming from the iron was intense, darkening the bark around them.

The metal continued to brighten until it blazed as brightly as Marcos's ring, forcing the watchers to look away. The torturous scream ended in a muffled boom that shook the ground.

When they looked back Marcos was leaning against the tree. His ring now dull and lifeless, sweat lay beaded on his brow and his breathing was labored.

Of the spikes there was no sign, they had simply vanished, all that remained were the two smoking holes in the tree's bole.

"There is much power in this wood," Marcos said once his own strength had returned. "Given time she will recover."

The ground trembled and roots crept up from the earth and pulled the cursed hammer deep beneath the stone.

Marcos nodded in satisfaction, "Even now the wood seeks to cleans itself." Marcos grew silent; he felt an alien awareness at the edge of his perception growing stronger. It was incredibly old and malignant. The pure malevolence of it assaulted his senses. "We must flee," he gasped, breaking off the mental contact. "Our enemy has sensed my use of power and the hunters are racing this way."

They needed no further urging, with reckless abandon they climbed down off of the Tor. Reaching their horses after what seemed an eternity they sped off to the north.

The path before them grew narrow and dark the trees no longer parting to allow them passage. They rode hard for the better part of an hour.

Marcos feared for the horses, their strength needed to be conserved. He allowed his mount to slow to a walk. He could see Casius looking at him from the corner of his eye.

"Questions?" He asked turning in his saddle to look at the young man.

"You have within you the power to destroy the Troll," Casius said cautiously. "Why did you not simply do so?"

Marcos nodded in understanding. "Do not judge me too harshly young man. Suni was capable of handling the Troll.

"Casius, the power I wield is known as the Phay'ge, and it has limitations. It is the power of life and creation. I cannot use it to cause a death. To do so would expose me to the influence of the Na Phay'ge.

"That is the source of Sur'kar's strength. As night follows day, death follows life. The Na Phay'ge is the antithesis of life.

"It corrupts even the noblest of men, should I open myself to it, I would become that which I fear the most. A willing servant to Sur'kar."

"You can sense our pursuers through their use of the Na Phay'ge?" Casius pressed.

Marcos shook his head. "No I am blinded to such power, to sense it you must know its touch. Sur'kar and his minions have no such liability. They know the Phay'ge and have rejected its limitations.

"What I did at Glin'eress sent ripples through the fabric of creation. As if I had thrown a large stone into a still pond. It is this that drew their attention." Marcos's eyes grew distant as he felt for the dark presence that was growing nearer.

"What seeks us now is not bound by the Phay'ge or Na Phay'ge. It is something far older and stronger, from a time before creation and order. I can feel its might tearing at the fabric of the world."

Casius shuddered, "Then what is it?"

"I do not know," Marcos answered. "There were many powerful beings in the days before light. They were overthrown by the creator and banished. The fact that one wanders free from their netherworld prison disturbs me greatly." Marcos rode in silence for a short while before speaking once more.

"Sur'kar's eye has marked us all," he announced. "I wish it were otherwise but I am certain of it."

"Just what do you mean by marked?" Connell asked, his conversation with D'Yana ending at Marcos's remark.

"Suni and I are known to him," Marcos answered. "D'Yana as well for she has shared in our venture for two years now." Marcos looked at Casius and Connell. "You were marked as well for he sent not one but two Naz'Haruk after you long before we met. He fears something in you Connell. Perhaps the same thing that made me seek you out."

"What would Sur'kar fear from us?" D'Yana asked. "You have your power and knowledge, but Connell is a swordsman."

"Sur'kar fears death," Marcos answered her. "He craves power and dominion, in death he would have none."

"Isn't he dead already?" Connell asked. "Did he not die in the breaking when the hammer fell upon Trothgar?"

"One as powerful as my foe does not easily die," Marcos answered. "The evil that Sur'kar is servant too has anchored his spirit to this world. His body was ruined by So'san's act but his spirit did not move on. He left the devastation of his seat of power and fled to the wild places in the west. After three millennia he has grown strong once more and has returned to his kingdom in both body and spirit.

"There are those that worship him as a god, the reptilians known as the Morne. They serve him blindly, and are the fodder of his armies. Their clerics proclaim him as the Storm God reborn, and the tribes are uniting under his bloody banner."

"The Morne are not idiots," Connell said. "They are a fierce and often barbaric people. Do not some resist his call?"

Marcos nodded, "Some do, but heretics die horribly on the altars of Sur'kar. There are some fates that are worse than death, even to the brutal Morne."

The Sun set and the forest's glow died, leaving them walking their mounts through the oppressive darkness. Marcos desired to move on, but it was too dangerous. In the pitch dark of the wood they could easily become separated and hopelessly lost.

They settled in for the night upon a low ridge crowned with thick thorny brush. Suni took the first watch allowing the others to catch what sleep they could in the coolness of the evening.

CHAPTER FIFTEEN

It was during the darkest hours of the night that the forest grew strangely quiet, a deep hush that was broken only by the whistling wind in the canopy high overhead.

Marcos sat apart from the others, his senses tuned to the wood. He could feel the strength returning to the trees. A subtle awakening was taking place, as Asua Tuell grew stronger and more aware.

The menacing presence he had felt was growing nearer with each passing hour. Marcos was concerned for it was tracking them, altering its passage to follow their progress.

As dawn approached the glimmer in the trees began to awaken, pushing back the darkness. Marcos stretched and jumped to his feet. The presence suddenly was gone, snuffed out as if it were a candle blown by the wind.

He knew it was yet there, but now it was concealing itself from him. Marcos tried in vain to find it, whatever this creature was it knew how to hide its presence.

"Wake quickly," he said urgently to the others, shaking them in their sleep. "Danger draws near and we cannot tarry."

They were riding in minutes, the concern in Marcos's eyes adding to their haste. They rode as fast as they could and yet remain quiet.

Through the gloom they pressed crossing small rills, and climbing steep embankments.

Marcos led them to the fallen bole of one of the largest trees of the wood. Its trunk was bone white and stripped of bark. A thick mat of green moss grew along its top. They circled around the giant's remains and took shelter in its shadow.

The horses were growing agitated, their eyes rolling in fear as they sensed something dire growing nearer. Marcos touched each of the horses. They calmed and stood still their eyes growing distant as if they bordered on sleep.

"Stay silent," Marcos whispered. "No matter how frightened you become, do not move or speak. If you do we will be discovered and our lives will be in jeopardy."

Marcos walked a tight circle around them, his ring emitting the faintest of glows. Barely visible in the forest's light the ring left a ribbon of pale light surrounding them. After a few moments it faded and was no longer perceptible.

In the distance they could hear the sound of cracking branches, and heavy footfalls. The sounds grew louder as whatever was making them closed the distance.

The forest darkened and a sense of dread hung in the air. A roaring crash sounded nearby as one of the massive trees fell to earth. A wave of intense heat swept over them bringing with it the smell of burning flesh.

Casius closed his eyes, he leaned his head against the fallen bole. Struggling to remember Marcos's warning. The fear was overwhelming; it tore into his mind tearing at the fragile walls of his reason. He wanted to scream and flee, to run away from the cause of such primal terror.

The ground shook violently, and a deep guttural roar caused him to jump. He bit his cheek, using the pain to help him focus his self-control. His heart pounded, he could hear the rush of blood in his ears. Another horrific roar tore through the air, sending loose bits of earth falling down from the trunk behind which they had taken shelter.

Casius felt as if his heart was being torn in two, the terror rending both body and soul.

As suddenly as the feeling had come it was gone. The ground shook and trees crashed to earth in the distance. What ever it was that had caused such fear was now leaving. Destroying any tree that stood in its path.

The metallic taste of copper filled his mouth. The burning pain of his cheek brought him out of his panic. He swallowed the fluid in his mouth, and breathed a deep sigh of relief. Opening his eyes to the brightening wood he was surprised to see the toll the aura of fear had taken on D'Yana and Connell.

Connell smiled and touched D'Yana's hand reassuringly. She gave him a quick nod, and with shaking hands she adjusted the braid in her hair.

Marcos breathed a sigh of relief, "We are most fortunate," he said in a soft voice that was barely above a whisper. "I was able to conceal us from its eyes. It pursues a shadow of my power I cast westward. It will not last long but will buy us some time."

Suni sheathed his staves, once again he appeared to be unaffected by what had just occurred. His face was impassive; no sweat of fear lay beaded on his forehead.

"Were you not frightened?" Casius asked, amazed at Suni's composure. He needed to talk; it was something to take his mind off of the memory of the terror that had held him.

Suni looked at him, as if puzzled by the question. "I do not fear death Casius," he replied. "The trials of blood teach us to control that which would inhibit our actions." He nodded his head to Marcos. "You would do well to trust Marcos."

"Do you?" Casius asked in response.

"I am Anghor Shok, I trust no one." Suni's impassive gaze hardened slightly. "If you or any of your companions would threaten Marcos I would be forced to kill you. Such is my duty, for I have taken the oath of the nine blades and have withstood the trials of blood. Long ago, upon the scarlet steps of Sorvahk Gohn I became Anghor Shok, defender of the last Warder. I live only to serve Marcos, my life holds no value other than this service."

"What are the trials of blood?" Casius asked, amazed that Suni had said more to him in one breath than he had since they first met.

"Since before the breaking, my people have journeyed the world protecting the Warders. It is the greatest honor to have won the right to swear the oath of service, and to be named Anghor Shok.

"The Jhed Adar, are considered holy men among my people. After many years under their instruction they select the most promising of warriors for the Trial. It is by combat our skills are judged.

"To become Marcos's guardian I slew twenty men." Suni said without emotion. "Before that I crippled a hundred more. Only the final challenge is to the death."

"That's barbaric." Casius said appalled that such a practice was allowed to continue.

Suni merely arched an eyebrow at his outburst.

Marcos gripped Casius's shoulder leading him away from Suni. "Do not mock him," He warned softly. "Their lands are high in the mountains, life is often short and harsh for his people. To the Anghor, honor is everything, besmirch it at your own risk." Marcos patted his shoulder. "Not all men live by the same code of ethics as yours."

Casius thanked Marcos for his advice, he found Suni staring off into the forest. "I feel I must apologize, I had no right to criticize your ways."

Suni turned his dark eyes onto the young man. "It is barbaric, but the world is an unforgiving place. At times the strength of a man's heart is all that stands between his failure or success."

Casius relaxed he knew his apology had been accepted. "It was my heart that failed me when the Troll attacked."

"There is fire in you Casius," Suni said. "You stood your ground when many a man would have fled screaming. It is only the skills you lack. The difference between fear and bravery is the sense of knowing what to do, and the will to attempt it."

He watched in awe as Suni turned away and effortlessly climbed the nearest tree. Casually walking out onto the lowest branch, the Anghor Shok eyed the way ahead.

"He must be above ninety feet," Connell remarked coming to stand beside Casius.

Casius nodded, "One wrong step and it will be his death."

Marcos chuckled at their concern. "He is Anghor Shok, they do not fall."

After a few minutes Suni climbed down out of the tree as easily as one would descend a broad stair. "The way to the north looks to be clear. There is a large track heading west and many of the trees are scarred by heat."

"We have waited long enough," Marcos said mounting his horse. "Let us ride as far as the remaining daylight will allow us."

They took flight to the north, moving at a swift pace across the forest floor. Weaving among the great trees, Marcos drove them onward. Even to Casius's eyes the wood was changing.

There was a subtle difference in the trees. They seemed more alert; it was as if a thousand eyes watched. Here and there a small branch would reach out and caress Marcos's robe as he rode past.

They rode hard throughout the afternoon, resting the horses only briefly. The ground became rougher and they were forced to slow their progress. Large boulders littered the forest floor. Scattered about the landscape as if they had been simply tossed onto the ground by some uncaring giant.

It was late afternoon when Marcos suddenly stopped. Reining his mount in, he spun the horse about to face southwest. Holding up his hand for silence.

Something had tickled his awareness, a feeling of wrongness that tugged at his perceptions. Now that he had stopped he could feel nothing. He sent his perception into the forest, and moving along their intertwined roots and branches he found what he was seeking.

Less than a mile away, the trees knew terror. A being of smoke and fire moved slowly among them. Searing bark, and boiling sap with abandon. The terror of the trees was such that Marcos was forced to break off contact and cling to his saddle to stay mounted. His eyes flashed deep purple as he shouted, "It is near!"

Turning his horse, he kicked its sides urging it to run as fast as its weary legs would allow. Through the ferns they raced, leaping over the lower boulders and dashing around those that barred their way.

They went perhaps a hundred yards when a wave of sheer malice hammered into them. The ground shook and strident horns rang out.

The hunters now gave chase; harsh barks joined the din as the pack of Fell hounds was released. The massive war dogs had found their prey's spoor, and with slavering maws they craved to rend flesh and crunch bone.

The horses could now smell the hounds, foam flecked their sides but they ran for their lives. Their great chests heaving with each breath they took.

In the forest's perpetual gloom Casius could see a bear sized animal approaching from the right.

It was long and lean, standing six feet at the shoulder. Its pelt was gray in color with dark bands across its back. The head was wedged shaped with a powerful jaw. Two huge canines, fully thirteen inches in length trailed streamers of saliva. The eyes of the beast were deep set and milky white, with a catlike pupil.

The Fell hound attempted to slash the horse's legs with its fangs. At the last instant the horse leapt to the side, nearly throwing Casius. The hound's teeth instead struck the ground. With a startled yelp it flipped over with the force of the impact. Rolling over, it was on its feet in an instant. With a startling burst of speed it closed the gap to Casius's mount.

Casius had used his moment of reprieve, and had drawn his sword. He let the horse have its head, confident in the animal's instinct to follow Marcos's lead. Closer the Fell hound charged, powerful muscles pumping beneath its pelt. Its long claws tearing deep holes in the loam as it tried to overtake the horse.

The horse was tiring and the Fell hound snapped at Casius's legs. Before the fangs could find his flesh, Casius's sword struck its head. The force of the impact stung his hand and for a brief instant the blade was lodged in the hound's skull. With a desperate jerk he freed the weapon in a spray of dark blood and gore.

The hound rolled, stopping in a heap of twitching limbs. Connell's horse leapt clear of the body. At his command it lashed out with its rear hooves. Striking his pursuer in the head. The strength of the blow shattered the Hound's neck killing it instantly.

Casius glanced back over his shoulder. He could see D'Yana and Connell riding side by side their swords flashing in the dim light. Behind them raced at least a dozen hounds, and in the distant shadows he could see the charging hulks of Rock Trolls.

Casius's heart sank; he could see no way that they were going to survive this. He did not dwell on this thought for long. From his left one of the hounds leapt into the air, its fetid maw seeking to remove his head.

Casius ducked, bringing his sword up he opened its foul belly. Loops of entrails spilled outward, a hot spray of bile and blood splashed over him. The hound was not dead but it would

soon die. It thrashed about on the ground wailing in agony. Staining the foliage with its blood.
Ahead of them the golden light of the afternoon sun shone through the trees. With their pursuers falling behind they raced into a large clearing filled with lush grasses, and wild flowers of almost every description.
The Sun's light beat down upon them warming their faces. Marcos led them to the clearing's center where a single massive stump covered with flowering vines stood.
"We make our stand here," Marcos said dismounting. He patted his weary steed's neck. "The forest will aid us."
Connell looked back to the tree line, the feral eyes of the Fell hounds glowed from within the gloom. "They're hanging back," he announced.
"They have no love of the light Connell," Marcos said. "To some of the dark servants, the touch of the Sun is deadly. To the Fell hounds it is merely an annoyance. They will come, and our wait will not be overly long."
Connell dismounted, he left the black unfettered. Taking his bow in hand he stood with the stump at his back. "If they are going to come," he set an arrow to string. "Then let's thin out the pack a bit." He let the shaft loose. The arrow flew straight, finding its mark in the head of one of the hounds. It was a long shot but Connell's skill with the bow was formidable.
The Fell hound dropped, it had died instantly, the barbed shaft driving deep into its brain. The other hounds milled about in consternation but they made no move to attack or retreat.
D'Yana smiled grimly, and dropped another hound with her bow as well.
They succeeded in killing a total of five before the remaining six were called away from the danger by the harsh blat of a Troll's horn.
In the darkness among the trees stood at least ten of the giants. The sun reflected dimly from the odd assorted pieces of armor they wore. The hounds paced about them snarling,

anxious to set their teeth into the flesh that was being denied them.

"Why do they wait?" Casius asked, his palms growing sweaty with fear.

"They wait for their leader," Marcos answered gravely. "The unknown horror, which has stalked us from Glin'eress."

For more than two hours the standoff continued. The Trolls spread out encircling the small clearing cutting off any chance of escape.

"The sky darkens, and yet they make no move," Connell commented. "Where is this leader of theirs?"

"It is near, closer than you think." Marcos answered. "It is merely waiting, savoring the fear that we feel." Marcos drew his sword, the light of the dying sun gleaming along its gold colored blade.

In the gloom a Troll shouted, a harsh guttural sound.

One of the Fell hounds charged, its patience at an end. Its lips were curled back exposing a mouth full of frightful teeth. It made four leaping bounds when Connell's arrow pierced its throat. With a bubbling howl it fell dead.

"It seems that they are growing restless," Connell said readying another arrow.

Before anyone could reply the ground trembled. The acrid smell of burning wood tainted the air and rolling plumes of dark smoke emerged from the trees to their right. The Trolls squealed and ran to clear the area.

"It has arrived," Marcos announced needlessly.

The ground continued to shake. Heavy and ponderous, the footfalls of the unknown creature rattled the clearing. Branches snapped and one of the giant trees burst into flame. Within the smoke and fire a massive form began to emerge.

Casius nearly screamed as the full force of its aura of terror slammed into him. He dropped his sword and scrambled to retrieve it. Through the roar of his blood in his ears he heard Marcos shouting.

"Stand fast, do not give in to your fear!"

Through the tree line it stepped, a demonic being that nightmares were made of. It stood on four cloven hoofs that burned the ground where they touched. Its head rose thirty feet above the forest floor. Crowned with four ebon horns wreathed in a mane of blazing fire that reached far down its back. The eyes were burning orbs of flame within a skull like face.

The demons skin cracked and peeled as it moved, each opening spouting a short-lived burst of fire.

The powerfully muscled torso of a man was fused to the body of a gigantic bull. In its right hand it held a long spear made entirely of flame, in its left it clutched a length of golden chain that was secured to a thick manacle about its wrist. A searing wave of heat blasted out at them, forcing them to protect their faces with up flung arms.

One of the Trolls stood too close to the beast and suddenly it burst into flame. Screaming in agony it raced through the clearing, falling to its death a few feet from the tree line on the opposite end.

"Ma'ul..." Marcos muttered.

The Ma'ul roared, its mouth a hideous furnace from which fire and smoke jetted.

Connell fought his fear and fired an arrow. Aimed for the monsters forehead. The shaft flared a brilliant golden color as the heat surrounding the beast turned it to ash.

The Ma'ul reared to its full height, and roared in fury at the puny man's insolence. The fiery mane flared brighter and a new wave of heat exploded outward from it.

Marcos warded off the heat with sheet of fiery power from his ring. "Your time is past!" Marcos shouted in anger. His eyes burned with power, the very ground on which he stood was aglow. "Return to the prison prepared for you in the first days."

The Ma'ul stepped forward and with a wave of its arm it sent the golden chain crashing into the ground. The earth bucked violently and the horses screamed while their riders fought to keep their feet.

The Ma'ul roared pulling its fetter from the soil. A huge smoking trench marred the grass, its end only a scant few inches from Marcos.

Marcos never flinched; he stepped over the trench and raised his hand. The golden band flared until it was brighter than the sun. "Be gone spawn of darkness," Marcos commanded, in a voice that shook the ground.

Beyond the trees the Trolls recoiled in fear, they could feel the might of the man who stood before the fire demon.

The Ma'ul gripped its chain tightly and with a powerful heave it sent the golden links down onto Marcos. The chain burst into a thousand fragments as Marcos deflected it with his might. The explosion of force knocked the Ma'ul back a few paces.

The Ma'ul's flaming orbs flared in anger. Grabbing its spear tightly it charged, seeking to run its opponent through.

Suni had had enough; he drew his staves and ran to Marcos's side.

Marcos saw Suni's approach, "Back!" he shouted.

Suni was lifted into the air and thrown back a dozen feet by the force behind Marcos's words. Marcos spun and thrust out his hand. Brilliant fire shot forth and struck the Ma'ul in the eyes.

The Demon screamed in anguish, dropping its spear. It clawed at the blinding light.

Suni was stunned and it took him a moment to recover his senses. As he climbed to his feet a sharp cracking sound came from the stump.

Casius and the others jumped aside as the stump suddenly tore itself free from the soil. Roots writhed and twisted forming powerful limbs. The stump took on the form of a giant its head created from knotted roots and large stones. Two branches erupted from it forehead, becoming thick horns that curled upward.

The giant towered over them and with lumbering steps it charged, building up speed until it slammed its shoulder into the Ma'ul's chest. The two giants rolled onto the ground pummeling each other. Wood burned and bones cracked. The Ma'ul screamed in both fury and pain. Blinded by Marcos's magic it was vulnerable, and it felt the pangs of fear for the first time in countless ages.

From the forest edge the Trolls screamed in terror as the trees came suddenly to life. Powerful limbs grasped the intruders lifting them high into the canopy. The Trolls were ripped apart, limbs still twitching with the remnants of life rained down onto the loam. The Fell hounds yipped in fear, gnashing teeth tearing at the branches that sought to ensnare them. They too were carried aloft to their death.

"Mount quickly," Marcos urged. "The forest has awakened a Wood King in her wrath."

The frightened horses spun about seeking to flee the clearing. Fighting for control of the terrified mounts they bolted northward into the line of swaying trees.

Through the wood charged a multitude of animals. Bears, wolves and great stags ran side by side, their eyes afire with rage. The wave of animals parted, passing the fleeing riders on either side. Attacking without caution the forest denizens threw themselves onto the Demon pulling it onto the ground by the sheer weight of their numbers.

Casius caught a fleeting glimpse of the Wood King clenching the Ma'ul's throat. Its back was ablaze and the wood of its arms burned brightly. Animals died in the heat of the fire by the hundreds and yet they attacked, heedless of the flames awaiting them.

Into the trees they passed, and rode unhampered for several hours before they were forced to rest. The horses stood on trembling legs, sweat lathering their heaving sides.

In the distance they could hear the sounds of combat. Resembling the rumbling of a summer thunderstorm. The two giants continued to assail one another, shaking the very earth with their vehemence.

"We were most fortunate," Marcos commented. "I had thought the last of the Wood Kings to have passed from this world."

"Wood King?" D'Yana said looking to Connell for an explanation. The swordsman merely shrugged in reply.

"Long ago, there was one solitary tree upon the earth." Marcos answered. "The first seedlings were not bound to the soil as are their offspring. They wandered far and wide spreading their seed to all the lands of the world. When their work had finished they returned to the soil.

In times of dire need they would rise up and defend the wood from harm." Marcos rubbed his eyes, clearly exhausted from his confrontation with the Ma'ul. "This is the tale taught to men by the forest, before the trees banished him. To the best of my knowledge we are the only Humans and Tal'shear to have ever seen one."

"Will the Wood King prevail?" Casius asked concerned for the strange ally they had found in the forest.

Marcos considered the problem for a few moments before answering. "I do not know," he answered honestly. "Both are ancient beings of immense power." Marcos said rubbing his goatee in thought. "No matter who the victor is we need to move quickly in case the Wood King fails."

"Aye," Connell said in agreement. "But the horses are nearly spent, to ride them further today would be folly."

"Then we walk," D'Yana suggested. The disturbing echoes of combat sounded too close for her liking.

"Until late afternoon," Connell patted his massive horses sagging neck. "A night's rest will do us all a world of good."

Suni led the way once more and it was only a short while later that they found a narrow track leading due north. Giant trees bordered the trail their lower branches forming an arch of thick leaves overhead. The sounds of combat faded until as they sat in their dark campsite only the faintest rumbles could be heard.

Marcos stood alone facing the south, his senses turned to the clearing where the titanic struggle was yet taking place.

"Any change?" Connell asked walking out of the gloom.

Marcos shook his head. "I cannot sense them clearly, the forces at work are formidable. It is akin to staring into the sun to watch the flight of a distant falcon."

"You used your power to free the tree." Connell continued changing the subject. "The Ma'ul sensed it and attacked. What of Sur'kar? Can he not feel it as well?"

Marcos nodded, "Perhaps, if his senses were turned this way. But it does not matter now. He knows where we are. For if it was his power that released the Ma'ul, then he must control it. Other wise it would go on a destructive rampage that would not suit his goals. The Ma'ul felt the power, and it was Sur'kar that forced its attack."

Connell turned and looked back at the sleeping forms of D'Yana and Casius. Of Suni, he could see no sign but he knew the warrior was nearby guarding them. "We don't have much of a chance for success do we?"

"No," Marcos sighed. "Long ago I stood upon the lush plains before the armies of Sur'kar. I was younger then and full of power, but even then, standing with my brethren, we were no match for his evil.

"Sur'kar is not restricted in his use of power. He has become a pure manifestation of all that is evil and it has given him almost godlike powers.

"In fact, to the Morne he is known as the Storm God and is worshipped fanatically."

"The sword you seek will be enough?" Connell asked full of doubt.

Marcos shook his head, "Not by itself."

"How then do we get close enough to Sur'kar to make use of it?"

"That is my task," Marcos said somberly. "While he deals with me, it is then that you must deliver the blow."

"Can he not simply strike us down?" Connell said in anger, he could see no way that they could succeed. "We wont even get the chance to strike a blow."

"Sur'kar will not pass up on the chance to capture me and turn me into one of his servants," Marcos said knowingly. "He will make my death slow and painful, until I am nothing more than one of the Balhain."

"You speak as if you know him well."

"I do Connell," Marcos answered. "At one time he was a Warder, before the evil turned him. I served the land at his side in those days.

"I only showed you a small part of what I have witnessed Connell. Sur'kar and the two Balhain were all warders in those times. The evil took Sur'kar, and in turn he enslaved the twin brothers that stood among our strongest members.

"Gre'Doth and his brother Gre'Koth were lured away from the path by Sur'kar's serpent tongue. With half-truths and promises of power he burned away their will and enslaved their spirits.

"They are forever banished to the shadows, the touch of light a poison to them." Marcos stopped speaking as a low rumble shook the ground. Causing the trees above to shed a small amount of leaves. "The battle continues," he said needlessly.

Straightening his robe he turned and walked past Connell. "I've said too much Connell," he smiled apologetically. "Dawn will be here in a few hours and we must travel far. Go get some rest, Suni will keep us safe."

"Doesn't he ever sleep?" Connell asked, searching the darkness once more for some sign of the Anghor Shok.

"Rarely," Marcos replied settling down on the loamy soil. "The Anghor Shok are not like other men."

"No one here is exactly what they seem." Connell quipped sarcastically.

During the night the sounds of battle had lessened, and only rarely did they hear anything of the monumental contest.

Twelve long days they rode, following the path provided for them by the forest. Without warning they found themselves passing beneath the canopies edge. The bright afternoon sun stung their eyes and warmed their faces.

The sky overhead was mostly clear with only a few light clouds in the east. A low grass covered hill stretched away to the north. At its crest stood a thick grove of birch trees surrounded by thick brambles.

The hilltop afforded them a view of the land ahead. Rolling fields of wild grain dotted with thick copses of trees. Small ponds in the distance reflected the sky above. It was late and at Connell's suggestion they made camp within the stand of birch trees. Using his sword Connell hacked a pathway through the Firethorn bushes and brambles.

Casius had little experience with the colorful thorn bushes. He soon learned however that within the plants, beneath the leaves of ochre and gold lay long wickedly barbed thorns. Bone white in color, they inflicted a burning pain that would last for hours. He sat rubbing his palm, waiting for the pain to lessen. It would be a long time before he would ever try and handle one of those branches again.

Connell built a small fire and made a thin stew of dried beef and a few small leeks D'Yana had dug up. "It's the last of our supplies," he said grimly. "Parin lies twenty or so miles to the north, across mostly open country. Perhaps we will sleep in proper beds tomorrow night."

"What?" Casius exclaimed. "And miss the luxury of sleeping on the hard ground."

His sarcasm brought laughter to the weary travelers. Even the normally stoic Suni grinned briefly.

Marcos stood with his guard a few paces away from the others. "These are brave people, Suni." He said softly. "Despite all that has befallen them, and the dark path that lies ahead. They still find it within them to laugh. With hearts such as these there is yet hope for mankind."

"They will need this strength before these days are passed," Suni replied before taking his place on watch.

Marcos joined them in their frugal meal as the sun set in a sky of vivid red and gold.

CHAPTER SIXTEEN

Gaelan rushed out of the tower fumbling with the leather chinstrap to his steel helm. Behind him Burcott was cursing as he fought to pull on a gauntlet. Once outside they could hear the strident calls of horns ringing in the pass. Two men stood nearby holding the reins to their horses. Torches blazed along the walls, casting long shadows across the bailey.

The Keep was alive with running men. Awakened from their sleep, the warriors were quickly taking their places along the battlements. Those atop the wall leaned out over the merlons, straining to see what was occurring in the pass.

Gaelan swung up into his saddle and blew into his numb hands. From the moon's position he judged the hour to be two past midnight. "Raise the portcullis!" he shouted over the din of running men in armor. "Burcott, this waking me with grave news is becoming a habit."

"I'll send a comely bar maid next time." Burcott grunted as he pulled himself up into his saddle.

Gaelan looked over the assembled men who formed the reserve. One hundred in number they sat in orderly ranks, the torchlight gleaming from their polished armor. They were ready, no fear shone in their eyes, only grim determination.

"Balar!" Gaelan shouted to a giant of a man standing upon the battlement. "You're in command until our return, seal the gate behind us."

Balar saluted his clean-shaven face beaming with pride.

Burcott smiled, "Mind that you don't lose the key little brother!"

Balar grinned, "Keep your head on your shoulders old man!" he yelled in response.

"Lets go!" Gaelan led the mounted charge out of the keep. The echoing horn blasts from the pass would not allow them any further delay.

Once through the portcullis, the men upon the wall let lose a great cheer. So loud was their cry that the mounted men could not hear the gate slamming shut behind them.

Hooves thundered against the stone, echoing from the cliff face. The warriors raced into the narrow confines of the pass. Their equipment jingled discordantly, over shadowed by the sharp blats of the distant horn.

The dim moonlight reflected in bright flashes from the lances held by the men. Beneath their helms their eyes burned brightly. The excitement of the charge driving away any discomfort from the freezing night air.

It was a dark night but the trail was well known by all. They made good time racing up the steep slope. A half mile ahead a fire was burning, its light reflecting from the walls of the narrow gorge that formed the heart of the pass.

The frantic shouts of combat and the scrape of steel upon steel could be heard echoing down out of the defile. Gaelan drew his sword.

"Sound the horns!" Gaelan shouted to his men.

Twenty bronze horns were raised, and a long clear note pierced the frigid air. Three times the call rang out, a reassuring note to the men locked in combat. Help was on its way.

Gaelan spurred his horse, coaxing more speed from the beast. The icy wind stung his cheeks and leached the warmth from his body. He was not properly dressed for this weather. Beneath his ring mail and padded shirt he wore only the thin tunic that he had slept in. He was cold now, but he knew he would soon be warm enough, too soon for his liking.

Up the final rise they raced with lances lowered, the men screaming their battle cry.

Bodies lay strewn across the narrow roadway. Twelve men of the guard were still alive, and locked in mortal combat with dark robed warriors that moved with amazing speed.

"Morne!" Gaelan shouted in anger. He rushed into the fray scattering the Morne. One of the reptilian warriors was slow to move, and it went down its skull crushed by Gaelan's mount's hooves.

The Morne were inhumanly quick, they rushed forward seeking to pull the men from their saddles. Outnumbered by more than three to one, they fought on as if possessed.

Gaelan lashed out with his sword and blocked a blow directed at his leg. Sparks flew when the blades met. The reptile sneered, its golden eyes narrowing as it redirected its blow.

Gaelan turned the blade aside at the last moment and countered the attack. His blade opened the Morne's forearm from wrist to elbow. The Morne dropped its blade and leapt forward seeking to pull Gaelan down.

Gaelan leaned back and kicked him in the throat. The Morne staggered, its thick neck nearly snapping. Gaelan struck the bruised Morne a savage blow that severed its head. Hot blood the color of tar sprayed outward.

Wiping the blood from his face Gaelan spun his horse around. Chaos reigned around him, men shouting and dying. While the Morne hissed and grunted. The weight of the mounted charge had driven them back to the east. They were forced backward until they could go no further.

The men had them pinned to the northern wall.

"Enough!" Gaelan shouted, halting the guards' advance. "The day is lost to you, drop your weapons and your lives will be spared."

One of the Morne hissed and licked his maw with a thick purple tongue that dripped with saliva. He shouted in their harsh language and they rushed the guardsmen with berserker like fury.

Swords clashed, the narrow gorge rang with the clamor of battle. Men cursed and the sharp ring of steel upon steel contended with the harsh barking shouts of the Morne. It was over quickly, none of the Morne survived the final onslaught but they had taken down many men with them.

Gaelan dismounted and cleaned the gore from his blade with one of the fallen Morne's cloak. Out of the hundred who had ridden with him into the pass, only thirty-two were left standing. He was appalled by their losses. The original guard posted here numbered forty now only twelve remained and six of them bore serious wounds.

Forty Morne lay dead; it was a miracle that the guardsmen had held the pass for any length of time at all.

"Sound the all clear," Gaelan ordered one of his buglers.

The single note hung in the air echoing for what seemed an eternity in the darkness.

"Forty Morne," Gaelan said to Burcott his face dark with barely contained rage. "Forty slew ninety six of our best."

Burcott nodded, "They are a terrible foe to face."

"We cannot afford these kinds of losses." Gaelan cursed and motioned for the watch commander to join him.

"What happened?" he asked the nervous man.

"They came upon us without warning sire. Moving as if they were ghost, they appeared out of the dark. Half our number died before we were aware of the danger." The Guard wiped the grime from his face with a shaking hand.

Gaelan nodded, "I would have done the same had I commanded the Morne."

"They're assassins with no sense of honor," Burcott grunted. "These men were ill prepared for such an attack. We had expected a few merchant caravans not a Morne patrol."

Gaelan looked at the guardsman. "Send a messenger to Carich. Have wagons brought to carry our dead and wounded back to the Keep. Inform Balar that I want two hundred men brought up here with stone working tools as well."

"At once milord," the man replied rushing off to fulfill his orders.

"You have an idea?" Burcott asked puzzled by Gaelan's request.

Gaelan nodded to the loose scree lining either side of the roadway. "We build a wall."

Burcott kicked aside one of the Morne swords. It was a long curving blade, with sharp saw like teeth running along its length. "What of the Morne?" He asked. "We cannot leave them here."

"Burn them," Gaelan suggested. "At the entrance to the pass. Their blackened bones may serve as a warning to any others who would attempt to come this way."

A wicked smile crossed Burcott's lips. "You learn quickly milord," he answered, standing tall in his stirrups. "Dismount!" he ordered the men who were still on their horses. "We have much work to do ere these bastards try to win past us again."

Some of the men were not pleased with the prospect of working through the night, but none would dare protest. Burcott had a reputation, and in the days of his youth he was known as the face splitter for a reason.

Sentries were posted and the dead gathered. The bodies of the Morne were piled upon a pyre of dried brush and set aflame. About the burning mound their weapons lay broken and twisted. The wagons arrived as the fire was lit and the dead and wounded were taken back to Carich.

An older man who had ridden in one of the wagons approached Gaelan. His hair was a tangled mass of snow white that stood out starkly against his sun-darkened skin. He bowed his head in respect to Burcott and the Prince. "My lords," he said in greeting. "I am Cias the Keep's stone mason. I came to see if I could be of some assistance." He stuffed his hands into the deep pockets of his leather apron to keep them warm. "When my tools were confiscated I decided to tag along. Without them I have little else to do."

Gaelan smiled at the man's remark. "There's work enough for all Cias, and your skills are sorely needed." Gaelan pointed to where the pass was narrowest, scarcely sixty feet across. "I need a wall, nothing fancy. Something we can erect quickly and that can be defended."

Cias looked at the loose rock lying about. "Easily done, with all these lads standing about it should not take long. It will have to be dry set, little more than a large pile of rubble."

Gaelan nodded, "I'll leave it to you then Cias." He said mounting his horse. With Burcott following they rode back to Carich. Over taking the wagons bearing the wounded and dead.

Cias watched the prince ride away. Looking about at the blood soaked stone he was thankful he was no longer a young man. From the foot of the pass a huge fire burned, the stench of burning flesh reaching him from time to time. He was curious, but after watching them load the bodies onto the wagons. He had no desire to see what it was that they had set afire.

Their return to the keep was a solemn occasion. Gaelan and Burcott led the slow moving wagons into the Bailey past ranks of silent men standing at attention. Burcott stood next to Gaelan, as the wounded were helped into the Hall. "There is a vale to the west, a hidden place where those who have died in the service of this Keep are laid to rest in honor."

Gaelan nodded, his eyes filled with sadness. "Have another group of two hundred sent to the pass after sunrise to relieve those who are working there. We will do so every five hours until the wall is completed."

Burcott knew Gaelan was feeling the sadness that comes with the loss of men you had commanded. "This whole business is going to be costly Gaelan." he said softly. "There will be many more before this is over."

"We have no choice in the matter, Burcott. The price will be higher should Goliad succeed. No man, woman or child would be safe from the Morne. If Trondhiem should become his."

That afternoon a procession of three hundred guardsmen marched out of the Keep's gate. At the end of the column came ninety-eight horses, each bearing a shroud wrapped body.

Gaelan and Burcott marched behind the horses, dressed in full armor. A black cloth tied about their left arm. Behind them a single drummer kept the pace. The resonant boom of his instrument drowning out the jingle of both harness and armor.

A mile down the road they turned off the path and entered the shade beneath the tall pines that crowded the mountainside. A thick carpet of nettles crunched underfoot as the column made its way deep into the wood.

The land rose higher the further they ventured. Until the steep slope they followed ended at the head of a deep valley. Lush amber grass carpeted the valley floor.

The thin Ribbon of a spring fed rill split it in twain. A few trees grew along its banks, their branches swaying in the gentle breeze blowing down from the heights above.

The northern end of the valley rose sharply, ending at the base of a high cliff. Nestled within the rocks shadow lay many earthen mounds. Most were small but there were a few that measured ten or more feet in height. Small golden flowers grew in abundance upon them.

Dar'lea, deaths blooms they are called, a rare flower that was planted on the burial mounds of the dead. An old way of proclaiming the honor of the men who lay beneath.

A freshly dug pit stood among the mounds. It was deep and broad. It was going to be a large mound, a mute testament to the damages inflicted by the Morne attack.

A group of twenty workers stood a respectful distance away, beside a mound of excavated earth and freshly cut sod. It was their labor, which had created the grave, and once the men had been interred it would be their task to cover their bodies.

The guardsmen formed a ring about the pit, and one by one the horses bearing the dead were led forward. As each man was lowered into the grave Burcott would announce their name, and the assembly would raise their swords and shout "Tel'lav an Amos!" An old phrase meaning for honor and glory, a tribute to those that have passed.

Gaelan stood rigid next to Burcott, a statue in glittering mail. When the last man was laid to rest he raised his sword and in a voice thick with emotion he repeated the tribute. "Tel'lav an Amos, may you find peace in the halls of your fathers."

The workers stepped forward and covered the bodies with the rich soil. When their labor was completed a new mound stood among the others, towering fifteen feet in height. Gaelan walked up its steep side and plunged a sword into the fresh sod, leaving two thirds of the blade exposed.

Reforming the ranks Gaelan took his place behind the rider less horses. With the first drumbeat they left the valley.

Gaelan took one last look over his shoulder down into the tranquil valley. The light of the afternoon sun was reflecting brightly from the blade atop the mound, a blazing beacon marking the first of many Gaelan thought darkly.

Burcott took his place at Gaelan's side; he too spared a quick look back onto the field of honor. "We've done all that we can for those men my prince," he said softly for Gaelan's ears alone. "The living have need of you now."

Gaelan nodded. He marched back to the keep in silence, the weight of responsibility smothering his spirit.

For two weeks the men worked upon the wall across the pass. During that time, men from all walks of life began to appear at the Keeps gate. From wealthy merchants to simple farmers they came. Armed with whatever was on hand, they crossed the plains seeking to come to their prince's defense.

They welcomed one and all, no one was turned aside and the Keep was becoming crowded. Burcott arranged training sessions in the bailey. The novice warriors were drilled in the art of warfare.

Gaelan and Burcott rode up to the wall upon news of its completion. They were pleased with the sturdy construct Cias had created.

The wall rose twenty feet, running arrow straight it spanned the sixty feet of the defile. A single narrow gateway pierced its heart, barred by a heavy wooden door banded in iron.

Although the wall was completed the work crews were still carting stone to the northern end.

Amid the workers stood Cias, the old stonemason directing the placement of each tone.

"Cias," Burcott said in greeting. "What are you making now?"

"Strong soldiers," one of the men quipped as he wrestled with a large stone. The comment drew a few laughs from the weary men; even the somber face of Prince Gaelan was brightened by the touch of a smile.

Cias bowed, "A shelter," he answered. "Nights tend to get cold up here. I figured we have stone enough and plenty of willing men."

"Good thinking," Gaelan said approvingly. "It will make the duty up here more palatable for the men."

"At the rate you're going we could have a fair sized Keep up here by summer." Burcott said jokingly.

Cias smiled as a few of the men nearby groaned at the thought.

Their visit was cut short by the arrival of a messenger from the Carich. The young man rode his horse recklessly through the workers. He was one of the newcomers, barely fifteen years old. "Prince Gaelan," he stammered suddenly unnerved by the thought of speaking to the lords.

"You have a message?" Burcott urged.

He ducked his head, "A rider has arrived from Timosh!"

Gaelan needed no further urging and with a parting nod he rode hard for the Keep.

They entered the hall of the tower and approached a trail worn soldier who was speaking with Balar. The weary warrior saw the prince approaching and dropped to one knee his fist striking his heart in salute. Raising a cloud of dust from his filthy tabard.

Burcott pulled him to his feet, "We're not much for formality here."

"My liege," he said with a short bow. "Lords Deneb and Neros send their respects, and have charged me to inform you that Timosh is yours to command."

Gaelan's heart skipped a beat, "That is good tidings indeed."

The messenger nodded, "It gets better, the force holding Timosh is seven thousand strong. Made up of free men from many of the noble houses."

"Hah!" Burcott exclaimed smacking his fist into his open palm with a resounding clap. "It would seem Goliad's plans have a few flaws."

"It would explain why they have not fallen upon us as yet." Gaelan mused. "He cannot leave Thorunder unguarded lest Deneb and Neros strike at his back."

"Caught in the middle," Burcott said with a smile. "He must be uncomfortable indeed."

"Mi lords," the messenger said drawing their attention. "I left Imnos eight days past. Taking the western path across the plains of Theranduil. Goliad has sent a sizable force southward. They are burning homesteads and putting entire households to the sword. I came across several on my trek here."

Gaelan's face reddened in rage, he clenched his fists and held his tongue allowing the man to continue.

"I encountered those fortunate few who have escaped. They claim Morne ride with the marauders." He looked to Burcott, "Can this be true?" he asked.

Burcott nodded, "Aye it is, Goliad has damned us all in his quest for the throne."

The Messengers eyes hardened, "Then he must be stopped."

"You have served honorably," Gaelan told the weary man. "Rest tonight, if you are up to it I will give you a message for Lord Deneb and Neros."

The man snapped to attention and saluted. "It would be an honor my Prince." With a quick bow he left the hall searching for a hot meal and a place to sleep.

Gaelan walked to the hearth and warmed his hands over the fire. "How many men do we now have?" he asked his advisor.

Burcott frowned in thought before replying. "Perhaps two thousand, our number grows daily and keeping an accurate count is difficult."

"Many of them have never seen combat."

"An untried sword is better than none," Burcott countered.

"Horses?" Gaelan asked.

"Seven hundred and thirteen at last count," Burcott answered. "That number is growing as well."

"Goliad is losing his control over the men," Gaelan said watching the fire dance along the sputtering logs. "He failed to consider the consequences of bringing the Morne into Trondhiem. No man of honor would willingly serve beneath his banner now."

"Where do you suppose he would gain the manpower needed to maintain the throne?" Gaelan asked, walking over to a table littered with maps.

"Morne," Burcott answered following him.

"With Timosh standing firm and our forces here," Gaelan said, laying his hand on an open map of the Kingdom. "There is but one way to get a sizable force into Trondhiem with any speed." He let his hand slide down the parchment to the southern border.

"That's ten miles of open ground between the Rahlcrag Mountains and Easterling Marsh," Burcott commented. "The rivers are shallow and easily forded in those lands."

"Could the Morne make a safe passage through the Gaul-Tyrian waste?" Gaelan wondered. He knew the fierce reputation of the nomads who called the shifting sands their home. The desert dwellers had a habit of killing any who dared violate their lands.

"Perhaps," Burcott nodded, "Given enough men. The greatest danger is the Randorien Forest." Burcott pointed to the wiggly line indicating the forests edge. "Any force entering that tangled mass would be cut to ribbons by the savage tribes within."

"We cannot count on them guarding our border," Gaelan said. "The wild men have no love of us." Gaelan touched a small tower drawn on a line of low hills. "What keep is that?" he asked somewhat embarrassed by his lack of knowledge of the southern borders of his father's kingdom.

"Ruins," Burcott answered. " A curtain wall and the broken foundations of a tower. It stands on the highest point of the Bal'Trae hills. A grim reminder of a war we fought with the forest men four hundred years ago. It is known as Fro'Hadume."

"Tower of the Damned?" Gaelan asked translating the name from the old language once used by all men.

"Aye," Burcott confirmed. "Not many men will even approach it during the full light of day. It is said that those who died there still man the walls."

"Our position is precarious at best," Gaelan looked away from the map. "Our strength grows daily and if we are to have any chance at disposing of Goliad and Vernal we cannot allow him to build his as well."

"What of your kin in Kesh?" Burcott reminded Gaelan. "The armies of the Spire may yet come to our aid."

Gaelan shook his head. "I do not think my uncle will come. We have sent three messengers to Kesh and none have returned with word, for good or ill. Goliad is no fool, the way to Kesh may be blocked by Morne."

"Or your Uncle has decided against you." Burcott added finishing Gaelan's thought. "Then we must assume no aid is coming."

Gaelan nodded, "I need that border sealed."

"Then I will lead an expedition south and see that it is done." Burcott volunteered.

"I would rather send someone else and have you at my side."

"We have no other option," Burcott answered. "I know those lands better than anyone. I have spent many months hunting Val Stags with my father in those hills."

Gaelan could see no other way. He knew Burcott would stay if he so ordered, but in doing so he would stain the old warriors honor. "Very well," he said reluctantly. "Take as many men as you deem necessary."

Burcott smiled, "Six hundred on horse, if we travel light and ride hard we can make it in three weeks time."

"Six hundred men will not be enough to hold those hills."

"We will travel through my lands, Gaelan. I will gather more men on the ride." Burcott folded his arms across his chest and tugged at his beard in thought. "More supplies will be needed than we can carry."

"I will send wagons south after you," Gaelan reassured him. "I would still rather send another in your place," he added.

"Duty to friends must always give way to your duty to Trondhiem. Ordering those closest to you to take great risk is part of the cost you must be willing to pay to wear the crown." Burcott tapped his forehead with his index finger to emphasize the point. "The crown you wear is a heavy thing. The weight of gold pales when compared to the cost of lives spent to defend it.

"Your father once said it was an anchor upon a king's soul, keeping his feet on the ground when his ego would have him soar across the heavens."

"My father also once said, tread lightly into the halls of war." Gaelan responded.

"Do not hold back," Burcott advised. "Men will die, a soldier knows this and accepts it. With the crown on Goliad's head our people will suffer. Men, women, and children will die at the hands of the Morne. There is no mercy in those cold-blooded hearts.

"There are tough choices to be made Gaelan, choices that will scar your very soul. Choose now what we are to do, but choose for the right reason. If you choose to fight this war for nothing more than vengeance and the crown, then to hell with you, for you will be no better than Goliad."

Gaelan blinked, surprised by Burcott's candor. "I have no wish to wear the crown," he protested.

"I know." Burcott said with a smile. "You have two options before you. Leave Trondhiem and forsake your people and birthright, or stay and fight. There are no other paths to be followed."

"We will stay and fight," Gaelan replied. "I will not leave these lands to that murderous viper."

"Then lock your heart away," Burcott said forcefully. "There are evil times ahead, and you cannot afford the luxury of grief." Burcott smiled brightly. "Besides I'm an old warrior and will not go down easily."

Gaelan smiled in return, "Go gather your men and gear. Tomorrow you will ride with the rising sun."

Burcott saluted and left the hall; there was a renewed spring to his step, and a deeply rooted smile across his craggy features.

Gaelan spent most of the night in the hall studying the maps. Sleep would not come easily to him, and it was no surprise when the first light of the rising sun brightened the parchment he was reading.

Before the sun had fully crossed the horizon the bailey was filled with men and horses. As to which group was protesting louder none could guess.

Through the milling mass stormed Burcott, his deep voice barking orders. Slowly the throng grew silent and order was restored.

Gaelan stepped out of the tower and pulled his cloak tighter. Damn its cold he thought. He could recall no other spring when the air had such a vile bite to it.

Burcott crossed the courtyard, his breath clearly visible in the crisp air. His cheeks were ruddy with the cold. "I see you're awake early this morning sire," he said with a grin.

"As if a man could sleep with all this racket," Gaelan answered sarcastically.

Burcott grasped the Prince's hand firmly his face growing serious. "Trust your instincts," he said. "There is much of your father in you."

Gaelan ducked his head at the compliment. "Look after yourself you old warhorse."

"Bah!" Burcott grunted climbing into his saddle. "You'll be taking all the risk while I waste my time waiting for an attack that will never come in the south."

The old veteran pulled on a tarnished steel helm adorned with outstretched raven wings on each side. "It's been a long time since I wore the helm of my father in service to the crown."

"Teach these Morne to fear it as had others in the past." Gaelan drew his sword and raised it high. The blade shone brightly, reflecting the light of the rising sun.

"Tel'lav an Amos!" he shouted. His voice echoing from the cold stonewalls.

The men raised their own blades and shouted in response, "For Trondhiem!"

At a nod from Burcott the herald placed a bronze horn to his lips and blew two sharp notes. The horns call was still echoing from the walls as Burcott led the long column of men out of the keep.

Burcott Fullvie rode to war, taking nearly half of the keep's strength with him.

Gaelan stood in the empty Bailey, and watched as the portcullis was lowered and the gates sealed. He sheathed his sword and made his way back into the warmth of the hall.

On the afternoon of the second day since leaving Carich, Burcott's men entered the town of Galtor. The rumor of war had spread, and a nervous populace lined the streets. Watching in awe as the force of men rode past.

At the columns head rode Lord Burcott, a powerful figure in gleaming armor wearing the winged helm of legend. Behind him came the standard bearers, the deep blue pennant of the house of Fullvie and the black and gold of Trondhiem's King snapped in the fitful breeze.

Burcott waved, and the crowd began to cheer. Few people in Trondhiem had never heard of Burcott. He was a living legend whose prowess in battle had earned him much fame. Once across the span he quickened the pace. They had a formidable ride ahead and time was not on their side.

So ends Blackthorn.
Book one in the Chronicles of the Dark Sword.

The Saga continues in

Aethir

Glossary

A

Aenos: Small city south of Graystone in Lakarra.
Aderis Rendir: Hero of lost Thelikor, slayer of the serpent Ysrex.
Ahalm Iban: Herald of the Sahri.
Ahmed: Nomads of the Gaul-Tyrian waste.
Ahmed Kai: Nomadic name for the Gaul-Tyrian waste.
Aethir: Greatest of the four swords forged by Ma'Rail also known as Blackthorn. Wielded by Thoron'Gil, lost following the breaking.
Aikinor: Ancient god of the sea, patron deity of the Cytheran Raiders.
Aithas: Warrior of the Mahjie.
Alagond: Storm biter, sword forged by Ma'Rail. Carried into battle by Caen, Captain of the armies of man.
Alcedoria: Island nation north of Ao'dan.
Amberoth: City in the land of Morne.
Ameldor Plain: Low lands in Kesh surrounding Red spire.
Amil Gallas: Rock of the south watch, southern entry into the land of the Mahjie.
Amothteir: Bell that is rung in Red Spire to welcome home a returning hero.
Amthur: Evil King who once ruled Kesh.
Anatha Di: Area of sand within the Gaul Tyrian waste that pulls anything that walks upon it down into the earth.
Anthail: Warrior of the Mahjie.

Anghor: Mountainous kingdom of fabled warriors. Its exact location a closely guarded secret, it lies west of the Gaul-Tyrian wastes.
Anghor Shok: Warrior from Anghor, sworn guardians of the Tal'shear warders.
Ansell: Village on the coast of Lakarra near the Copper hills.
Ao'dan: Nation on eastern edge of continent.
Arkett: Guardian of Amberoth's well.
Armon'oth: Bells of the Mahjie forged to herald the selection of the sword bearer.
Arn: Island lying between Kale and Cythera.
Ash'Kelon: Marcos's real name among the Tal'shear.
Asua Tuell: Mother of all trees, lies within the heart of the Nallen Forest.
Aytor, Stone of: Artifact given to the Kings of man by the Tal'shear. It has the power to reveal all falsehoods with its light.

B
Balar: Younger brother of Burcott Fullvie
Balhain: Servants of Sur'kar, Tal'shear warders enslaved by his power.
Baln Longwyrm: Lord of Kale and Founder of New Hope.
Bal'Trae Hills: Low group of hills rising above the fork where the Evtor Wash and the Songart River meet.
Bel'Lendil: North wind, sword forged by Ma'Rail. Carried into battle by Ce'Loth, Warrior of the Tal'shear.
Bel'Vir: General who slew king Amthur.
Bjorn Ironfist: Lord of Cythera also known as the Raider king.
Blackthorn: Sword also known as Aethir.
Blackwatch: Mountain range forming the eastern barrier to Tarok nor.
Black Trumpet: Flower from which a powerful narcotic is made.

Braelin Wood: Forest bordering the fields near Graystone.
Bri'Amor: Lake to the west of Rodderdam.
Brymir: Scarcely populated land east of Trondhiem.
Burcott Fullvie: Veteran warrior of Trondhiem and lord of the largest house in the Landsmarch.

C

Cal'Arev: Hill upon which the city of Rodderdam was built.
Caleph: Small area of land on Lakarra's western coast.
Carec Mountains: Chain of mountains that run west from the Copper hills forming the northern wall of the Varsus valley. Also known as the Carec mounds.
Calriss: Warrior of the Mahjie.
Carich: Fortress that wards the Tro'marg pass leading into Brymir.
Carl Dunburrow: Farmer who lives near Ansell.
Carthos: Sparsely populated land south of Trondhiem on the shores of the Southern Sea.
C'arl Finnerson: Keeper of the bridge across the Koran.
Casius Rhaine: Son of Urold Rhaine ship thane of Kale.
Cewyn Rhaine: Mother of Casius, Urold's Wife.
Chaobol: Legendary land in the far west, reputed to be the home of Warlocks.
Cias: Stone Mason of Carich Keep.
Connell Malkor: Prince and heir to the throne of Kesh. Superb swordsman unsurpassed by even his legendary father. Known as the eagle, for a brand he gave himself as a child.
Creators hammer: large asteroid that nearly destroyed Sur'kar during the war of the breaking.
Copper hills: chain of low mountains on the eastern coast of Lakarra. Named for the rich veins of copper found there.
Cyndra: Capital of Lakarra, located on the north east coast.
Cythera: Island, home of the Raiders. A nation ruled by Ruthless cutthroats. They patrol the seas ransacking coastal villages and merchant ships.

D

Dal'Entor: Fields south of the town of Tor on the edge of the Nallen wood.
Darkling Sea: The void between worlds, space.
Darkwater River: River that flows out of the copper hills into the sea, water is dark with sediments from the Mountains.
Dar'lea: Death's blooms, small golden flowers that grow only in Trondhiem. They can only be found on the graves of the honored dead.
Delin' Tor hills: Heavily forested outcrop of the Rahlcrag Mountains laying to the south of Timosh.
Demilion: Statue before the entry into Red Spire.
Dragord: King of Ril'Gambor.
Dulrich: Cytheran Raider, member of G'relg's crew.
D'Yana: Man hunter and consort of Connell, Nicknamed Dy by him.

E

Easterling Marsh: Swamp that lies between Trondhiem and Carthos, fed by the Waters of the Evtor Wash River.
Edwall: Son of Lord Eyahn of Whiten.
Elain: Wife of Gayn.
Elkrun: City on the shores of the Darkwater River.
El'radrien: Sacred hill in the center of the isle of Eol.
Elrendil: Queen of Kesh, Mother of Connell.
Enchanter: Human who wields the Phay'ge.
Eol: Mist shrouded island of perpetual spring. It lies in the southern sea. Adopted home of the Tal'shear and Marcos's refuge.
Eramat: House of Hurin located on the northern shores of Lake Valdecar.

Evtor Wash: River that runs north to south through central Trondhiem to the southern border. Beginning in the Delin' tor hills and ending in the expansive mire of the Easterling Marsh.
Eyahn: Lord of the house of Whiten.

F
Fa'lain wood: dense forest that surrounds the hill of Ga'ron.
Fel'Tuin: Large bear that lives in the upper reaches of the Carec Mountains.
Fell Hound: Huge wild dogs of the northern wastes. Not quite tamed they are often found in the company of Trolls. Used by Sur'kar as trackers they are relentless when pursuing prey.
Forest Lord: Taur Di name for a Wood King.
Fro'Hadume: The Tower of the Damned, a ruined Citadel in the Bal'Trae hills. The Savages of the Randorien forest destroyed it four hundred years ago.

G
Gaelan: Prince and heir of Trondhiem, cousin of Connell Malkor.
Gal'adori: Legendary home world of the Tal'shear.
Galloglass Hall: Ceremonial chamber used by the King of Trondhiem, famous for its walls constructed of stained glass.
Galtor: Town on the shores of the Rildrun River.
Ganduil: Tal'shear vessel that crossed the darkling sea.
Ganeth: Usurper of Lakarra's crown, a Brutal tyrant who is allied with the Cytheran Raiders and a servant of Sur'kar.
Gared: Connell's older brother, the heir of Trondhiem who died in an accident. Thrown from his horse while on a hunt.
Ga'ron: Hill on the isle of Eol, where the standing stones ring the well of Sa'ramir.
Gaul-Tyrian wastes: desert lying southwest of Tarok-nor, Home of the Ahmed.
Garoul: Also known as Naz'Haruk.

Gayn: Nephew of Carl Dunburrow, scribe in Graystone.
Gellan: Murdered King of Trondhiem, father of Gaelan.
Gil'Galdov: Red spire in the days before the Tal'shear left the world.
Glin'eress: the Lake at the heart of the Nallen Forest.
Goliad: Usurper of Trondhiem, one of Sur'kar's Balhain.
Gorcrahlg: Pass through the Black Mountains.
Graymane: Mountain from which emerges the Delin' Tor hills, and the plateau of Delin' Tor.
Graystone: City in Eastern Lakarra, On the Taelus River.
G'relg Halmfist: Cytheran Raider, leader of the attack on New Hope.
Gre'Doth: One of the Balhain, also known as Lord Vad Goliad.
Gre'Koth: Brother of Gre'Doth also known as Vool.
Grel'in: Possessed heroes who serve Sur'kar.
Gren'dour: Legendary bow of the Keshian Kings.
G'thur: Member of the Keshian Home guard.
Guall: Yellow leaves, mild stimulant chewed by men of Caleph.

H
Haego: Small kingdom conquered by the Lakarrans.
Haft: Keshian cavalry unit of 1500 men.
Havoc'Mor: Forest north west of Trothgar.
Hurin: One of the Lords of Trondhiem, Member of the Landsmarch.

I
Illuminai: Metallic spheres fashioned by the Mahjie that Generate light and heat.
Imnos: Settlement on the shores of the Evtor Wash in central Trondhiem.
Irson Qual: One of Burcott's trusted officers serving Gaelan.

Isembahl: Temple in Anghor, it is where Suni was trained and tested to become Anghor Shok. Also known as the crystal palace.

J

Jehnom: Warrior from the Randorien forest.
Jerud: King of Thral'duras, a kingdom of the old world. Lost during the breaking.
Jerudan: Son of the King of Ril'Gambor.
Jhed Adar: Holy men of Anghor who teach the arts of combat. They are responsible for the testing leading to the selection of the Anghor Shok.

K

Kadril steppes: Northern most region of Kesh, famous for the warhorses bred there.
Kale: Island east of Ao'dan
Kalmari: Iron staves, only weapons wielded by the Anghor Shok.
Ka'rich: Throwing knives used by the men of Caleph.
Kesh: Kingdom north of Ao'dan east of the Dragon Spine Mountains.

L

Lakarra: Island nation south of Ao'dan.
Lakarrans: People of Lakarra.
Landsmarch: Formed of eight houses, they are the greater nobles of Trondhiem, and form a council advising the king. Each of these is comprised of several lesser houses. Together they form the basis of the king's power.
Larkoth: Carnivorous apes from the western lands.
Lenar: Bard of Ril'Gambor, famous for his heroic epics. His works survive long after his death.

Lon Hawsell: Butcher of New Hope on the isle of Kale.
Lo'Wyren: Dawn Singer, sword forged by Ma'Rail. Carried into battle by Na'Boal, Warrior of the Tal'shear.
Lycian Mountains: High peaks within the heart of Cythera.

M
Mahjie: Last of the high men, Guardians of the resting place of Thoron'Gil. They are small in number but fighters who are only surpassed in skill by the Anghor.
Majik: Human name for the power wielded by enchanters and Warlocks, Also used to describe any ability that defies explanation.
Ma'ul: Demons from the time before the world was created. Powerful and utterly evil they stand thirty feet in height. They have the bodies of bulls with the torsos of a muscular man. The face is skull like with flaming orbs for eyes and great horns wrapped in flame about the heads and backs.
When the world was created they were cast into the abyss of the netherworld, a prison to hold them until the end of days.
Ma'Rail: Tal'shear metal smith who forged the four great blades used during the war of the breaking.
Marcos: Last of the Tal'shear warders, his true name is Ash'Kelon.
Moinas Ard: Range of Mountains, claimed by the Mahjie as their own.
Moinar-Thur: Wild lands that lay between Morne and Trondhiem.
Morne: Arid lands that lay to the west of Tarok nor, realm of the Morne warriors, worshipers of Sur'kar. It is an inhospitable lands filled with deep canyons and rocky plains.
Morne Warriors: Non-human inhabitants of Morne, superb swordsmen who wear black robes over dark chain. They are merciless foes slaying men, women and children alike. They worship Sur'kar whom they have also named the storm god. To die in his service is the highest honor in their society.

The Morne live in scattered tribes ruled by a chieftain who is also their spiritual leader, sacrificing the old and sick to the storm god on altars constructed from the bones of the dead. Warfare among tribes is not uncommon, daring raids are looked upon as opportunities to hone their skills. It is only in rare of circumstances that they unite, often under the banner of a powerful chieftain.

They are short between 4 and 5 feet in height, powerfully built weighing over 250lbs. Their skin is a dark mottled green with a pale yellow belly. The eyes are large and golden in color with narrow slits for pupils. Their mouths are broad stretching from ear to ear and filled with small shark like teeth. From their necks hangs a brightly colored fleshy mass that is inflated as a threat display.

The Morne females lay their eggs in warm dry sands. The females jealously guard these areas. It is death for a male to enter them. Among the Morne there is no greater delicacy than dining on the eggs of ones foe.

Muel'Don: Volcanic waste land to the southwest of Trothgar.

N
Na Phay'ge: The dark side of the Phay'ge. Power of destruction wielded by Sur'kar and his minions.
Nahl wood: Forest on the island of Kale.
Nall: Largest Lake in Lakarra, its northern shore borders the Nallen wood.
Nallen wood: Forest in northern Lakarra, Supposedly haunted few men ever venture far within its borders.
New Hope: Village on the Isle of Kale.
Naz'Haruk: Creature created by Sur'kar. It is a relentless tracker that mindlessly pursues its prey until it is destroyed. Also known as a Garoul in the tongues of man.

O

Ogorum: Tal'shear word for Ice Trolls and Rock Trolls, Ice Trolls are one-eyed giants that haunt the frozen north. Ranging from 12 to 15 feet tall heavily muscled with large canine teeth and a snout like mouth. Their hair is thick and matted sprouting from the shoulders and upper back. The skin of the Ogorum is thick and arrows find it difficult to penetrate. Rock Trolls are slightly smaller than their northern kin reaching 8 to 10 feet in height, their bodies devoid of hair.
Otess: Steward of the King of Trondhiem.

P
Padwen: Lord Vernal's brother.
Pelatus: King of Ao'dan.
Parin: Coastal town in Northern Lakarra.
Phay'ge: Power of creation wielded by the warders, also known as Majik in the lands of men.
Peyetor Dunburrow: Son of Carl and Winowa, murdered by raiders at an early age.

R
Rahlcrag Mountains: Mountain Range that forms the Western Border of Trondhiem. Snow clad year round, it is a daunting barrier that is not easily crossed.
Randorien Forest: Vast woodland south of Trondhiem, Home of tribes of men known as savages by the people of the north.
Raobahn Mountains: Mountain range forming the northern border of Trondhiem.
Ravenslaugh: Swamp in Moinar-Thur, poisoned by waters from Tarok-Nor.
Ravin Suni: Anghor Shok, guardian of Marcos.
Redeff: Owner of the Fouled net inn.
Re'lith: Eastern watchtower in Moinar-Thur.
Rildrun: River in north Trondhiem.
Ril'Gambor: Land west of Kesh.

Rodderdam: City about the keep of Thorunder.
Rukash: Giant hawk that lives in the lands of the Mahjie making the high mountain crags its home. Forty foot wingspan with razor sharp talons and a fierce beak. They are white, banded with light gray stripes.

S

Sa'ramir: Well in the center of the standing stones on Eol, Enchanted keeper of the rings of the Warders.
Sahrencor: Oasis destroyed by the Morne in the Gaul-Tyrian waste.
Sahri: Leader of the Nomadic tribes of the Gaul-Tyrian wastes. Revered by his people, to be almost godlike. Also known as the Sahri kahlamm.
Senatum: Enforcers of King Ganeth of Lakarra, Corrupt officials who are nothing more than hoodlums and murderers.
Se'estra: Blind seer and leader of the Mahjie.
Seh'ja: Family or clan of Mahjie.
Shardwall: Line of mountains forming the eastern border of Trondhiem.
Ship Thane: Title given to an individual who is the foreman of a shipyard.
Shoffal: One of G'relg's crew, who attacked New Hope.
Sirel Tellius: Captain of the guard serving the house of Fullvie.
Songart River: River that flows south along the foothills of the Rahlcrag Mountains in western Trondhiem. At its southern end it joins with the Evtor Wash as it remerges from the Easterling Marsh and flows into the Randorien Forest.
Sorvahk Gohn: Arena of testing in Anghor. It is where those selected are tested to become Anghor Shok. The scarlet steps at its heart, is where the sacred oath is taken.
So'san: Tal'shear warder who nearly destroyed the world in desperation during the war of breaking.

Sur'kar: Tal'shear warder, who was corrupted by evil. Seeks dominance of mankind and believes himself to be a god.

T

Taelus: River in Lakarra on whose banks stands Graystone.
Talen: Gold coin used in all kingdoms of the east, emblem of an eagle's claw stamped into them. Minted in Ao'dan.
Tal'shear: Race of immortal beings who crossed the darkling sea on three ships.
Tanuth the axe: Legendary hero of northern Lakarra. Slain in treachery by his friend and companion.
Tarok nor: Cursed land of fell beast and poison, Sur'kar's realm.
Taur Di: The name the forest dwellers of Randorien forest call themselves.
Te'Caleph: Language of Caleph.
"Tel'lav an Amos": an old phrase meaning for honor and glory, a tribute to those that had passed in combat, the battle cry of the house of Fullvie.
Tel'Ganduil: Ship of the Tal'shear, upon which Marcos was born.
Tharlas: River originating beneath Trothgar and headwaters for the Ravenslaugh marsh.
Thelikor: Island nation that sunk into the sea before the war of the breaking.
Theranduil: Lowland Plain located in east Central Trondhiem. At its heart stands the Capital of Rodderdam.
Thral'duras: Kingdom founded before the breaking, destroyed during the disaster caused by So'san.
Timosh: Keep that wards the entrance to the lands of Moinar-Thur. In the old tongue it was known as Timosh Kahlen Ahned, Shield of the east.
Thraldur: The gateway into Trothgar, also named the gate of skulls.

Thoron'Gil: Wielder of Aethir, Hero from the lands of what is now known as Ao'dan. A farmer who grew to greatness, undefeated in battle he was chosen to slay Sur'kar.
Thorunder: Half brother of Thoron'Gil, He survives the breaking and builds Thorunder keep to protect the eastern lands should Sur'kar ever return. Only his descendants can sit upon the throne of Trondhiem.
Thorunder Hall: Keep located in the city of Rodderdam, Residence of the King of Trondhiem.
Towers of Torinth: Twin towers that guard the entrance to Cythera's Harbor.
Tor'lith: Western most watchtower in Moinar-Thur.
Trothgar: Volcano within the heart of Tarok nor.
Trondhiem: Kingdom bordering on the wilds of the west.

U
Un'eldur: Pass through the Black Mountains leading into Tarok-Nor.
Urbas Ugei: Caravan master from Caleph.
Urold Rhaine: Ship thane of New Hope and father of Casius.
Ursai Do: Mahjie guardian of the way, protector of the borders of their lands.

V
Vaelan Wall: A rugged plateau marking the southern frontier of Trondhiem.
Valdecar: Lake in northern Trondhiem.
Valliness: The white city of Ril'Gambor and its capital.
Varsus Valley: Valley in Southern Lakarra carved by the Darkwater River.
Vell: Lake in Ril'Gambor.
Vel'Gallum: A range of mountains destroyed during the war of the breaking.

Vi'Erud: The keep of the damned, destroyed during the war of the breaking.
Vi'Eruk: Fortress guarding the entrance into Tarok nor.
Vool: Balhain one of two Tal'shear enslaved to Sur'kar.
V'rag: Tower of Sur'kar, erected within the Calderas of the volcano Trothgar. It now stands in the land of Tarok nor, a great crater created when the hammer fell during the first age. It is the seat of Sur'kar's power and his sanctuary.
Vurgwall: Range of mountains forming the rim of the ancient crater about Tarok nor.

W
Wahlen: Blacksmith of New Hope.
War of the Breaking: Fought during the first age, when Sur'kar tried to conquer the world.
Warder: Member of an order of Tal'shear mages, sworn to the protection and preservation of the earth.
Warlock: Human skilled in the use of the Na Phay'ge. Evil by nature they care nothing for normal men and see them as a lesser being.
Westerling Trail: A narrow track that winds out of the town of Low fall, and down into the southern edge of the Nallen Forest.
Weyass: Princess of Trondhiem and sister of Gaelan.
Weyre Mountains: Long chain of mountains that run north through the heart of Lakarra.
Whiten: One of the lesser houses of Trondhiem.
Whitenshire: Wine producing region ruled by the house of Whiten.
Winowa Dunburrow: Wife of Carl Dunburrow.
Wolhan: King of Kesh, Connell's father.
Wood King: Fabled seedlings of the first tree. They were not tied to the earth and wandered the world spreading the forests throughout the lands. They sleep for millennia beneath the earth, rising only to defend the wood in which they dwell.

Thought to have passed from the earth long before the coming of Man and Tal'shear.
Wyremounds: Tombs in the garden surrounding Red Spire.
Wyrenatt: A single tomb within the Wyremounds.

Y
Ysrex: Sea serpent slain on the shores of Thelikor.
Ythia: Great Lake of ancient times that once surrounded the hill on which Rodderdam was built.

ABOUT THE AUTHOR

Born in 1964 at a U.S Military installation in France, DeWayne M Kunkel has served in the U.S Navy and has widely traveled the world. Painting and writing are two of his passions. He currently lives on the Space Coast of Florida.

DeWayne can be contacted at
dewaynekunkel@me.com

Made in United States
Orlando, FL
26 March 2022